This book is dedicated to the men and women of the Air Force Personnel Center, who work countless, often thankless hours to promote the careers of AF military and civilian personnel around the world.

ACCLAIM FOR THE BLOCKBUSTER MILITARY ROMANCES OF MERLINE LOVELACE

DUTY AND DISHONOR

"Exciting. Powerful. Fans of Tom Clancy and Scott Turow will love Merline Lovelace."
—*Affaire de Coeur*

"Sizzles with excitement."
—Nora Roberts

"A great yarn told by a masterful storyteller. It could have happened!"
—Brigadier General Jerry Dalton, USAF Ret.

"Fresh and unique . . . powerful, passionate, and guaranteed to appeal to a wide audience!"
—*Romantic Times*

LINE OF DUTY

"Merline Lovelace is poised to create a unique and powerful storytelling niche for herself."
—*Romantic Times*

"This is strong, action-packed stuff."
—*Publishers Weekly*

"Lovelace has created an interesting background for this sizzling romance. The sparks flying explode off the page."
—*Rendezvous*

CALL
OF
DUTY

Merline
Lovelace

AN ONYX BOOK

ONYX
Published by the Penguin Group
Penguin Putnam Inc., 375 Hudson Street,
New York, New York 10014, U.S.A.
Penguin Books Ltd, 27 Wrights Lane,
London W8 5TZ, England
Penguin Books Australia Ltd, Ringwood,
Victoria, Australia
Penguin Books Canada Ltd, 10 Alcorn Avenue,
Toronto, Ontario, Canada M4V 3B2
Penguin Books (N.Z.) Ltd, 182–190 Wairau Road,
Auckland 10, New Zealand

Penguin Books Ltd, Registered Offices:
Harmondsworth, Middlesex, England

First published by Onyx, an imprint of Dutton NAL,
a member of Penguin Putnam Inc.

First Printing, August, 1998
10 9 8 7 6 5 4 3 2 1

 REGISTERED TRADEMARK—MARCA REGISTRADA

Printed in the United States of America

ACKNOWLEDGMENTS

With special thanks to:

Major General Susan Pamerleau, Commander, AF Personnel Center, for her friendship, her enthusiasm, and her willingness to let an officer-turned-author inside the doors to the Center.

Lieutenant Colonel Kenneth DeKat, Chief, Military Personnel Law, AF Personnel Center, for keeping me straight on the ramifications of unprofessional conduct.

Captain Mike Rein, Chief, Public Affairs, AF Personnel Center, for escorting me around the Center and patiently answering my steady stream of E-mail.

Mr. Gary Emery, Chief, Public Affairs, 82d Training Wing, Sheppard AFB, TX, who didn't bat an eye when I walked in off the street and told him I was including his base in my next thriller.

And most expecially to:

Brook, Jim, Chuck, Mint Newman and all the officers and enlisted personnel I worked with at the Center so many years ago. Those were some of the most fascinating, challenging, and rewarding years of my AF career.

Chapter One

Jennifer Varga had made a number of really dumb mistakes in her chaotic thirty-one years. Two in particular had reached epic proportions.

The first was dropping out of college to marry her jerk of an ex. The second was joining this chickenshit outfit otherwise known as the United States Air Force.

She'd recovered from her short-lived involvement with Danny Varga. That little hormonal power surge had cost her seventeen months of marital misery and four years of working two jobs to dig out of the avalanche of debt her irresponsible husband had brought down on them both. Along the way, Jen had managed to complete her undergraduate degree, but she'd never quite learned to curb the impulsiveness that had gotten her into her disastrous marriage in the first place.

If she had, she might not have downed one too many fuzzy navels on a night out with friends and ended up accompanying a bleary-eyed Diane Parmentier to the Air Force recruiter's office the next morning. Nor would she have taken the officer qualifying test just for grins. She *certainly* wouldn't have jumped at the promise of travel and adventure, not to mention advanced schooling, and signed on the dotted line. That world-class blunder had cost her another six years in a turbulent, up-and-down Air Force career.

As she reported to her supervisor at the Air Force Personnel Center on a chill November morning, she couldn't know that it might soon cost her her life.

The temperature inside the first-floor office of the sprawling stucco building that housed the Personnel Center matched the chill outside. San Antonio's warm, sunny fall had gone south last night. So, apparently, had Jen's brand-new Jeep Cherokee. At least that's what the police had speculated when she reported the vehicle missing earlier this morning.

As if the loss of her car weren't bad enough, she now had to face her boss. Trying not to think of the as-yet-unpaid first installment of her absent Cherokee, Jen waited for Lieutenant Colonel Michael Page to get on with it. She'd been called into his office often enough in the past four months to know the drill.

He'd let her stand and wait for the ax to fall. Which she was now doing.

Then he'd lean back in his armchair and zap her with those twin gray lasers. Which he now did.

Finally, he'd nod to the chair in front of his desk and order her to sit down in that gravel-laced voice of his.

"Sit down, Captain Varga."

Tucking her dark blue uniform skirt under her thighs, Jen made herself comfortable. From the expression on the colonel's face, she was in for a long session.

"This is the second time in as many weeks you've been late."

"Yes, sir."

He waited for an explanation.

Jen waited back. She'd learned a thing or two in her dealings with Lieutenant Colonel Page.

His jaw tightened another notch.

One of these days, Jen mused, the damned thing was going to crack like a slab of granite hit at just the right angle by a sledgehammer. She very much hoped she was there to see it.

"What's the story this time?" he got out at last. "Did you lock yourself out of your apartment again? Or did your roommate borrow your car without telling you?"

"Someone borrowed it," she replied coolly. "It was stolen last night."

He lifted a sandy brow in patent disbelief. "You'll have to come up with a better tale than that, Varga. No self-respecting thief would bother with your heap of rusted tin."

"If you're referring to my Camaro, I traded it in last week."

Actually, she'd paid the Jeep salesman fifty bucks to have the Camaro towed to the salvage yard, but Iron Jaw Page didn't need to know that.

God, she disliked the man! Well, maybe disliked was too strong a word. She had to admit he was fair enough in his own tunnel-visioned fashion. And he'd been known to crack a smile on occasion, although rarely when Jen was in the general vicinity. Still, she might have made more of an effort to appear suitably repentant in these little sessions if he hadn't represented everything about the Air Force that rubbed her exactly the wrong way.

Take his office, for instance. It was as precise and spit-shined as Page himself. Not one of the dozens of colorful squadron plaques decorating the walls tilted a single degree off center. A neat stack of messages sat beside his phone. Even the papers in his in and out boxes appeared perfectly aligned. There wasn't a hint of the chaos that seemed to invade every facet of her life.

Jen shifted her gaze from the clean, orderly desk to the clean, orderly man behind it. His sun-streaked, toffee-colored hair wouldn't dare give in to the curl hidden in its close-cropped layers, any more than his starched, knife-creased blue uniform shirt would display a single wrinkle. Granted, the shirt molded muscular shoulders and a flat stomach. And, yes, his tanned face gave ample evidence of a man more used to the outdoors than an office environment. But his tough, uncompromising build only emphasized his equally tough, uncompromising personality.

In the four short months since he'd arrived at

the Center, he'd lived up to the reputation that had preceded him. A communications engineer by background and training, he'd worked his way up through the ranks, from a slick-sleeved no-striper stringing wire at remote sites to chief of the combat communications team that went in as part of the advance landing in Grenada. He'd been commissioned soon after that, and subsequently pulled assignments at every level from base to major command to the Pentagon.

In the process, he'd made major and lieutenant colonel ahead of his peers. Everyone predicted he'd make full bird early, too. Maybe even get a star eventually. The fact that he was divorced wouldn't kill his chances, as it might have a few years ago, when a wife was considered a requirement for general officer rank. According to the office scuttlebutt, Michael Page possessed the credentials that today's Air Force considered essential in its future leaders.

He also, Jen had discovered, possessed a sadistic determination to extract every last ounce of blood from anyone unwise enough to get on his bad side.

Like her.

Page leaned forward, his rugged face creasing just enough to give a casual observer the totally erroneous impression of concern. Jen hardly qualified as a casual observer.

"Are you trying to tell me that your car really was stolen?"

"I'm not *trying* to tell you anything." At the

sudden icy glint in his gray eyes, she tacked on a grudging, "Sir."

Across the expanse of polished wood, they locked glances. In the ensuing silent battle of wills, the computer terminal on his desk hummed. Heels scuffed as someone walked down the corridor outside. Jen curled her fingers into her palms. Just a little. Not enough to let Page know how much he got to her.

She felt a short-lived flush of triumph when he broke the small standoff. "Let's start over. You were late this morning because . . . ?"

His deliberate, grating tone spiked her too-ready temper. Lifting a hand, Jen ticked off the morning's disasters, one after another.

"Because I had to wait for the police to arrive and take my statement. Because I had to report the loss to my insurance company. Because I then had to call half a dozen rent-a-wreck agencies before I found a clunker I could afford, because my frigg . . ."

She caught herself just in time. Colonel Page flatly refused to tolerate unprofessional language or off-color jokes in the workplace. It was one of the few things about him Jen really admired.

"Because my insurance policy doesn't cover rentals," she finished on a tight note.

She eyed the man across from her, knowing better than to expect sympathy. Sure enough, he didn't offer any.

"And it didn't occur to you to call the office

while you were spending all this time on the phone?"

Jen couldn't help herself. She curved her mouth in a saccharine-sweet smile.

"I did call. Several times. Your private line was busy and you don't want to know how many voice mail menus and submenus I had to wade through before I got the usual busy signals for the other lines."

As expected, Page stiffened. For weeks now, he'd been waging a fierce, no-holds-barred war with the weenies who'd designed the Personnel Center's automated phone-answering system. Usually, the mere mention of the layer of options every caller had to endure to reach a real-live person was enough to make him fire off another scorching E-mail to the system's designers.

To Jen's intense disappointment, he refused to rise to the bait today. Instead, he leaned forward and pinned her with a look that evaporated her sugary smile.

"Careful, Captain," he growled. "You're on thin ice here. Very thin ice."

He was right. Jen had been in trouble often enough in her less-than-stellar Air Force career to understand the consequences of her failure to appear this morning. Page could lay a letter of counseling on her, maybe even a letter of reprimand. For sure, he'd zing her on the efficiency report due in a few weeks. Another black mark on her record would kill her admittedly slim chances of promotion.

The possibility she might not make major

didn't bother Jen as much as the lack of control over her life. It was time, past time, she returned to the civilian world. She wanted to work on projects that fired her interest, not those she was assigned. She wanted the freedom to walk off a boring job if she chose. She wanted to wear jeans to work when the mood struck her, and let her thick, unruly chestnut hair tumble down her back instead of cramming it in a loose twist on top of her head every day.

In short, she wanted out of the military.

Leaning forward, she tried to convince Page that it was in the best interests of the United States Air Force, the Air Force Personnel Center, and him personally to end their respective misery.

"Look, we both know that I'm not Air Force material. I never have been."

"We've been through this before. No one forced you to hold up your hand and take the oath."

"I've told you. I made a mistake. I realized that my first morning at Officer Training School, when some idiot flipped on the lights at four a.m. and played reveille on a tin whistle."

He wasn't impressed. "Yet you managed to graduate from OTS with honors."

"Only because I tripped the second day I was there and sprained my ankle! They put me to work in academics, where I—"

"Where you got to play on the computers. I know the story, Varga. How you designed a simple, user-friendly program to sequence training modules. How your program became a standard for the Air Force. How you earned an Achievement Medal as a result."

"I didn't want the medal. I only wanted out."

"So you've told me. Instead of releasing you when they had the chance, however, the misguided officials at OTS dangled the promise of a master's degree in front of your eyes."

"Yes, well . . ."

"The Air Force paid for that degree, and for the various computer schools you've attended since . . . including that very long, very expensive course in digital optic displays you wrangled a slot for last year."

"I didn't 'wrangle' that slot," Jen protested indignantly. "It was offered, and I accepted."

She suspected her previous boss had tempted her with the opportunity to spend six months at the University of Texas in Austin as much to get her out of his hair as to further her technical skills. Whatever his motivation, she had jumped at the offer. Unfortunately.

"You also accepted the additional active duty service commitment that went with those courses," Page reminded her, unnecessarily.

Jen gave a huff of frustration. They'd come around to the same sticking point they always reached. Trying hard to keep her voice even, she pointed out a fact well known to both her and her bullheaded supervisor.

"The military is drawing down. The Air Force is waiving active duty service commitments right and left."

"Forget it. You're in a critical skill."

"Right! So critical that I spend all day reviewing error reports that any entry level clerk could handle."

"Do I need to remind you that you volunteered for this task force?"

She slumped back in her chair. "No, you don't."

When the word went out that the Personnel Center's commander was bringing in an outsider to spearhead an independent, far-reaching look at the personnel systems necessary to support tomorrow's Air Force, Jen had welcomed the chance to be part of the task force. Given her record, she'd been lucky to get on the team. Her years of experience in the Data Systems Directorate had done the trick. Now she was a member of the team charged with evaluating Phase II of the Automated Records Management System.

ARMS II represented the next generation in personnel data management. Eventually, the information now being stored on optical discs and updated daily would eliminate all paper and microfiche records. Jen had been dying for a chance to see the guts of the new system up close and personal.

To her intense disappointment, her role so far had consisted of endless boring hours in front of a remote terminal, analyzing results of test runs and recommending changes to the programmers. Within a day, she'd wanted off the detail. Badly. Page's response to that unwise request had singed the ends of her hair.

Never one to go down without a fight, Jen made one last plea. "Just think about it. If you approve my request for separation, I'll disappear from your life forever and you can stop popping Rolaids every time you see me walk through your door."

She was exaggerating, of course. Lieutenant Colonel Mike Page wouldn't resort to medical aids to quell a rebellious stomach. His stomach wouldn't dare rebel.

He studied her, his silvery eyes masked behind the screen of his lashes. For a few, heady moments, hope flared in Jen's chest. Maybe, just maybe, she'd finally gotten through to the man!

He soon sent that hope into a nosedive. Shifting his shoulders under the tailored blue shirt, he leaned forward and capped her already dismal morning.

"You have a habit of quitting whenever you get bored or things don't go your way, Captain Varga. Get this straight, once and for all. I'm not letting you quit this team or get out of the Air Force. You owe us another eleven months for all those expensive schools we sent you to, and I intend to see that you serve them."

Jen's fingers curled into her palms.

"In view of what happened with your car, I'll excuse your tardiness this morning."

She bit back an involuntary and completely inappropriate comment on his magnanimity.

"Just make sure you call in when the next

disaster strikes . . . as I'm sure it soon will," he added dryly. "That's all."

She was halfway across the room before she remembered to salute. She turned to find Page watching her with an expression that told her she was lucky she hadn't reached the threshold. She jerked her hand to her forehead, and a moment later closed the door behind her with just enough emphasis to let the man understand that she was *not* happy.

Jen stalked down the hallway to the front entrance and hub of the Personnel Center, as frustrated as she could remember being in a long, long time. Damn Page. Damn the Air Force. And damn the idiot who invented the all-too-potent combination of vodka, triple sec, and peach schnapps that constituted a fuzzy navel, a concoction she hadn't touched since she put on a uniform.

Nodding with something less than her usual friendliness to the receptionist manning the front desk, Jen took the quarter-mile passageway that connected the front of the building with the rear wings. As always, a steady stream of people in and out of uniform traveled the narrow umbilical corridor. Charged with providing support to the Air Force's military and civilian personnel worldwide, the Center maintained a twenty-four-hour operation. At any time of the day or night, computers hummed, phones rang, assignment RIPs flowed, and personnel were reported missing, captured, or imprisoned.

Her anger still simmering, Jen pushed through the glass doors that opened onto the small alleyway leading to the three-story building labeled D wing. Misty air nipped at her cheeks and frosted her breath. Shivering, she climbed the half flight of steps to the rear entry.

Inside, another long hallway traced a path through a maze of workstations and offices. Metal Leiktrievers filled with paper records sat like massive gray behemoths amid clusters of the latest state-of-the-art computers. The juxtaposition of the old and the new tickled Jen's irrepressible sense of the ridiculous on her better days.

This wasn't one of them.

A few moments later she entered the partitioned area occupied by the ARMS II test cadre. Rolling her chair away from the desk, Jen sank into the seat with a long, frustrated sigh.

The grizzled, gray-haired civilian at the next workstation swiveled to face her. "Uh-oh. Sounds like your session with the colonel didn't go well."

"An understatement if I ever heard one."

Her coworker chuckled sympathetically. A San Antonio native, Ed James had worked at the Personnel Center for more than twenty years. He'd started as a data entry clerk and had risen in both pay grade and responsibility. Now, he served as one of the few trusted agents at the Center with the authority to go into an individual's Master Personnel Files and make the changes directed by the Air Force Board for Correction of Military Records. With his wealth of experience in personnel systems, he'd been a natural for the team.

He and Jen had worked together for weeks now. She'd duly admired the photos pinned above his workstation of a much younger and slimmer Ed with his wife and kids. The kids were adults now. The daughter lived in California with his three grandchildren. The son owned a videocassette rental business in the North Texas city of Wichita Falls. Ed still grieved for his wife, who'd died of lung cancer two years ago, although his grief hadn't put an end to his own nicotine addiction. Despite a wracking cough that started in his lungs, rattled around his chest, and rasped through his throat with alarming frequency, he stepped outside every thirty minutes, no matter what the weather, for a quick smoke.

A cigarette pack stuck out of his plaid shirt pocket now as he bent both elbows back, rested his palms on his chair arms, and gave Jen a commiserating smile.

"You look like you got dragged through an obstacle course by your heels."

"That bad, huh?"

"Nearabouts."

She propped her elbows on her desk and her chin in her hands. "I feel even worse than I look," she admitted.

"Page give you a rough time?"

"He's never given me anything else."

Ed chuckled again. Jen's thorny sessions with

her boss had become a topic of lively discussion among the rest of the team.

"I covered for you the first time he called this morning. Guess I was out taking the air the second time he called."

"Yeah, well, thanks for trying."

Absently, Jen tugged on a stray tendril that had worked free of her loose twist. Her heavy mass of hair slipped free of its brown plastic clip and tumbled down around her shoulders. Grumbling, she twisted it into a rope and clamped it back on her head.

Her annoyance over the requirement to keep her hair off her shoulders was such a petty thing, she knew, but somehow it had come to symbolize her urgent need to shuck all these silly, restrictive rules. When she got out of the Air Force, she'd wear her hair hanging down to her knees!

If she ever got out of the Air Force.

Releasing her pent-up frustration in a gust of breath, she turned to her keyboard.

"Guess I'd better hit the keys. If I finish the rest of these error analyses in the next day or two, maybe I can get back to some real work."

"Records management is real work, missy," Ed replied primly. "These screens represent living, breathing people. They expect to get paid or promoted or retired based on the information in the system. It's up to us to make sure it's entered correctly."

Ashamed of herself for denigrating the work

Ed had devoted his life to, Jen nodded. "Yes, you're right."

Two clicks of the mouse brought up the first display, which filled half the computer screen. Another click brought up a second display. Jen skimmed the second report to identify the data error. She made a swift, on-screen annotation to the programmers to check the lines of code that would allow base-level scanners to enter the United Nations Service Ribbon into the system, then double clicked the mouse again.

Both windows disappeared instantly.

One more test record down. Five or six hundred to go.

With more than thirteen million bits of data stored in the ARMS, no one had expected the test of Phase II to go without a hitch. In fact, the low error rate had surprised everyone. Still, Jen could think of several things she'd rather be doing than sitting here double clicking a mouse all day.

Like programming some changes in these clumsy screens so that they'd scroll faster.

Or sticking long, sharp pins into a doll with straw-colored hair and lieutenant colonel's oak leaves on its shoulders.

Or calling the police to ask what they were doing to find her missing vehicle.

Damn!

How long would it take them to locate her car? she wondered glumly. And what kind of shape would it be in when they did?

Sighing, she hit the mouse again.

*   *   *

After her aggravating morning, Jen was sure her day couldn't get any worse. She was wrong.

At two-fifteen that afternoon, the San Antonio police called to tell her they'd found her vehicle in a southside chop shop. The Cherokee had been stripped of every removable part, and the chassis was in the process of being cut into scrap. Jen hung up, dropped her head into her hands, and silently ran through every oath in her rather extensive repertoire.

At three-twenty, Ed James gave one of his lung-rattling coughs, stiffened, and clutched at his chest.

Jen spun around, gasping when she saw his pasty white face. "Oh, my God! Ed! Ed, what's the matter?"

With an agonized grunt, he fell out of his chair.

She threw herself down on her knees beside the stricken man and felt for a pulse. Screaming for help, she tilted his head back and started CPR.

Team members came running. Another civilian took over breathing air into Ed's mouth while Jen pumped on his chest. Someone called 911.

It could only have been minutes until the EMT unit arrived, but it seemed like centuries. With swift competency, the paramedics shoved her aside and took over. Shaking, Jen watched as they labored over Ed for another eternity.

They couldn't revive him.

In stark silence, the medics bundled Ed's still

form onto a stretcher and wheeled him away. The white-faced major who served as the team's second-in-command hurried away to inform the colonel.

For a long while, no one spoke. The strained silence stretched endlessly. What was there to say in the face of such swift, devastating finality?

At last, everyone wound their way back to their workstations. Alone and shaken, Jen stared numbly at Ed's empty chair. Slowly, her gaze lifted to the photographs over his flickering terminal. Her stomach clenched as she thought of the calls someone would make to his kids in the next few hours.

She reached out a trembling hand. Long habit prompted her to back up the files the civilian had been working on. Not knowing his user ID, she labeled the backup file with her own ID. Tears stung at her eyes as she turned off Ed's computer terminal for the last time.

Although Jen couldn't know it at the moment, she would bitterly regret that simple, instinctive act.

Chapter Two

The soft, muted ring of the phone pulled Russell Murdock from a dreamless sleep. He held himself still for a few seconds, adjusting to full wakefulness.

Evie lay in her customary facedown sprawl at his side. She'd flung one arm across Russ's chest. Her left knee dug into his thigh. When he eased out of her loose embrace, she muttered irritably and curled into a tight ball. After almost forty years of sharing a bed with Russ, Evie still didn't take kindly to his late night calls.

A second low ring brought Russ rolling onto his hip. Noting the time displayed by the digital clock on the nightstand, he reached for the phone. He knew the identity of the individual at the other end of the line. Only three people in the world had access to this number. Only one would call him this late at night.

"Murdock here. What's up?"

His chief of staff wasted no time on preliminaries. A brusque, impatient man with a network of white scars mapping the left side of his face, the former Special Forces commander served as the perfect foil for Murdock's more amiable public persona.

"I thought you'd want to know. We lost Ed James."

Russ went perfectly still. "How?"

"He had a heart attack. He was at work at the time. Didn't even make it to the hospital."

"Ahh . . ."

A wave of sadness washed through Murdock, ebbing and flowing like a slow-rolling tide. Ed had been a good man. One of their best.

"It happened this afternoon," his chief of staff said tersely. "I didn't get word until a little while ago. That particular communications glitch won't happen again."

And it wouldn't, Russ knew. George "Andy" Anderson would make sure of that.

"I assume everything's been taken care of?"

"Yes, sir."

Russ was silent for a few moments, thinking of the man he'd personally recruited so many years ago.

"Are Ed's kids doing okay financially?"

"They could use some help. His daughter's a single mother with three kids. His son runs a video shop in North Texas."

"Make the usual arrangements."

"Yes, sir. And I'll fax a slate of candidates to replace Ed to you tomorrow . . . correction, today."

"Fine. I'll talk to you after I've reviewed them."

Russ replaced the receiver, still gripped by sadness. The loss of any of his handpicked band left an emptiness in his heart.

Taking care not to disturb Evie, he eased out of bed and scooped up his robe. Radiant heat flowing under the floor tiles warmed the soles of his bare feet. The undraped, three-story windows that formed the east wall of his Rocky Mountain retreat spilled enough moonlight into the room to guide him.

The open windows constituted a distinct benefit of living atop one of Colorado's most majestic peaks. The spectacular views constituted another. Even now, in the dead of night, the panorama grabbed at Russ's chest. Millions of stars splashed across the velvety sky. A low-hanging moon bathed the surrounding, snow-covered Rockies with light.

Russ shoved his hands in the pockets of his robe. The aesthetic in him could appreciate the awesome vista outside his windows. The husband in him took comfort in the stark isolation, even while he decried the need for it. Since the attack on Evie, though, he'd sworn never again to take any chances.

The mere thought of attack curled his hands into fists. Russ accepted the risks that went with power and wealth. He'd known since making his first million that he'd become a target for everyone from kidnappers to kooks wanting to strike at the establishment. What he couldn't accept was the fact that four men could spray terror and bullets across a busy shopping mall in broad daylight, killing Evie's bodyguard and five innocent bystanders, and escape.

If Russ hadn't already been convinced of the rightness of the operation he'd begun years before, that incident would have fired his determination into tempered, unbreakable steel. Since the bloodbath at the shopping mall, Special Programs had moved from a small piece of his worldwide responsibilities to the main focus of his life.

Ed James had been a part of Special Programs from the earliest days. A quiet, dedicated crusader like the others Russ had recruited, Ed had played a pivotal role in building and training the cadre of elite men and women who carried out Special Programs' secret mission.

Ed would be a hard man to replace, Russ thought. Not only because of his intimate knowledge of the Air Force's personnel systems, but because of his single-minded belief in the cause they served.

They'd have to find someone to take over his role quickly, though. Someone with his skills. His dedication. His concern for the future of this country.

Chapter Three

After a night made restless by thoughts of Ed James's tragic death, Jen hit the snooze button three times in succession. Stuffing her face into the pillow, she closed her eyes and re-lived again the traumatic events of the previous day.

As they had for most of the night, haunting questions tumbled through her mind. Had she reacted fast enough? Could she have done more? She hardly knew the man, but death had somehow bonded them more closely than their shared work on the ARMS II team.

Finally, she dragged herself out of bed with even more reluctance than usual. She wasn't a morning person. She never had been. She barely functioned as a human before nine or ten. Unfortunately, the Air Force didn't make allowances for distinctions in character and physical metabolism.

She showered as quietly as possible to avoid waking her roommate. A junior high gym teacher, Patricia Scanlon usually got up an hour later than Jen did. With her coaching duties and active social life, Trish stayed out a lot later in the evenings, as well. The two women rarely saw each other, which, in their considered opinions, made them perfect roommates.

Retrieving a uniform shirt from her closet, Jen pulled it on and stuffed the tails into the waistband of her tailored navy skirt. After a frantic search for her blue wool Air Force sweater, she finally found it under her bed. She dragged it out by one sleeve and dislodged the animal nested in its folds. The small, wiry almost terrier gave her a look of profound reproach.

"Don't give me that sad-eyed routine," she grumbled. "You know you've got a perfectly good bed downstairs."

In response, Commodore pulled back his gums in the tongue-lolling grin that had stolen Jen's heart during a moment of insanity a year ago. She'd been between roommates then, and lonely. Impulsively, she'd stopped by the Animal Shelter and driven home with this lop-eared mixed breed. When she'd seen the blinding speed with which the mutt could devour anything that looked, smelled, or sounded like food, she'd named him for her heroine, Commodore Grace Hooper, discoverer of the nanosecond.

"Jeez, to think I actually believed that guy at the pound who swore you didn't shed."

While she plucked vainly at the short, stiff hairs decorating the blue sweater, the terrier jumped onto the unmade bed and circled two or three times. A few scrapes of his front paws pulled together a new nest. He sank into the mound with a blissful sigh.

"Oh, sure," Jen said sarcastically, tugging the still hairy sweater over her head. "Sleep in, why don't you?"

The dog showed every evidence of doing just that.

"Get Trish to take you out before she leaves. Any more accidents and you're history, pal."

With that totally useless warning, Jen hurried through the darkened apartment. She didn't dare stop to make coffee, much less pop a slice of bread in the toaster. She'd be lucky to get to work on time as it was. Digging in her purse for her keys, she stepped out into a gray morning.

The rental vehicle waited for her in her assigned slot. Jen winced when she saw it. The driver's side window wouldn't go all the way up, the paint peeled on the roof, and the bumper had more dents and dimples than a golf ball. With a stab of regret for her new and now deceased Cherokee, Jen unlocked the door.

Despite its shortcomings, the rented wreck got her around San Antonio's northeast loop and to the front gate of Randolph Air Force Base in good time.

More or less.

She had just stopped at the red light a few yards from the gate when a bell clanged and the railroad crossing guards started to drop. Jumping half out of her sweater, Jen hastily checked to make sure the rental car's nose was clear of the tracks. The last thing she needed was to make another call to her insurance company today.

Drumming her nails impatiently on the plastic steering wheel, Jen waited while a freight train lumbered by. Rush-hour traffic into the base backed up for miles behind her along Pat Booker Road. Finally the bell stopped clanging, the gate lifted, and Jen flattened the tensionless gas pedal. Her rented vehicle shot across the tracks and screeched up to the stuccoed main gate.

A disapproving security policeman waved her to a halt and took a close look at her ID card. "Is this your vehicle, Captain?"

"No, it's a rental."

He gestured to the small building to the right of the gate. "You'll need to pull into Vehicle Registration and obtain a temporary pass."

Jen groaned. She'd intended to do that yesterday. She really had. The traumatic events of the day had driven it right out of her mind.

"Can't I do it later?" she pleaded, not above groveling when necessary. "I have to get to work. I'll register the car this afternoon, I promise."

The cop eyed the backed-up traffic, then gave her a resigned salute and waved her through. Thankfully, Jen joined the flow making its way down the flag-lined boulevard.

Built in the thirties as an aviation training center, Randolph Air Force Base boasted red-roofed stucco buildings and a beautiful Spanish-style chapel that was listed on the registry of National

Historic buildings. At the far end of the main boulevard stood the base's landmark headquarters building. A six-sided, round-topped tower protruded straight up from the low, sprawling headquarters. Known throughout the Air Force as the Taj Mahal, the odd-shaped water tower always reminded Jen of an erect penis.

The distinctive shape loomed ahead of her now, bringing an appreciative grin to her lips. She could use an erect penis with the Taj's magnificent proportions in her life. She'd been experiencing something of a dry spell in that department lately. Commodore constituted her closest thing to a male companion.

Oh, she had her share of dates. And she hadn't remained celibate after her disastrous marriage, by any means. One laughing, blue-eyed maintenance officer in particular had almost convinced her to take another stab at the long-term relationship business. But he'd shipped out to Korea last year, and long-term didn't pass the long-distance test for either of them.

Which was another reason why Jen wanted out of the Air Force. She didn't like forming friendships, only to have them constantly broken.

Slanting a final, fond glance at the Taj, Jen peeled off the traffic circle in front of the headquarters and headed for the west side of the base. With a stroke of rare luck, she found a parking space in the Personnel Center's main lot. She twisted the key and pulled it out of the ignition, then waited while the rented clunker rattled and wheezed for an embarrassing stretch of time. Heads turned. Brows rose. Finally, the engine died.

Cramming her flight cap on her head, Jen dashed across the street. Once inside the front entrance to the Personnel Center, she shot a quick glance at the clock above the receptionist's desk. Seven twenty-six and a half.

She'd made it!

With a buoyant sense of victory, she strode down the long, narrow corridor to the back of the building. Her pace slowed as she passed through the glass doors and stepped into the alleyway. The reminder of what had happened yesterday killed her brief euphoria.

She stopped at the entry to her work area. Chewing on her lower lip, she eyed Ed's empty seat and blank terminal screen. Slowly, her gaze drifted to her own terminal. A yellow sticky note hung on the top edge. Even from where she stood, Jen could make out the brief message.

Colonel Page wanted her to report to his office when she arrived.

She groaned. What now?

Stashing her purse and her hat in a desk drawer, Jen retraced her steps to the central entrance. From there, she took the hallway that led to the commander's wing. For the duration of his special analysis, Page had been given a temporary office just outside the command suite. Puffing slightly from the brisk walk, Jen poked the stubborn strands of her hair back into place and smiled at the secretary behind the desk.

"Hi, Dee. I had a note that the boss wants to see me."

"Hi, Jen. Go right in. He's been waiting for you."

Fortifying herself with a deep breath, Jen rapped on the doorjamb. "You wanted to see me?"

"Yes, Captain Varga. Come in."

He indicated the chair in front of his desk with a wave of one hand. Jen's brows lifted in mild shock. No standing at attention? No steely-eyed stare?

"Major Cernecki called me last night," he informed her, his eyes watchful behind their sandy lashes. "She told me about what you did for Mr. James."

"What I tried to do. I didn't help him much."

"From what I understand, you administered CPR until the ambulance arrived. That took cool nerves and a good deal of courage, Jen."

She didn't know what surprised her more, his quiet praise or the unexpected use of her nickname. She didn't think Page even knew it. Pleasure percolated through her for a few moments. A few short moments.

"Major Cernecki also wants me to extend you on error analysis effort," he told her, "until we can fill the void left by Ed James's death."

"You said no, right? Anyone can click on those screens and batch-code the errors. I want to get into some hardcore programming."

She knew the answer before she asked the question. Page's concept of duty would put the mission first and Jen's personal preferences dead last.

Sure enough, the colonel shook his head. "I agreed to the extension."

So much for her boss's brief descent into near humanity. Her reaction to his decision must have showed plainly on her face.

"You have a problem with that, Captain?"

"I really think I could be of more use to the Air Force doing something else."

Like anything else.

Colonel Page didn't even bother to comment on that one. "Major Cernecki will keep me apprised of your progress."

"Is that all?" she asked tightly.

"No, it's not." His jaw worked as he raked her with a disapproving glance. "Either get that sweater cleaned or get a new one. Today."

"Yes, sir!"

She shut the door behind her with her usual statement.

Mike Page didn't move until the noise of the busy Personnel Center had swallowed his subordinate's angry footsteps. Even then, he sat still for another few moments, willing himself to calm.

Willing didn't work.

It never worked where Captain Jennifer Varga was concerned, not since the day he'd chosen her for the team over the advice of her previous boss. The woman could drive any supervisor to drink, Major Hal Benson had warned. Or to murder.

Mike had considered both in the past four months. In his own way, though, he was every bit as stubborn as the captain. He wasn't about to let her wriggle out of repaying the Air Force for the training she'd received. And he was damned if he'd palm her off on another unsuspecting supervisor. Mike believed in handling his problems, not passing them on, and Captain Varga headed his list of problems.

She reminded him too much of himself, Mike thought. She was too cocky by half, and too damn smart for her own good. What's more, she had a bad habit of shooting off her mouth . . . just as Mike had before age and experience had tempered him. Age and experience and, he recalled, a bruising, bare-knuckled session behind the comm center with an irate sergeant determined to teach the wiseass airman respect for authority.

Mike had learned that lesson well. Along the way, he'd also acquired the discipline and drive needed to accomplish his assigned tasks. Varga, from what Mike had observed, had acquired neither.

She'd aced every school the Air Force had ever sent her to, but the same bright, inquiring mind that questioned and probed in an academic environment had a tendency to question and probe in the duty environment, as well. Although a tireless worker, she let her irritation with what she termed Mickey Mouse rules and regulations sidetrack her. All too often, she lost sight of the big picture in her annoyance over the small stuff.

In her first few Air Force jobs, her intelligence and extraordinary capabilities had overshadowed her impatience with the rules. At the Personnel Center, where she'd worked in a succession of positions within the Data Systems Directorate, just the reverse occurred. Lately, she'd gained a reputation as a troublemaker. Mike could understand why. Captain Varga could be, to put it mildly, a real pain in the ass. Her last two performance reports reflected that fact.

She was too bright and too talented to end her military career on this kind of a downward spiral, though. From the first, Mike had considered her a personal challenge. He refused to let her give up on the Air Force, and he refused to shirk his responsibilities to her.

As he had with Lisa.

Suddenly the walls of his office seemed to close in on him. Shoving his chair back, Mike moved to the window. The cold, drizzly day outside called to him. He needed to feel its bite. To breathe in something other than the recirculated air of the Personnel Center.

Dammit, he wasn't a deskman. Never had been. Until the past few years, he'd spent most of his career in the open air. He couldn't count the number of times sweat had streamed down his bare back as he trenched cable at some remote desert site. Or the ice that had nipped at his face as he and his crew rigged satellite dishes in subzero temperatures. Even as an officer, he'd been more of a hands-on supervisor than a desk jockey.

His years at the Pentagon, first on the Air Staff and then in Congressional Liaison, hadn't resigned him to paper shuffling. He could handle the staff work and the constant pressure of dealing with one top-level crisis after another. He didn't particularly enjoy it, but he could handle it. What he didn't like was this constant feeling of being cooped up . . . and his running battle with Captain Varga.

He wasn't giving in, he vowed in grim silence. Or giving up on her. No matter how much she wanted out of the Air Force, he wasn't approving her request to waive her active duty service commitment.

Feeling decidedly hostile toward the military rank structure in general and gray-eyed lieutenant colonels in particular, Jen pulled off her sweater and stuffed it in her desk drawer. Major Cernecki showed up a moment later and handed her a slip of paper.

"This is Ed James's password. Log onto his terminal and transfer his data error files to your system."

"All of them?" Jen yelped.

"I know, I know. It's a huge workload. I'm trying to get someone else in to help."

"Try real hard," Jen muttered as the major turned away.

Slowly, she crossed the small cubicle and

paused in front of Ed's chair. A reluctance to take his seat percolated at the surface of her consciousness. It didn't seem right, moving in on his turf so soon. The funeral wouldn't take place for a few days, and Air Force business had to go on in the meantime, but still . . .

Jen trailed her fingers across his keyboard. The cross bar on the "T" was gone, worn away by hard use, as was the upper curve on the "P." Ed had spent most of his life hitting these keys, or similar ones.

Swallowing, she slipped into his chair and toggled the power switch on the keyboard. While she waited for his system to boot up, she eyed the bare spaces above the terminal. Someone had already taken down the pictures of his family. Major Cernecki, Jen guessed. No doubt she'd give them to his kids, along with the rest of his personal effects.

Feeling unsettled and uncomfortable, as though she were invading Ed James's personal space, she typed in his password.

The screen went blank.

Jen blinked in surprise. Flipping the power switch off, then on again, she rebooted the system and reentered the password. The screen darkened once again.

"What in the world . . . ?"

Frowning, Jen made one more try. When that, too, failed, she pushed the chair back and went in search of the major.

"Are you sure this is the right password?"

"I pulled it off the registry myself a little while ago."

"Every time I enter it, the screen goes blank."

"Huh?"

"I don't even get a user authorization failure notice."

"Did you boot up and log on properly?"

"Yes, Major," Jen drawled, "I did."

Cheryl Cernecki held a master's degree in computer systems integration. She also tended to resent Jen's frequent and all-too-vocal criticism of the way she ran the ARMS II review. She pushed her wire-rimmed glasses up on her nose with one finger and frowned at Jen.

"Try again," she instructed abruptly. "That password should take you right to Ed's electronic desktop. Let me know if you can't get in."

She'd get in, Jen decided. One way or another.

Three attempts later, she stared at the still blank screen. Okay. All right. What was the problem here?

Ed's password hadn't been deactivated. She'd gone into the master registry herself to verify that fact. But it wouldn't open his desktop. She couldn't transfer his data to her system without accessing his desktop.

Or did she need to?

Suddenly Jen remembered the backup she'd made yesterday using her own ID instead of Ed's. With a few quick taps, she keyed in her own password, then searched the directory contents for the most recent addition to her files.

Aha!

Grinning, she clicked on the backup file and waited while a colorful desktop painted across the screen. There it was. The ARMS II test icon, with a subdirectory of files Ed had been working with, and a few others as well. Resting her fingers on the keyboard, Jen eyed the little symbols. Most she recognized as identifiers for standard AF programs. A couple represented popular commercial programs. One or two she'd never seen before.

The presence of non-Air Force programs didn't surprise her. Jen herself kept a few innocuously labeled files on her desktop. Okay, so she was a solitaire junkie? So she kept track of her personal finances on a government computer? Worse abuses occurred every day. Much worse.

She couldn't take the chance that these non-Air Force icons represented only games or personal information, however. As Ed himself had reminded her just before he died, real people got promoted or paid or separated from the military based on the data in the system. She'd better verify just what was behind those little symbols.

When she clicked on the first icon, it blossomed into a colorful, action-packed, shoot-'em-up Rambo-type game. The three-dimensional graphics grabbed Jen instantly. She got her near naked, muscle-bound hero through three bloody ambushes and an attack by a horde of vengeful Mongolians before quitting.

The second icon opened an electronic "to do" list. Biting her lip, Jen scanned the entries Ed had compiled.

Pick up shoes at the repair shop.
Get birthday card for Betts—7 yrs? 8?
Check date of last oil change.

Jen's fingers gripped the mouse. How sad to think that a living, breathing man had sat here just yesterday, wondering about the date of his vehicle's last oil change. Feeling a loss she couldn't explain, Jen hit the mouse again.

The third icon opened to reveal half a dozen standard Air Force personnel records. Swiftly she skimmed through them. All the records appeared to relate to people in training.

Captain Steve Warner, currently taking a course at Sheppard Tech Training Center.

Technical Sergeant Rosalie Tobias, just finishing up a seven-week Satellite Communications course at Keesler.

Staff Sergeant Gerald L. McConnell . . .

Jen leaned forward. Strange. Only half of the data fields in this record contained any information. Even stranger, neither the name nor the social security number on the record resulted in a match when Jen fed them into the master personnel system.

Her interest piqued, she tried to match the other data. Only one bit of information clicked. A projected school start date.

Staff Sergeant McConnell, whoever he was, was scheduled to attend advanced explosives ordnance disposal training at Eglin Air Force Base in Florida starting January 10.

Curiouser and curiouser.

Why the heck couldn't she find McConnell in the Air Force Military Personnel Data System?

Thinking he could be a reservist activated for training purposes, Jen decided to bump his social security number against the Guard and Reserve files. The responses came back within minutes. Neither the Guard nor the AF Reserve listed a Staff Sergeant McConnell or anyone else with that particular SSN on its rolls.

Thoroughly intrigued now, Jen formatted several more queries. One went to the Explosive Ordnance Disposal course requirements manager at Air Education and Training Command, located just across the base. Another went to the course manager at Eglin.

Eglin responded first. They showed no one with that SSN or name slated to attend the January course, but indicated that several slots had just been made available to the commands for short-notice fills. McConnell could have been tagged to fill one of these slots, and his data just hadn't flowed yet.

The reply didn't satisfy Jen at all. How could Staff Sergeant McConnell be slated to fill a short-notice training slot when he didn't even exist on the Master Personnel File?

Her natural inquisitiveness fired, she waited impatiently for AETC's response. The course manager got back to her a little while later. He didn't manage people, only requirements, but he could send a query to Eglin about this SSgt. McConnell if she wanted.

Jen declined his offer and considered her next

move. She *should* get back to the error analysis. She *ought* to turn Gerald L. McConnell's intriguing file over to the major. But this little puzzle constituted the first real mental challenge she'd encountered in weeks. She didn't want to let go of it. Not just yet.

This McConnell character could be in another branch of the service, she reasoned. The Army, maybe. Or the Navy. Other services often sent members to Air Force schools, and vice versa. Or he could be a civilian from another governmental department who'd been tagged with an equivalent rank designator. Stretching her authority just a bit, she formatted an intergovernmental query and zinged it off.

Knowing it would take a while to receive replies, Jen closed McConnell's file. She'd better get to work on the more mundane tasks she'd inherited from Ed or she'd never get off this detail!

Fifteen hundred miles away, a coded message flashed on another screen. Immediately the watchful operator keyed in a response. His brows slashed downward as he read the politely worded request for verification of status on Gerald L. McConnell, SSN 031-34-4486.

"Hell!"

Scowling, he printed a copy of the request and hurried out of the communications center. A swift, silent elevator carried him from the basement to the seventeenth floor of the granite tower that housed the corporate headquarters of

Murdock Enterprises, Incorporated. Tall glass
windows gave spectacular views of Denver's
skyline and the snow-covered mountains beyond, but the operator paid no attention to the
dazzling vistas. Intent only on the paper in his
hand, he headed for the glass doors that
guarded the MEI executive suite.

He slipped his ID into the security scanner
and waited impatiently while a camera matched
his image to the hologram on the ID. When the
doors whirred open, he pushed through and by-
passed the smiling receptionist and veered
toward the chief of staff's private offices.

The chief's assistant glanced up at his entrance. With his buzz-cut hair and dark conservative suit, the man could have been a clone of
his boss.

"I need to see Mr. Anderson."

"He's in a meeting with Mr. Murdock."

"Call him out. Tell him this is a Code
Yellow."

The assistant verified his ID and lifted the intercom. Moments later, the communications specialist entered the inner office.

Shoulders square and scarred face tight, the
chief of staff greeted him with a brusque, "What
have you got?"

"I just intercepted this query from the Air
Force Personnel Center."

Anderson skimmed the brief message. When
he lifted his eyes again, the operator felt a sudden hollowness in the pit of his stomach.

"I thought you told me you'd taken care of Ed James's files."

"I did. I used our standard protocol to delete the unfinished files he was working on from the Air Force system. The active files I transferred to his replacement. I even altered his password in the official directory as a backup security measure. No one can get into his desktop, let alone his files . . . if they still existed, which they don't."

"Obviously, someone got to them *before* you deleted them."

The razor-sharp lash of his voice sent the operator back a pace. "It's not my fault we didn't learn of Ed James's heart attack until several hours after it happened."

Anderson crumpled the paper in his fist, controlling himself with a visible effort. "No, it's not."

The operator let out a breath of relief. He'd been with MEI for five years now, and had worked Special Programs for almost eighteen months. Like the others in the small, handpicked headquarters cadre, he absolutely believed in Mr. Murdock's vision. Like most of the others, he also admired and feared the chief of staff empowered to carry out that vision.

Anderson could raise a person's sweat with a single glance. Some said he could terminate a person's membership in the elite Special Programs unit just as easily, but that was only speculation, since no one ever left the cadre. Not by choice, anyway. Oh, they'd lost a few members to natural causes, like poor Ed James, and more than a few during dangerous missions. But no one in his memory had ever opted out of the unit.

"You were right to bring this straight to me," Anderson told him flatly. "I'll take it from here."

The door closed behind the operator, leaving Andy Anderson alone with his racing thoughts and the communiqué crumpled in his hand. How the hell had this happened? They'd never had a compromise like this, not since he'd taken charge of Special Programs.

They'd had a few close calls. Once, a dogged reporter had dug a bit too deeply into Mr. Murdock's past connections to the CIA and had to be . . . discouraged. Another time, an inquisitive auditor from the Securities and Exchange Commission had questioned a certain transfer of funds. But this was the first time queries about one of their recruits had ever floated through the system.

A man of action, Anderson didn't waste time. Picking up the phone, he pressed a button to scramble the transmission so that only those with access to MEI's secure satellite codes could receive it. His brief call completed, he rose, brushed a hand over his close-cropped, graying scalp, and returned to the conference room.

The vice president for marketing still had the floor, his bald head shiny with perspiration as he outlined his strategy for MEI's next satellite launch.

As the world's third largest supplier of communications equipment, MEI sold its products to every major defense contractor and almost as many private concerns. Now, thanks to Russ Murdock's friendly persuasion, some hard-headed bargaining, and an inside tip that Congress would pass by a close vote a hefty increase in foreign military sales money to several of MEI's best customers, the corporation was poised to leap into the lead.

Murdock nodded imperceptibly in response to the silent signal his chief of staff telegraphed. Anderson slipped into a seat at the foot of the conference table and waited for his boss to conclude the meeting.

Russ did so a few moments later, dismissing the others with his usual smile and a promise to get back to them later that day about the proposed strategy. When the conference room emptied, he sat back in his chair, steepled his fingers, and listened to Anderson's terse report without interruption. As always, he displayed no outward sign of anger, but his voice grew dangerously quiet as he asked the question Anderson had anticipated.

"How could a compromise like this occur if our people followed the standard protocols?"

The scarred tissue on the side of Anderson's face pulled into a grimace. "Someone must have accessed Ed's files before we deactivated them."

"Do we know who?"

"Not yet. But I've contacted our senior operative on-site. We'll find out soon enough."

Murdock rested his chin on his peaked fingers and held his deputy's gaze. "No leaks, Andy. I gave my word when we started this operation that there wouldn't be any leaks."

"There won't be, sir."

Jen was still waiting for responses to her query at the end of her duty day. She lingered at her workstation, hoping to satisfy her curiosity about Gerald L. McConnell before she headed home.

Major Cernecki stopped by around six. Obviously surprised to find Jen still at the keyboard, she said again that she'd try to get more help. Jen didn't feel even a twinge of guilt about letting the major think that she'd stayed late to work the ARMS II test data.

She gave up just a half hour later. The lack of response to her queries surprised her. Someone out there in the vast government bureaucracy should have answered by now. Impulsively, she transferred Ed's files to a floppy disk and slipped it into the side pocket of her purse. She'd play with this McConnell guy's record a bit more at home, tap into a few databases she couldn't—well, shouldn't—access via the government's computers.

Pulling on the sweater she'd forgotten to take to the cleaners, Jen walked out the front entrance of the Personnel Center to the vehicle she'd forgotten to register with Pass and ID. The rented car huddled forlornly in the rapidly descending dusk. It looked even more decrepit in the gloom than it had in the early morning light.

Digging through her purse for the car keys, Jen thought about food for the first time that day. Trish probably wouldn't be home yet, so she couldn't count on her roommate's talents in the kitchen. Maybe she'd order in a pepperoni and pineapple pizza to share with Commodore. Or drive over to Miguelo's, just a few blocks from her apartment. She and the Commodore both loved the spicy tamales, although Jen took the time to remove the corn husk wrappers before she wolfed hers down.

Shivering in the damp chill, she unlocked the car and slid behind the wheel. A quick twist of the key resulted in . . . nothing.

Her heart sinking, she tried again.

Not a sputter. Not a cough. Not even a hiccup.

She stomped the accelerator to the floor and twisted the key once more.

Stone cold silence.

Great. Just great!

Calling down evil curses on the rental car agency, she fumbled under the dash for the hood release and climbed out of the car. Holding up the hood with one hand, she stared at the engine. She could identify the major components and knew where to put oil, but that was about the extent of her mechanical skills. Propping the hood on its support, she poked a tentative finger at the battery cables. That futile exercise resulted in nothing more than a grease-tipped nail. A gust of icy air swept straight up her skirt, which didn't exactly improve either her mood or the situation.

Nor did the voice that came at her out of the gathering darkness.

"Captain Varga?"

Startled, Jen jerked upright. Her head whacked against the hood. Bright pinpricks of light pinwheeled across her vision.

She whipped around, her heart pounding, to confront a dark, shrouded figure.

Chapter Four

"Got a problem?"

Jen recognized both the voice and the face under the dark hood at almost the same moment. For the first time in four long months, she was actually glad to see her boss.

"As a matter of fact, I do."

"Why doesn't that surprise me?"

Before she could come up with a suitable response to that one, Colonel Page shoved back the hood of his sweatshirt and strolled toward the car.

"What's the situation here?"

"I think the battery's dead. You don't have some jumper cables in your car, by any chance?"

"I do, but why don't I take a look first? That might not be the problem."

He poked his head under the car hood and got his first good look at the engine. A long and low whistle sent Jen's last hopes plunging.

"You don't need jumper cables, Captain. You need a tow truck. Or a lawyer. You ought to sue whoever rented you this vehicle."

"If I could afford a lawyer, I wouldn't have rented it in the first place." She crowded close to his side and peered into the gloom at the engine. "What's wrong?"

"What's not wrong? The fan belt's frayed to a thin wire. The battery connections are corroded. There's sludge all over the engine, which probably means a cracked block or a—"

Groaning, Jen cut him off. "Don't tell me any more. I don't think I want to know. Just help me get it started, will you?"

"I'll try. Hang tight while I retrieve my car. It's parked at the gym."

Jamming her chilled fingers under her arms to warm them, she watched the colonel lope toward the row of hangars that lined the flight line west of the Personnel Center. One of the hangars contained a well-equipped fitness center, which Jen conscientiously avoided as much as possible. She wasn't into sweat.

Page, on the other hand, obviously was. He must have been running for some time before he stopped to help her, Jen surmised. Darker patches arrowed down the back of his navy sweatshirt and formed a small triangle just above his buttocks. His *very* trim buttocks, she noted.

She caught herself with a small start. Good grief! What was she doing, ogling Iceman Page's buns? Okay, okay, they definitely merited an ogle or two. In fact, they sparked a completely inexplicable curl of heat in Jen's belly. All she had to do to douse that spark instantly, however, was remind herself of the hard head and starched mind that went with those neat, tight buns.

Shivering in the growing darkness, she hunched her shoulders and awaited his return. A few moments later a purring, low-slung MG pulled up beside the rented wreck. Jen eyed the beautifully restored car in some surprise. If she had thought about it at all, she would have put Page behind the wheel of something bigger and more immovable, something that matched his personality. A bulldozer, maybe. Or a Bradley Fighting Vehicle. Certainly not this sleek little beauty that looked as though it had been hand-polished every week of its life.

He angled the MG nose to nose with the rented vehicle and dug a set of neatly coiled jumper cables out of the trunk.

"Are you sure you want to hook your car up to this thing?" she asked doubtfully. "What if it drains your battery, too?"

"From the looks of that engine, I doubt if the battery's the problem. We'll give it a shot, though. Try to crank her up when I signal."

Repeated infusions of power failed to produce even a small sputter from the wreck. After the third try, Page signaled her to stop.

Jen grabbed her purse and climbed out. Resisting the urge to give the unresponsive vehicle a swift, hard kick in its metal shins, she turned to the colonel. "Thanks for trying anyway. Guess I'd better go back inside the Center and call that tow truck you mentioned."

Page disconnected the cables and slowly coiled them. "Where will you have it towed?"

"To the rental agency."

"Think they're still open?"

"If not, I'll leave the thing parked in their yard and call a cab."

Jen slung her purse strap over her shoulder and turned toward the Center. Cables in hand, Page blocked her way.

"Look, I don't like leaving you stranded in the cold and dark like this. Why don't I give you a ride home tonight? You can take care of the car in the morning."

"No, thanks. I don't want to put you to so much trouble."

"It's no trouble. Your place is on my way home."

She blinked up at him in surprise.

"You live at the Spanish Oaks apartments, don't you?" he asked calmly.

"Yes. How did you know?"

"I looked up your address the first time you failed to show for work. I thought you might be sick or something. As I recall," he drawled, "that was the day you locked yourself out of your apartment wearing nothing but an embarrassed smile and—"

"I remember the occasion!"

How could she forget? That was the *last* time she'd hauled a protesting Commodore outside against his will. The darned mutt had darted back into the kitchen, knocking the door shut behind him and leaving Jen stranded in the apartment's minuscule backyard wearing only bikini panties and a midriff baring cutoff T-shirt. The apartment's high wooden fence provided privacy, but that didn't help much when she'd had to shout to a neighbor for help, then wait for the complex manager to arrive and unlock the back door. To this day, she couldn't face the smirking manager.

Page pulled open the MG's passenger door. "Get in. It's too cold to stand here arguing. That sweater isn't much protection against the damp."

As if reminded of their conversation earlier this morning, he frowned and took a closer look at the garment under discussion. Hastily, Jen slid into the passenger seat and slammed the door. With any luck at all, the dim interior would hide the wiry dog hair still adorning the blue wool. She sank into buttery soft leather and a welcome warmth. While Page stowed the jumper cables, Jen admired the car's rich, wood-grained instrument panel and well-appointed interior.

The moment he joined her inside, the MG suddenly lost its luxurious feel and seemed downright cramped. The colonel took up more than his fair share of airspace, Jen observed. Keying the ignition, he glanced back over his shoulder and moved the gearshift into reverse. In the process, his knuckles brushed her thigh. Disconcerted, Jen edged her leg aside.

If Page noticed either the brief contact or her reaction, he didn't show it. He kept his right hand on the gear knob and his eyes on the road as they headed for the west gate. Wet pavement hissed under the tires. Lights from oncoming vehicles illuminated the interior, then passed in a blurred blaze.

A stream of warm air from the vents brushed Jen's cheeks. She squirmed in her seat, more than a little uncomfortable with this whole situation. She didn't like accepting favors from the man who headed her hit list.

The MG was out the gate and heading for loop 1604 before Page's deep voice broke the stillness. "How did it go today?"

"What?"

"How did it go? Having to fill in for Mr. James?"

Jen stared out at the slick pavement. "It was kind of sad, really. I didn't know him very well. No one did, it turns out. He pretty much kept to himself. Yet you'd think that after twenty plus years on the job, his death would leave more of a . . . a void."

"Maybe that was Mr. James's special gift," Page suggested quietly. "He performed his duties so well and so thoroughly that his passing didn't result in chaos. That's not a bad legacy, when you think about it."

Jen shot him a sideways look. She might have known Page would ascribe to the do-your-job-and-heaven-will-be-your-reward philosophy of life. For a moment she toyed with the idea of telling him about the puzzling files Ed had left behind, but quickly squashed the impulse. She wanted to play with the files a little more before mentioning them to anyone in authority. Besides, Page's nearness was proving too distracting to talk about much of anything.

In the close confines of the car, she could pick out his scent above the damp wool of her sweater and the rich aroma of waxed leather. His combination of faint, tangy aftershave and healthy male disconcerted her . . . almost as much as the smooth, pumping action of his leg every time he pushed in the clutch to change gears.

This was her boss, she reminded herself sternly. The man who intended to hold her to every blasted hour of her service commitment. A familiar resentment bubbled up. Jen slumped lower in her seat and stared out at the night.

The little MG pulled up at her apartment complex less than twenty minutes later. Jen directed the colonel through the labyrinth of two-story, Spanish-style buildings and reached for the door handle as soon as he'd pulled into her vacant parking space.

"Thanks for trying to jump-start the rental and for the ride home. I really appreciate it."

"No problem. I'll pick you up at what? Six-thirty tomorrow morning."

Six-thirty? She wasn't even alive at six-thirty, let alone awake!

"No, thanks," she replied hurriedly. "I don't want to inconvenience you any more than I have. I'll get my roommate to bring me in to work."

"It's not an inconvenience."

Jen groped for the handle. "Really, I . . ."

The driver's side door slammed on her protests. Walking around the back of the car, the colonel opened Jen's door and held out his hand. She hesitated, strangely nervous about making contact.

For heaven's sake! She was acting like a total twit. Just because the man scraped on her nerves like fingernails across a blackboard was no reason to refuse his help. She took his hand and climbed out of the low-slung sports car with more haste than grace.

"Okay, six-thirty it is. If you're sure it's not . . ."

"It's not," he said firmly. "Come on, I'll see you to your door."

His calm assumption that she needed an escort to walk twenty yards annoyed Jen considerably, but it was difficult to put a man down for acting like a perfect gentleman. Especially when that man was your boss.

Tall, wrought-iron lamps made puddles of light on the walk that led to the two-bedroom end unit she shared with Trish. Jen fished around in her purse for her keys and pushed open the heavy metal front door, designed and painted to look like paneled wood. Turning, she offered what she hoped was a grateful smile.

"I'll see you tomorrow morning."

"At six-thirty."

"Right. Six-thirty."

"And Captain Varga?"

"Yes?"

"Lose the sweater."

He turned to leave, and the words slipped out of Jen before she could stop them.

"Colonel Page?"

"Yes?"

"Get a—"

She'd never know how he would have reacted to her blunt suggestion that he get a life. The sudden yank of the door cut it off in mid-sentence.

"Jen!"

Her roommate's soft West Texas drawl spilled into the drizzly night.

"It's about time you got home, girl. The mutt and I are starving. I'll spring for tamales if you . . ."

She broke off, her aquamarine eyes widening as she caught sight of the colonel. Propping a hip against the door, she gave him a very slow, very interested once-over.

"Hel-lo."

Page returned both her greeting and her glinting approval. "Hello."

What was not to approve? Jen thought, observing his reaction to the supple body covered in turquoise spandex and a bright, gaudy tank suit that was cut high on the hips and low everywhere else. Trish not only taught physical fitness to her giddy, prepubescent students, she lived it. When she wasn't at school or refereeing some athletic event or another, she was at the spa or out running. There wasn't an ounce of cellulite on her disgustingly trim body. Her pale cornsilk hair hung in shining waves to her shoulders, and she didn't need makeup to accentuate her glowing complexion. The only thing that kept Jen from totally hating the woman was that her cheerful personality more than made up for her stunning good looks.

Trish flicked another glance over his navy sweats. "I'm glad to see Jen's finally bringing home someone whose idea of strenuous exercise isn't clicking through all the TV channels twice."

"I didn't bring him home," Jen corrected quickly. "He brought me."

"That's even better," her irrepressible roommate replied with a waggle of pale blond brows. "Come on in and get cozy. I'll disappear for a few hours."

Jen flashed Trish a warning glance as she led the way into the lighted foyer. "This is my boss, Colonel Page."

Her roommate had her eyes glued to Page's torso-hugging sweats and missed the signal.

"Well, well," she purred. "So this is Iron Jaw Page."

Jen decided that she wouldn't strangle her roommate in front of the colonel. She'd wait until he left, then do it slowly. She wanted to enjoy every exquisite moment.

"The rental car wouldn't start," she said tersely. "The colonel gave me a ride."

Unabashed, Trish slid her gaze back to Page. "So you and Jen aren't, shall we say, bringing your work home?"

"The Air Force tends to frown on that sort of thing," he replied easily.

"Does it?"

"It does."

Page bent to knuckle an inquisitive Commodore's head. The mutt promptly plopped down and rolled over, presenting a pink and black speckled belly for attention.

"Unprofessional conduct and fraternization with a subordinate run close seconds to murder or desertion in the face of the enemy these days," Page replied, hunkering down to stroke the animal's quivering stomach. "After the Navy Tailhook episode and the scandal with the Army's drill instructors, the Air Force expects us all to walk a very straight, very narrow line."

"We've got rules like that in the public school system, too," the teacher tossed back with a cat-like grin. "To my knowledge, they've never proved the least bit effective as a deterrent to good old-fashioned lust."

"Trish," Jen groaned. "Give it up, will you?"

"All right. But even very straight, very narrow colonels have to eat. You want to join us for tamales? Unless . . ." She turned a limpid look on Jen. "Unless you two stopped on the way home? To eat. Supper, that is."

She was dead! As soon as Jen got the colonel out the door, her roommate was dead!

"No, we didn't stop to eat," Jen snapped.

"And no, I can't," Page added, abandoning a boneless, drooling Commodore. "But thanks for the invitation. I'll pick you up at six-thirty to-morrow morning, Captain Varga."

Thankfully, Trish waited for the door to close behind Page before she pounced on that one. She trailed Jen into the sunken living room, crowing all the way.

"No fraternization, huh? He just gave you a ride home because your rental car wouldn't start, huh? Tell me another one, Jenny-girl. Like how the man has ice water for blood. Like how he wouldn't recognize a human impulse if it bit him in the butt. Like—"

"Okay, okay!" Jen tossed her purse aside and collapsed onto the sofa. Commodore landed in her lap before she hit the cushions. "Maybe he's not quite as inhuman as I painted him. But he's still got his backside firmly planted on my request for a waiver."

Trish worked her eyebrows again. "And a very nice backside it is, too."

"I didn't notice."

Her roommate snorted. "Then your case is more desperate than I'd realized."

Jen stifled a groan as Trish picked up what was becoming a frequent refrain.

"You've gone too long with only that sorry excuse for a dog as company, Jen-girl. You need a male of the two-legged variety to play with."

"Tell me something I don't know," Jen muttered, tickling the dog's warm belly.

Trish folded her legs under her with fluid grace and sank to the floor. Shoving aside the papers she'd been grading, she propped her chin in her hands. "Seriously, though, this guy Page isn't bad. Not bad at all. Are you sure you couldn't interest him in something other than a waiver?"

"No, I couldn't."

"Have you tried?"

"Page wasn't kidding about this fraternization stuff, Trish. Fooling around with a subordinate is a big-time no-no."

"Only if you get caught."

"I'd get caught," Jen tossed back with a grimace. "I always get caught."

"You're probably right there," her roommate admitted. "You're the unluckiest person I know. Trouble seems to follow you around like a hungry dog. Speaking of which, your hound and I are both starved. Want to go grab something to eat?"

Jen gave Commodore's belly a final rub. "I'll get changed."

They left the apartment ten minutes later and piled into Trish's Camry. Commodore made nose prints all over the windows, much to the owner's disgust.

"Can't you control him? Or at least teach him not to drool all over the upholstery?"

Distracted by the dog's antics, neither woman noticed the vehicle parked five spaces away. Or the silent watcher in the front seat.

He waited until the taillights had disappeared, then mentally ticked off ten more minutes. Satisfied that they were gone, he extracted a small, leather-wrapped tool kit from the glove compartment.

The front door lock gave on the first twist of a slender tool. His footsteps silent on the carpet, he crossed the sunken living room and headed for the stairs. From his earlier calls to the management, he knew that this floor plan included two bedrooms and two baths on the upper level.

The first bedroom reflected the personality detailed in the report he'd received a few hours ago. All soft colors and faintly perfumed air. Stunningly framed artwork from various Olympics that celebrated the human spirit. Clean. Organized.

Not the room he sought.

There was no question that the target occupied the second bedroom. Scattered shoes and panty hose vied for floor space with an assortment of magazines, textbooks, and an empty pizza box. Cosmetics and electric hair appliances dangling twisted cords crowded the bureau top. An Air Force sweater and blouse had been tossed atop an unmade bed. The coffee-colored bra lying beside the blouse caught his attention. Trimmed with lace and fitted with little push-up pads inside the cups, it conjured an instant erotic image of mounded breasts overlaid by layers of uniform.

The concept of lush femininity straining at the bounds of military regulation stayed with him as he systematically, thoroughly, searched the clutter. He didn't find what he sought among the scattered clothes or in the jumbled bureau drawers and closets.

After a few moments, he moved to the desk. Swiftly he examined the library of floppies in a plastic case next to the computer. In contrast to the chaos atop the rest of the desk, every disk bore a neat, dated label that detailed its contents. None of them appeared to contain the files he wanted. Just to be sure, he turned on the computer and methodically inserted the disks, one after another.

When none of the floppies produced the files he sought, he searched the hard disk contents. Frustration added a jagged edge to the grinding tension that came with any mission. He stared at the flickering screen, replaying in his mind the scenario he'd pieced together with the director of Special Programs.

The target must have copied Ed James's files last night, before the originals were destroyed. Obviously, she'd played around with them today. That was the only explanation for the queries about McConnell she'd sent out this afternoon.

He hadn't found the copied files on her computer at the Center. He'd searched that earlier this evening, soon after she left. It hadn't taken much brainpower to realize she had transferred the files to a floppy disk.

If she had, it wasn't here. He could only conclude that she still had it with her. Probably in her Air Force purse. The black bag had been slung over her shoulder when she left the apartment tonight.

He'd have to come back later to search the purse, he acknowledged grimly. In the meantime, though, he'd take out a little extra insurance.

His gloved fingers slipped on the plastic keys as he entered the proper sequence. When a coded file downloaded, a small smile played at the corners of his mouth. He moved the file to the system folder, where it disappeared. That task done, he turned off the computer and went downstairs and played with the back door lock. He tested it twice before he was satisfied that he could gain entry with a simple twist.

Damp mist filled his lungs as he walked back to his car. Hunching his shoulders against the cold, he settled down to wait for the target's return.

Some thousand miles away, Andy Anderson entered the control booth that gave access to MEI's underground command post. After his palm print, voice patterns, and infrared heat signature had been scanned and verified by the secure computers, the inner doors whirred open. Instantly the world Andy felt most at home in welcomed him.

Here, there was none of the posturing or gamesmanship that characterized the financial empire Russ Murdock ruled from his seventeen-story offices.

Here, there was only action. Direct. Sometimes forceful. Necessary.

His eyes went instantly to the backlit digital display status boards that gave him up-to-the-minute information on current Special Programs operations. The scarred skin on the side of his face pulled as a small frown formed.

"No word from our San Antonio operative yet?"

The senior command post operator on duty shook her head. "No, sir."

Anderson's gaze flicked to the bank of clocks above the screens. He'd much prefer to wait here in the control center until a report came in, but he had to make an appearance at a special charity performance of the Denver opera in his capacity as chief of staff of MEI. The opera, for Christ sakes! "Notify me as soon as he reports in."

"Yes, sir."

The target and her roommate drove into the parking lot of the apartment complex just before nine-thirty. The watcher gave a grunt of satisfaction.

They dawdled on the front stoop while the dog nosed around the front of the apartments, spraying bushes and the neighbor's steps indiscriminately. Finally, the trio went inside.

The dog didn't worry him. He'd neutralized far more vicious animals than that little runt. Flipping open the glove compartment, he pulled out the small canister he'd brought along for just that purpose. Idly, he tipped the canister end over end in his palms.

The blonde's bedroom lights went out first. The target's room plunged into darkness a few moments later. He let another thirty minutes go by, then pulled a black ski hood over his head and left the car. He'd just reached the corner of the building when light spilled from the bedroom windows once more.

Cursing, he flattened himself against the wall.

The front door opened a few moments later, and his target emerged. He watched her hike a hip onto the iron railing. Tucking her hands into the pockets of a tan raincoat, she called inside.

"Come on, Commodore! Get out here, and get serious this time, will you?"

He weighed his options and chose instantly. Slipping around the back of the building, he gained entry to the apartment within seconds. Surefooted, he raced noiselessly up the stairs.

He found the black leather Air Force purse on the chair beside the bed. The disk nestled in a side pocket. He slid it out and stood still, listening intently. He heard her voice, thin and querulous, warning the dog that he'd better get on with it or she'd leave him out all night.

A surge of something close to disappointment swept through him. It had been easy. Almost too easy.

He had just stepped out of the bedroom when the door across the hall opened.

"Jen? What are you doing still . . . ?"

The blonde saw him and froze in shock.

He swung before she could recover, calculating exactly how much force to put behind the blow. He didn't intend to kill her. Just disable her until he made his escape.

She jerked back at the same moment his fist connected. Her own momentum as much as the force of the blow slammed her against the doorjamb. Her skull hit with a small, brittle crack, then she crumpled slowly to the floor.

Chapter Five

The phone shrilled as Mike stepped into the shower. Leaving the hot water to steam up the bathroom, he caught it on the third ring.

"This is Page."

"Lieutenant Colonel Michael Page?"

"Yes."

"This is Detective Gutierrez from the San Antonio Police Department. I apologize for calling so late."

Mike didn't need to glance at the clock on the nightstand to know it was almost one. Since dropping Varga off at her apartment, he'd been too restless to sleep. Nor had he been able to concentrate on either the Spurs exhibition basketball game he attended earlier or on the work he'd brought home with him. As a last resort, he'd watched talk shows until the inane philosophy expounded by a tattooed rock star had finally driven him to the shower.

"I was awake. What can I do for you, Detective Gutierrez?"

"We're investigating an incident that just occurred at the Spanish Oaks apartments."

The Spanish Oaks apartments? A combination of annoyance and resignation rippled down Mike's naked back. What the hell had Varga gotten herself into now? The way she attracted trouble, it could be anything. The possibilities flashed in his mind like cluster bombs detonating on the horizon.

Drunk and disorderly?

Mouthing off to a police officer?

Mike couldn't see it. Varga, for all her other faults, hadn't shown any signs of problems with intoxicating or illegal substances. Maybe she'd locked herself out of her house in her underwear again and now faced a charge of indecent exposure.

The image that had danced around the edges of Mike's consciousness since the day Varga had lain that lame excuse for being late on him suddenly exploded onto center stage. His mind filled with a vision of the irksome, annoying, alluring Captain Varga in skimpy panties.

Just as suddenly, Mike went hard. His muscles locked. Heat streaked into his groin.

The unexpected reaction surprised the hell out of him. He couldn't remember the last time he'd felt such an unfettered, uncomplicated surge of male lust, but he knew damn well he shouldn't be feeling it for Jennifer Varga. She was under his supervision, for God's sake. His responsibility.

As Lisa had been.

The deliberate reminder banished the erotic

mental image instantly and acted on the fire in Mike's groin like a bucket of cold water.

"What kind of an incident?"

"An apparent burglary and assault."

The muscles he'd just forced to relax went stiff again. Every sinew and tendon in his body seemed to tighten.

"Who was assaulted?"

"A woman by the name of Patricia Scanlon."

Mike didn't have time to appreciate the relief that rushed through him before he connected Patricia Scanlon with the blond, laughing Trish.

"What happened?"

"At this point, our best guess is that Ms. Scanlon surprised an intruder and was injured during the struggle. We won't know for sure until she regains consciousness. If she regains consciousness."

The detective's flat, emotionless voice suggested that the possibility was remote. Mike swore under his breath.

"Ms. Scanlon's roommate, Jennifer Varga, indicated that you were here at the apartment earlier this evening."

"That's right."

"We'll need you to come down to Seventh District Headquarters on Rittiman Road tomorrow to provide us a set of prints, so we can eliminate yours from others we might find on the scene."

"Seventh District Headquarters. Got it."

"We'll also need you to confirm your whereabouts at approximately ten-thirty tonight."

Mike stiffened. "Why?"

"We consider everyone whose prints are found at a crime scene a suspect," the detective replied coolly, "until or unless they're eliminated from the list of potentials."

"I was at the Spurs exhibition game until almost eleven."

"Can anyone confirm that?"

"The three other officers I went with."

"Keep their names handy. I might need to talk to them."

Cold bastard, Mike thought, but thorough. The first quality didn't bother him. He appreciated the second.

"Is Captain Varga there?"

"Yes."

"Let me speak to her."

Cool air prickled Mike's bare skin while he waited. He heard voices in the background, and a popping noise he couldn't identify.

"Hello."

The ragged whisper sounded so unlike his smart-mouthed captain that Mike's jaw clenched. "Jennifer? Are you all right?"

"Yes. No. Yes."

"Which is it?"

"No."

"What happened?"

"I was outside. With the dog."

Mike bit off a scathing comment about idiot women who walk dogs late at night. "Where was Trish?"

"Inside the house. I found her. Upstairs." She

made a small choking sound. "There was so . . .
so much blood."

"Is she okay?"

"I don't know. They've taken her to St.
Mary's. I need to go, too. After the police finish
and I . . . I call her parents."

She sounded dazed and totally unfit to drive
anywhere. Assuming she had a vehicle to drive.
For the second time that night, Mike took
charge.

"How long will the police be there?"

"I don't know."

"Put the detective back on. Jennifer? Let me
talk to Gutierrez."

The police officer confirmed Mike's estimate
of the captain's condition. "One of the medics
checked her out. She's not actually in shock, but
she's pretty shaken. I'll see that she gets to the
hospital when we're through here."

"How long are you going to be there?"

"Another half hour forty-five minutes at most.
The lab guys are dusting the place now."

"I'll be there in thirty."

It took him just over twenty.

Mike pulled on the jeans and sweater he'd
discarded on his way to the bathroom and
jammed his feet into worn, comfortable boat
shoes. Snatching up his wallet and keys, he took
time to shut off the shower before heading for
the door.

The MG squealed out of the garage and ate
up the dark, deserted streets of the quiet sub-

division. Moments later, it spun onto Highway 281 and sped south.

When he'd reported to his new assignment four months ago, Mike had chosen to rent where San Antonio ended and Texas hill country began. The wide-open vistas and rolling hills covered with twisted, silvery green live oaks satisfied his need for space. Normally, he didn't mind the forty-minute drive to the base. At the hour he went in to work each morning, the road hadn't yet choked up with traffic. Dawn mist usually curled through the hills, and white-tailed mule deer grazed on the scrub beside the roads.

Tonight, the empty miles seemed to stretch forever. Driven by a mounting sense of urgency, Mike kept a wary eye out for deer and wove through the light traffic with controlled, contained aggression. The hills flattened. The darkness disappeared as carefully developed residential areas gave way to glass-and-granite corporate headquarters, trendy strip malls, and neon-lit restaurants. Jaw tight, hands clenched on the leather-wrapped steering wheel, Mike skimmed through one amber stoplight, then another, before intersecting the inner loop.

As the commercial buildings lining each side of Loop 410 flew by, Mike tried to dissect the urgency that kept his foot so heavy on the gas pedal. Part of it—most of it—he ascribed to an ingrained, instinctive concern for a subordinate. He'd been a supervisor since the day he'd sewed on his second stripe and taken charge of a three-man crew. Responsibility for greater numbers of personnel had come with each promotion. As he'd learned through both training and experience, if a leader took care of his people, they'd take care of any job.

But the kick to the gut he'd felt earlier when he thought of Varga bothered him. Big-time. For a few seconds there, he'd skidded right past supervisory concern and smacked butt-first into lust.

Characteristically, he broke the situation down into workable pieces. All right. That unexpected hard-on wasn't so difficult to understand. Even fully clothed and not precisely spit-shined, Varga could turn a few heads when she traveled the Personnel Center's long hallways . . . Mike's included.

The problem, he decided, was that he hadn't yet made an effort to develop social contacts here in San Antonio. It was time, past time, that he did. Maybe he'd give that long-legged, doe-eyed accountant he'd met a few weeks ago a call. Later. After he'd done what he could for Captain Varga and her roommate.

The memory of Jennifer's voice when she described finding Trish twisted Mike's stomach into hard, tight knots. Cursing, he bore down even harder on the accelerator. The exit for Harry Wurzbach caught him sandwiched between two semis. He floored the accelerator and swung right. Air brakes hissed. A blast from a horn shattered the night. Mike ignored the piercing shriek and swept down the curving access road that led to the Spanish Oaks apartment complex. Leaving the MG parked behind a black and white cruiser, he took the shallow steps to Jennifer's apartment in a few swift strides. The doorbell roused a series of shrill barks.

It was answered by a uniformed officer who jotted down Mike's name and address in a log and had him wait in the foyer while he summoned the detective in charge. Moments later, a thin, dark-haired man in a rumpled gray suit and a Daffy Duck tie came forward.

"I'm Gutierrez." He had to raise his voice to be heard over the noise of the barking. "Good timing, Colonel. The team from the lab is still here. They can save you a trip downtown by taking your prints tonight."

"Fine."

The high-pitched yelps rose to a crescendo, then the stubby, brown and black terrier whose hair decorated Varga's uniform sweater darted between the detective's legs. Gutierrez glanced down in disgust.

"Damn mutt. We tried to lock him in the bathroom, but he raised such a stink we had to release him."

As he had earlier, Mike stooped down to knuckle the dog's head. The dog promptly rolled onto its back and presented its liver-spotted stomach.

"Looks like he knows you," the detective observed.

Mike rose. "We met earlier this evening."

"Only this evening?"

"That's right."

Having lost Mike's attention, the little dog scrabbled to its feet and leaped onto a chair. It dropped down, resting its muzzle on its front paws while it kept the two men in sight.

Gutierrez led the way into the living room. Mike skimmed a quick look around. The room looked the same as it had when he'd glimpsed it from the hall earlier tonight . . . except for the black smudges on the walls and the smooth surfaces of the furniture. Fingerprint powder, Gutierrez explained, noticing his frown.

"Where's Captain Varga?"

"She's on the phone in the kitchen. Talking to Ms. Scanlon's parents."

Mike's stomach did a quick roll. He had a good idea of the shock and disbelief Jennifer was dealing with now. He'd had to notify families of a service member's injuries or death a few times himself.

Beside him, the detective pulled a thin, spiral-bound flip notepad from his suit pocket. "I might as well take your statement while we're waiting." He flipped through the pages. "According to Ms. Varga, you gave her a ride home from work tonight when her car wouldn't start. Do you remember what you touched while you were here?"

"The doorknob," Mike said succinctly. "The dog. Maybe the wall in the entryway."

"That's it?"

"Yes, that's . . ." He caught himself. "No, that's not it. I also shook Ms. Scanlon's hand."

Mike watched Gutierrez scribble that information in his little book. He had no idea whether the cops could lift prints from skin, but the thought of anyone having to lift them from Trish Scanlon's flesh made his own stretch tight across his chest.

The police officer flipped back a page to check his notes. "As I understand it, you're Captain Varga's supervisor at Randolph Air Force Base."

"Yes."

"And this is the first time you've been to her apartment?"

The casual question triggered a flicker of wariness in Mike. Even without the implications relating to tonight's incident, he didn't like the suggestion that he might be a regular visitor to Jennifer's apartment. It came too close on the heels of his totally inappropriate reaction a short while ago.

"Yes," he replied curtly. "This is the first time. Why?"

Gutierrez tapped his pen on his notebook. His brown eyes measured Mike with professional detachment. Whatever he read in the other man's face seemed to satisfy him. That, or Mike's alibi. His replies became less cautious and more informative.

"From what we've been able to piece together so far, whoever assaulted Ms. Scanlon was in and out of the apartment within a few minutes. That means he knew his way around the place, and knew exactly what he was after."

"Which was?"

"We don't know. Captain Varga didn't notice anything missing, but she was too upset to give the place more than a cursory look. She's promised us a more careful search later."

"Maybe Trish—Ms. Scanlon—surprised the burglar before he could take anything."

"Maybe."

When Gutierrez had nothing more to add, Mike raised the possibility that had nagged at him during the drive to the Spanish Oaks. "Did Captain Varga tell you that her car was stolen a few days ago?"

"Yes, she did."

"Could there be a link?"

"There could." Gutierrez flipped the notebook shut. "I'm going to pay the owner of the chop shop a personal visit tomorrow morning. He has only a vague recollection of what the scumbag who brought it in looked like. Maybe his memory will improve when I suggest he could be named an accessory to an assault."

The detective had just slipped his notepad into his pocket when Jennifer appeared in the archway that led to the kitchen.

She looked awful, Mike thought, as awful as anyone with a wild mane of chestnut hair and a ripe, curving body precisely detailed by a clinging red T-shirt and tight, faded jeans could look. Her olive-hued skin had a gray cast to it, and the stark expression in her eyes made Mike's hands fist at his sides. She acknowledged his presence with a small nod.

"I just talked to Trish's folks. They'll . . . They'll get here as soon as they can."

At the ragged catch in her voice, the little dog launched itself off the chair and aimed for its owner. She dropped to her knees and scooped it in her arms. Her thick, honey-brown hair fell in an impenetrable curtain around them both as she buried her face against the animal's wiry body. She rocked back and forth on her knees, making no sound.

Crossing the room, Mike wrapped his fingers around her upper arm and brought her gently to her feet. The tears streaking her face bit big chunks out of his self-control.

He'd handled tears before, both men's and women's. Few commanders or supervisors with his years of experience hadn't. He'd offered his shoulder while a widow sobbed out her grief, and tried to comfort a father who'd just learned his only child had leukemia. Yet he'd never felt this driving need to take the sufferer in his arms before.

"Jennifer . . ."

As it turned out, he didn't take her in his arms. She put herself there. Still gripping the dog, who aimed wet, worried swipes at her neck and chin, she slumped against Mike's chest.

He held her loosely while his senses registered the feel of the body against his. She was shorter than she appeared in the heels she wore with her uniform. Her hair just brushed the underside of his chin. The heavy mass carried a faint, damp scent, like wildflowers after a rain.

With the dog and her arms scrunched between them, her breasts didn't touch his chest, but her hips notched against his in a way that made Mike swallow. Hard.

Her soundless, wracking sobs subsided almost as quickly as they'd begun. She hiccuped once or twice, then lifted her face. The tears gave her eyes a silvery sheen, like a layer of thin, crystallized sugar over caramel candy.

Another man might have been tempted to forget that the candy was forbidden. Another woman might have let him.

Not Jennifer Varga. She blinked, as if realizing for the first time who held her, and jerked out of his arms.

"Good grief." A wave of embarrassed color took some of the gray from her face. "I'm sorry. I don't usually fall apart . . . or fall over my boss like that."

"I know."

He did, Jen realized. He had to understand that she'd thrown herself into his arms only out of a mindless need for human contact. She would have done the same if Gutierrez had stepped forward instead of Page.

Maybe.

She couldn't think about that now, though. At that moment she had more urgent matters to deal with than the shock of finding herself curled against Page's chest.

"I've got to get to the hospital. I promised Trish's folks I'd stay with her until they get there."

"I'll take you whenever you're ready," her boss said.

She threw the detective a questioning look.

"I'll check on the lab folks."

Gutierrez disappeared up the stairs, and Commodore took advantage of Jen's distraction to lick at her chin again. She set him down and regretted immediately the loss of his warm, wriggly heat. Wrapping her arms around her sides, she waited in silence for the detective to return.

He came back a few moments later with two men trailing at his heels. "We've dusted everything we think might raise a print. Colonel Page here is going to give us a set of prints, like you did, so we can eliminate them from the possible suspect's, then we're out of here."

With swift competence, the lab team printed Page. Gutierrez took a look around and handed Jen his card.

"We'll let you know what we find. I might see you at the hospital later. If I miss you, and you think of anything to add to your statement, give me a call."

She tucked the card in her jeans pocket without looking at it. When the door closed behind the detective, Jen was suddenly overwhelmingly grateful for Page's presence. The awkwardness she'd felt at finding herself in his arms dissolved, along with her not-particularly-latent hostility toward the man. For the moment she was willing to ignore the stubborn male at the core of his solid strength.

"Ready?" he asked quietly.

"I'll get my purse."

She turned and headed for the stairs. Halfway across the living room, a queasy sensation started in the pit of her stomach. By the time her foot hit the bottom tread, the tamales she'd stuffed down for dinner were threatening to make another appearance.

She stared up at the lighted landing, her fingers clenched on the ornamental iron railing. The thought of what she'd see upstairs made her feel sick.

She couldn't go up there. Not yet. Not with Trish's blood spattered across the walls and floor of the hallway. The police hadn't cleaned it up, she was sure. That wasn't their job. Jen would have to do it herself.

Later. After this awful night was over. After Trish was out of danger. Right now, though, she couldn't go up there.

When a hard hand closed around her arm, Jen jumped. Gently, Page moved her aside.

"I'll get your purse. Where is it?"

"In my bedroom. It's the one on the left."

When he came back downstairs a few moments later, deep grooves creased his taut, unsmiling face. Unspeaking, he handed Jen her purse, then held out a fleece-lined windbreaker. She slipped into it with a shiver of relief. Her skin was icy under the thin T-shirt and jeans.

To her surprise, Page scooped Commodore up and tucked him under his arm.

"We'll take him with us and leave him in the

car," he said tersely. "I've got a blanket in the trunk. He'll be warm enough."

"But I might be at the hospital awhile."

"It's better not to leave him here. I'll take him home with me, if necessary."

She started to protest, but the words got lost in a sudden, sick rush of understanding.

Commodore might get into the . . .

He might track . . .

Jen whirled, her jaw locked as tight as Page's had ever been. Later! She'd clean up the blood later! Right now she'd only let herself think about getting to the hospital and to Trish.

The ride to St. Mary's through San Antonio's darkened streets passed in silence. Neither occupant of the front seat spoke. Commodore huddled in a tight, subdued ball in the back.

This time, Jen didn't notice the MG's smooth glide or the warmth of the interior or even the colonel's proximity. She stared unseeing at the white pools made by the streetlights and prayed that the physician attending Trish would greet them with good news.

She didn't.

Her face seamed under a short cap of iron-gray hair, the doctor accepted Jen's rushed explanation of her relationship to Trish and led them to the ICU family consultation room.

"As you're aware, Ms. Scanlon sustained a severe trauma to her skull. The blow caused massive edema . . . internal bleeding. Some of the blood escaped, but enough remained within the cranial cavity to swell the upper brain stem and cerebrum and push it against the skull. We've put in a shunt to drain the swelling, but . . ."

Jen's nails bit into her palms. "But what?"

"But so far she's exhibited only minimal reflex responses to stimuli."

Despite her best efforts to control it, Jen's voice spiraled upward. "What does that mean?"

"She's in a coma. We won't know how much, if any, damage she sustained until we run more tests."

"Oh, God!"

"Do you know her next of kin?"

"Yes," Jen whispered. "Her parents. They live in Lubbock."

"Have they been notified?"

"I . . . I . . ."

Mike Page picked up when Jen couldn't finish.

"They were called about an hour ago. They'll be here as soon as they can."

Her face grave, the physician nodded. "Good."

Chapter Six

"**I**'m not happy about this."

Russ Murdock put no special emphasis into the quiet words. He didn't have to. His message came through with thundering clarity.

Andy Anderson squared his shoulders. "It was an accident."

Murdock sat silent for several moments, his pale blue eyes on his chief of staff. Anderson kept his face impassive while the seconds ticked by, measured audibly by the priceless gilt and silvered bronze mantel clock the French president had presented to Russ on the culmination of his tour as ambassador to that country. The clock sat on an ebony platform supported by crossed elephant tusks, the gift of an African dictator friendly to the U.S. whose shaky regime Murdock had saved with a quiet infusion of cash and arms.

Normally, Andy enjoyed his visits to Murdock's private office. Like everyone else who made it to the inner sanctum high atop MEI's Denver-based headquarters, he always marveled at the mix of sleek, contemporary furniture, advanced electronic displays, and priceless mementoes marking the diverse career and philanthropic interests of his extraordinary boss.

He wasn't enjoying this visit.

How the hell could someone like Murdock, who'd never fired a shot or faced an enemy in combat, convey such lethal danger with a few quiet words?

It was his money, Andy reminded himself, as he had uncounted times before . . . and the awesome brain beneath the thinning strands of rust-colored hair. That was the same powerful combination that had mesmerized Anderson from the day Russ Murdock had braved hostile ground fire to deliver honey-glazed hams and five sacks of mail to the restaging hospital where Anderson and the other casualties of the so-called peace mission to Somalia awaited airevac. Murdock had used his own private fleet to bring the mail and the meals halfway around the world . . . as a simple gesture of gratitude from one citizen. He refused to accept the thanks of everyone from the president to the legless grunt in the bed beside Andy's.

Russ Murdock might not stand as high as the top button on Andy's white shirt, but he had balls. Cast-iron balls. And a patriotism that was as awe-inspiring as it was single-minded. The day Andy had received his medical discharge from the Army, he'd hauled his scarred carcass onto a plane and flown straight to Denver. Murdock had hired him the same afternoon.

In the years since, Anderson had reached the point where he could count on both his boss's ear and his absolute confidence. In return, Murdock expected results.

"It was an accident," he said again, breaking the nerve-shriveling silence. "Our operative didn't intend to cause serious injury to the Scanlon woman, only incapacitate her long enough to exit the scene."

The explanation didn't appease Murdock. Rising, the shorter man splayed all ten fingers on the slab of polished ebony that was his desk.

"You know the rules of engagement our field units operate under. I refuse to tolerate accidents to innocent civilians. Terminate this man immediately."

Andy had anticipated the order. He'd seen the devastation the attack on Russ's wife had wrought in Murdock, both personally and professionally. Ever since that day, the president and CEO of Murdock Enterprises, Incorporated, had devoted an ever-increasing portion of MEI's commercial resources to electronic security. Similarly, he'd directed that the secret Special Programs units operate under tighter and tighter parameters. Hell, the field teams had gotten so good they could enter a hostile area in the dead of night, extract a hostage or take out a target, and be back in the States while the bewildered locals were still scratching their heads and pointing fingers.

For the most part, Andy agreed with his boss. Their tight rules of engagement left no room for accidents or needless civilian casualties. But he'd recruited this operative himself. He knew him personally, and used him for special missions on more than one occasion. He wasn't ready to lose his unique skills.

"Our man retrieved the disk and planted the virus, as ordered," Anderson said evenly. "Considering the irreparable harm he may have averted, I think you should reconsider your decision."

Murdock didn't like hearing his authority questioned, even by his trusted chief of staff. His head went back, and he gave Andy one of the cold, penetrating stares that could raise the hairs on the back of a dead man's neck.

The scarred tissue on the side of Andy's face pulled tight as he held his boss's eyes.

"All right," Murdock conceded finally. "I'll accept your recommendation this time. Just make sure our operative doesn't get careless again. And see that the Scanlon woman's family is taken care of."

Chapter Seven

"Mr. Scanlon?"

The warm, rich voice penetrated the silence of the ICU waiting room. Head back against the wall, neck aching, Jen opened her eyes a slit. Her tired gaze settled on Pierce Brosnan's profile. Or if not his, she decided after a second look, his twin's.

Inky black hair waved back from the stranger's forehead. His tanned skin formed a startling contrast to vivid blue eyes. Even this early in the afternoon, his lean cheeks and square chin showed the beginnings of a very faint and very sexy five o'clock shadow.

"I'm Harry Waterman," the newcomer said, introducing himself to Trish's father.

Donald Scanlon's gnarled, arthritic hands gripped the chair arms. Slowly, he levered himself out of the seat he'd occupied for the past twenty-eight hours, between visits to his still comatose daughter.

"Are you a friend of Trish's?"

"I'm a business acquaintance. Look, I know

this is a rough time for you and your wife. I thought it might help you to know that any medical care your daughter requires is fully covered."

Jen's heart ached for the thin, gray-haired Don Scanlon and for the woman who rose to stand beside him. The few times she'd spoken to the Scanlons over the phone, they'd always sounded so proud of Trish and of the fact that she'd become a teacher, as they had both been.

After Jen's wrenching call, Trish's parents hadn't waited for morning to catch a flight to San Antonio. They'd sped more than three hundred miles through the Texas countryside to reach their daughter's bedside. Jen had met them for the first time yesterday morning in the waiting room just outside ICU. After sharing the day and most of last night with them, she now understood Trish's devotion to her parents.

"I'm sorry," Don Scanlon said to the stranger. "I didn't catch your name."

"Harry Waterman. I'm with Western Mutual."

A sort of numbed confusion registered on the older man's tired face. "We . . . that is, Jen here . . . found Trish's medical insurance card in her wallet. She's covered through the school where she teaches, with Blue Cross."

"She took out a supplemental policy with us a few years ago to cover any costs Blue Cross doesn't."

Don Scanlon rubbed a hand over cheeks stubbled with gray. "Do you want us to fill out some forms or something?"

"No, I'll work with the hospital. That's why I'm here." Waterman's voice gentled. "I read about the attack on your daughter in the newspaper. In cases of serious injury requiring possible long-term intensive care, the hospital usually files a notice to all insurers. When I didn't hear from St. Mary's, I realized they—and you— might not know about the supplemental coverage. I just wanted to take any worry about the cost of your daughter's care off your shoulders."

Listening to the conversation, Jen could only contrast Waterman's compassion with the hassle her own company had given her over the stolen Cherokee. It was time she changed insurance companies, she decided. She'd look into it . . . after Trish got well and the days and nights stopped running together.

While Waterman engaged the Scanlons in quiet conversation, Jen drifted once more toward the hazy state that comes after an extended period without sleep. Her head tilted back against the wall again. Her lids scraped like sandpaper over burning eyes.

A telephone rang at the nurses' station down the hall. The squeak of crepe soles on tile sounded in the distance. Jen suppressed a yawn that brought with it the stinging scent of antiseptic. She'd promised the Scanlons she'd stay with them as long as she could, but she'd already missed two days of work. Major Cernecki was probably having a fit. At least tomorrow was Saturday. She didn't need to think about work for two more days. After that . . .

Maybe she should call Colonel Page and arrange to take leave next week. Or ask him about it when he came by tonight.

She didn't doubt that he would. He'd stayed with her all through that first, horrific night. Consumed with fear for Trish, Jen hadn't exchanged more than a few sentences with him. She'd felt his presence, though. He'd become her anchor in the surreal world of the ICU, where the universe narrowed to a collection of beeping monitors and time was measured in fifty-minute increments.

Jen had been allowed in to see Trish for only ten minutes every hour. The rest of the time she'd paced. Back and forth across the waiting room. Up and down the halls. Around the cafeteria, where Page had insisted on taking her just after dawn. She'd forced down a few bites of toast and a half cup of coffee and returned to the ICU.

Page left yesterday morning just before the Scanlons arrived, taking with him Commodore and Jen's promise to call if there was any change in Trish's condition. He'd returned last night, on his way home from work.

At the sight of him striding down the hall in his starched, knife-edged uniform, Jen had experienced an unfamiliar sensation. It wasn't quite pleasure. Her distress over Trish blocked anything resembling pleasure. But neither was it the combination of irritation and hostility she usually felt when she confronted her boss.

Their relationship had certainly shifted in the

past few days, Jen thought tiredly. When she had more energy, she'd have to think about the way Page had held her and let her sob all over his chest.

"Would you like some coffee?"

As it had a few moments ago, the deep masculine voice pulled Jen from a near trance. Her eyes opened and locked with Waterman's piercing blue ones.

Good grief! Up-close and personal, the man's blatant masculinity carried twice the firepower it had from a distance. He even smelled like something the angels would sing about.

Belatedly, Jen realized that the heavenly scent tingling her nose was fresh-brewed coffee. She pushed herself upright again and accepted the foam cup with the closest thing to a smile she could manage.

"Thanks." She took a sip of the steaming blend and glanced around the waiting room. "Where are Mr. and Mrs. Scanlon?"

"In with their daughter."

One more ten-minute increment. Don Scanlon would come out after seven or eight, Jen knew, to give her time to talk to Trish. She took another swallow of the hot liquid and hoped it would infuse the energy she needed to carry off a cheerful, one-sided conversation with her unresponsive friend.

Waterman settled in the chair next to hers, unbuttoning his suit jacket to give himself ease. Jen couldn't help but notice the blunt-tipped, well-manicured nails and the flash of a blue stone on his ring finger. A *big* blue stone.

"Is that a sapphire?" she asked, mesmerized by the color, which, she noted, matched his eyes.

"Actually, it's a blue diamond."

So that's where all those insurance premiums went, she thought with an inner grimace. Waterman sported a diamond the size of a basketball, while she drove a rented wreck that rattled and wheezed like a whooping crane with an attitude.

Correction. She *had* driven a rented wreck. To the best of her knowledge, it still sat, unmoving, in the parking lot in front of the Personnel Center while she paid a daily fee she couldn't afford. Reminded once again of her grievances with her own insurer, Jen tipped her companion a sideways glance.

"Does your company also provide auto insurance?"

"Sure."

"Do you have a card? I'd like to give you a call to talk about a policy."

He slipped a silver case out of his inner pocket and extracted a richly embossed card. Jen reached for it, glancing up in surprise when he held on to his end.

"Better yet," he said with a smile that curled Jen's toes, "why don't I give you a call?"

"I beg your pardon?"

"Insurance is pretty dry stuff unless you wash it down with a fine merlot, and a fine merlot calls for a steak char-grilled to perfection."

Ordinarily, Jen wouldn't have hesitated.

Gorgeous-looking hunks in tailored suits and blue diamonds didn't exactly offer her steak every day of the week. That anyone would offer her dinner when she was wearing the same faded jeans and baggy sweatshirt she'd worn for the past twenty-eight hours was a miracle in itself.

She was tempted. Very tempted. As much as she wanted to accept his offer, though, Jen couldn't bring herself to arrange a date while her friend lay just yards away, her every bodily function measured and monitored. She tugged the card from Waterman's hand. It joined Detective Gutierrez's crumpled card in her jeans pocket.

"I'll call you," she said firmly. "When Trish is better."

Trish didn't get better. Not that day.

From the grim prognosis the doctors gave the Scanlons later that evening, there was no way to predict when—or if—she would. Shattered, Trish's parents left the ICU for the hotel room the hospital had arranged for them.

Jen accepted a ride home from Colonel Page. He'd stopped at the hospital after work, as he had the previous evening. He'd also, she discovered when they pulled into the Spanish Oaks apartment complex, arranged a replacement for her rented wreck. A late-model Taurus sat in her parking space.

"I had the other car towed to the rental

agency," he said, handing her the keys. "This one's from a more reputable firm."

Jen couldn't summon the energy to worry about the cost or the fact that he'd made the arrangements without so much as consulting her. At this moment, all she felt was relief that she didn't have to depend on an undependable vehicle for transportation.

"Thanks."

"I'll bring Commodore by later," Page said, accompanying her to the door. "So you won't be alone."

Guilt flooded Jen as she fumbled in her purse for the front door key. Once Page had assured her that Commodore had made himself at home in his new quarters, she'd forgotten all about the terrier. No doubt every piece of furniture in her boss's house now carried a coating of brown and black hair just as Jen's did. Even worse, she'd bet her last dollar that the mutt had left his signature on the carpet a few times. Her sloppy, gregarious pet had probably driven every-picture-perfectly-square Page up the wall. No wonder he wanted to return him right away.

"I'll come get him tonight," she said hastily. "Just give me your address. I'll drive out as soon as I clean up and change."

"The house is a little hard to find in the dark. Why don't I wait, and you can follow me out?"

"Okay."

Once inside the apartment, Jen headed for the stairs. She paused at the foot and glanced up at the landing. Once more, dread coiled in the pit of her stomach.

"It's okay." Page's voice sounded behind her, deep and quiet and infinitely reassuring. "I called the manager. He sent in a cleaning crew."

Jen spun around. Surprise and gratitude tumbled in her chest, but she didn't express either. Instead, she frowned up at the man she'd considered her personal nemesis until a few days ago.

With his knife creased uniform, precisely knotted tie, and glittering silver oak leaves on his shoulders, Page represented the unyielding authority she'd butted against all too often. Yet he'd shown more concern, more humanity, in the past week than she'd ever thought him capable of.

How could one man be so considerate, and so damned hardheaded at the same time?

"Thank you. Again."

"You're welcome. Again."

Her fingers curled around the iron banister. "I seem to be doing that a lot lately. Thanking you, I mean."

His lips twitched. "Does that bother you?"

"I'm too tired for anything to bother me right now."

She took the bottom step, then paused. All right, maybe his consideration did bother her a little. More than a little. Sometime during the past few days, Iron Man Page had slipped out of the niche Jen had carved for him in her mind. Now, she didn't quite know where to slot him.

"It goes with the job, right? Taking care of the troops?"

He stood so close, Jen could see the faint tracery of lines webbing the outer corners of his eyes and the banked concern behind the smile in their gray depths.

"Yes, it does."

It occurred to Jen that she could use his concern to press once more for the waiver of her remaining service commitment. As swiftly as the notion came, she dismissed it. She wouldn't use Trish's injury to play on her boss's sympathies, any more than she'd arrange a date with a Pierce Brosnan look-alike while her friend hovered in some dark void.

Besides, her battle of wills with Colonel Michael Page had become too personal to drag Trish or anyone else into. Jen would wear him down, she was sure. Hopefully sooner rather than later.

Hurrying up the stairs, she paused briefly outside Trish's room. The bloodstains on the walls and carpet had disappeared. From the faint tang of turpentine that lingered in the still air, Jen guessed that the cleaning crew had retouched the walls, and perhaps replaced a portion of the carpet. They'd made Trish's bed, too. No one surveying the neat bedroom could tell that a vital, vibrant woman had almost died here.

Her mouth grim, Jen turned into her own room. Gutierrez hadn't yet turned up a clue as to the identity of Trish's attacker. As he'd told Jen over the phone, he was still working with the possibility that the break-in was tied to the theft of the Cherokee.

Thinking of her lost car, Jen shucked off the ripe sweatshirt and jeans. She'd call her insurance company tomorrow. They should have received a copy of the police report she'd faxed them. They'd better not try to give her any more bull. She wanted a replacement for the Cherokee, so she could turn in the rental . . . and call Waterman.

Scooping up the discarded jeans, Jen retrieved the two crumpled cards from the pocket and tossed them atop a pile of unopened letters on her desk. She took a quick shower, pulled on a red chenille sweater and matching red leggings, and went downstairs to tell Page she was ready to reclaim her dog.

The moment Captain Varga stepped inside his front door, Mike realized that inviting her to his house was a mistake. A big mistake.

Until now, he'd defined their relationship in strict, structured terms. She was his subordinate. His irritating, smart-mouthed subordinate. Single-handedly, she caused him more headaches than all of his other people.

Up to this point, Mike had honestly believed that he stayed on Varga's case because it was his duty as an Air Force officer to extract the best from his people, and because he felt a private, almost paternal determination to see that she faced up to her obligations.

He'd even rationalized the unexpected surge

of lust he'd experienced a few nights ago. For all her annoying traits, Captain Varga possessed a body and a flashing smile that would tempt a monk. Since Mike had no desire to join the priesthood, he'd reacted. Period.

Recognizing the danger in that brief, electric response, he'd called the red-haired accountant he'd met a few weeks ago. After stopping by the hospital last night, he'd joined her for dinner. She was smart, sexy, and intriguing. Mike had enjoyed her company and the promise of more than just company conveyed by her kiss. He'd fully intended to call her tonight and arrange another date.

But watching Jennifer drop to her knees to receive the terrier's wet, ecstatic kisses drove all thoughts of the accountant from his mind. With her hair tumbling in unruly waves down her back and her brown eyes alight for the first time in days, she looked very little like the pale, exhausted woman at the hospital and nothing at all like his mulish subordinate. The dog's leaping joy brought a flush of color to her face. The sound of her laughter filled the stone-walled foyer.

Mike hadn't heard her laugh before. The spontaneous, rippling waves of merriment generated another, wholly inappropriate reaction.

Dammit!

By the time she tucked the dog under one arm and rose, he'd recovered enough to issue a casual invitation for her to come in for a few moments.

"No, thanks. It's late. I'm sure you want to get out of your uniform and relax."

"I can relax in uniform as easily as out," he replied with a shrug.

"Somehow, that doesn't surprise me." The corners of her mouth tipped up in a quicksilver grin. "I'll admit I can't picture you in anything but starched uniform shirts and spit-shined shoes."

"During my early days stringing cable, I spent more hours than I want to remember up to my knees in mud. I didn't wear a shirt then, and certainly not shoes. Although," he admitted with a slow, answering grin, "I did spit-shine my field boots after every job."

"I knew it! Tell me, Colonel, do you wear oak leaves on your pajamas?"

"I don't wear pajamas, Captain."

The drawled rejoinder slipped out before Mike could stop it. He bit back a groan as a speculative gleam sprang into Jennifer's eyes.

A discussion of what he wore or didn't wear to bed could only easily led to the kind of sexual banter that got too many male—and a growing number of female—supervisors in trouble. He cut off the question he saw in her face before she could ask it.

"Commodore wouldn't eat the dog food I picked up, so I bought some ground sirloin to mix with it. You might as well take both with you."

"Ground sirloin!" She turned an accusing look on the terrier. "You little mooch!"

The dog grinned up at her.

"At home, all he'll eat are tamales and pizza and an occasional can of tuna fish."

No wonder his digestive track was so unpredictable, Mike thought wryly.

"Come on into the kitchen. I'll get the leftovers for you."

Jen followed him through the huge great room. Its stunning proportions awed her almost as much as its well-ordered luxury.

High above her, a wood-paneled ceiling soared to a peak. A natural stone fireplace dominated the far wall, with windows on either side that offered what she guessed was a magnificent view of the rolling Texas hills during the day. Built-in bookshelves stretched the entire length of the opposite wall and contained an impressive library of books—all precisely aligned, of course. In the center of the shelves, a drop-down desk housed a late-model PC that made Jen's mouth water.

She skirted an L-shaped hunter green leather sofa and chairs grouped around a man-sized coffee table. The sofa cushions, Jen noted, sported a film of brown and black dog hair. She didn't have the nerve to check the natural-colored Berber carpet for stains.

As she expected, the kitchen matched the great room in magnificence and orderliness. Beautiful copper pots that could only have come straight from a Turkish bazaar hung above a center cooking island. Interspersed among the pots was an array of herbs that would have done Martha Stewart proud. Jen sniffed appreciatively at the tantalizing aroma of garlic and onions and oregano.

"Do you actually use all this stuff when you cook?"

"Not all at the same time."

She hitched a hip on one of the tall oak stools in front of the cooking island while Page extracted a package of meat from the fridge. Commodore danced around, obviously thinking he was about to be fed.

"A man who cooks and buys ground sirloin for animals," Jen murmured as Page slid the meat into a plastic sack and placed it on the counter. "How can you . . . ?"

She caught herself just in time.

"How can I what?"

"Nothing."

Something that could have been amusement lit his gray eyes. "Are you subscribing to the adage that discretion is the better part of valor at this late point in your career, Captain?"

"I doubt I'll ever subscribe to that particular adage," Jen admitted. "I don't believe in holding back or bottling things up."

"So I've noticed."

Fascinated by the laughter in his eyes, she plunged ahead. "As a matter of fact, I was just wondering how you can be so human during nonduty hours, and so obstinate at work."

"I could ask you the same question."

"Me? I'm not obstinate."

A sound that hovered between disbelief and derision rumbled up from his chest.

"I've got a lot of faults," Jen conceded, a little annoyed by the way he'd turned the tables on her, "but obstinacy isn't one of them."

"No?"

"No."

Page's hands dropped to his hips. Jen's gaze dropped with them. Like Harry Waterman's, his nails were blunt-tipped. Unlike Waterman's, they weren't buffed and manicured. The knuckles on his right hand bore a tracery of white scars. Page had worked with his hands, Jen acknowledged. Worked hard.

"Then what would you call this stubborn determination to quit the Air Force?"

Her head jerked up. All traces of amusement had disappeared from his face.

"I'm not quitting," she replied. "I only want to take advantage of the same waiver provision everyone else does and get on with my life."

"Did it ever occur to you that this *is* your life?"

"The Air Force?" She hooted. "Not hardly."

"Listen to me, Jennifer. I saw your precommissioning record of employment. It read like the yellow pages. You've held more positions than a professional wrestler."

Jen's annoyance took a sharp turn into stubborn pride. She could have told Page that she'd worked two, sometimes three different jobs simultaneously to extricate herself from the sinkhole of debts Danny Varga had left her with, but she wasn't about to bring up that sorry mistake.

Her chin jutted. "So what?"

"So you've followed the same pattern in the Air Force. You've never held the same job longer than a year."

"Maybe I've never had a job that really held my interest."

"You can't change careers every time you get bored or annoyed at your supervisor or want to try something different."

"Who says?"

His pontificating irritated her as much as her belligerence set up his back. His voice took on an edge Jen recognized all too well.

"Sooner or later you have to stick with something in life."

She slid off the stool and stood toe to toe with him.

"Careful, Colonel. You're not the only one with access to personnel records. And I'm not the only one who's made a few mistakes in life."

His eyes narrowed. "You want to tell me which of my mistakes you're referring to?"

Jen could have pointed out that his divorce put him on a equal playing field with her when it came to life-sized blunders. She didn't want to throw a broken marriage in his face, however, any more than she wanted to talk about her own.

"Not particularly," she snapped.

With a few clipped words of thanks for his care of Commodore, she turned and strode out of the kitchen. The dog followed, thank God. A moment later, so did Page. She had the front door half open when his voice cut through the air like sharpened steel.

"Captain!"

She spun around. "What?"

Both her stance and her tone of voice dared him, absolutely dared him, to pull rank. They were on neutral ground now. Off duty. She didn't have to take any more snide comments or lectures or orders from Iron Man Page tonight. Luckily for him, he didn't try to issue any. He simply held out the blue plastic bag.

"You forgot the sirloin."

Jen hesitated, sorely tempted to tell him what he could do with his sirloin.

A nervous Commodore must have sensed that the hostility swirling between the two humans was about to cost him his dinner. Leaping straight up, he snatched the bag from Page's hand and scampered out the door. Jen followed a moment later.

She shoved the key in the ignition of the rental car and glowered when the engine turned over immediately. Her resentment at Page's unfair attack spilled over to the Taurus. Where the hell did he get off renting this car for her, anyway?

The long drive home calmed her down enough to recognize that pettiness for what it was. Page was only trying to help one of his troops out of a jam. She'd give him that much. And she needed transportation.

But hell would ice over before this particular troop would ask for his help again.

Or accept it.

Not two hours later, Jen tossed her silent vow to the winds. Her fingers trembling, she dialed Page's number.

"This is Jennifer," she said in a breathless rush when he answered.

"Yes?"

His voice held the same steely quality it had when she'd stalked out of his house. Jen ignored this evidence that he hadn't quite gotten past their argument. She hadn't, either, but their personal differences would have to take a back seat to a new, more urgent concern.

"Can I stop by for a few minutes tomorrow after I leave the hospital? I need to use your computer."

"My computer?"

"Mine just developed a terminal illness."

"Is that supposed to be a joke?"

"No." She glanced at the glowing, multicolored worms crawling across her computer screen. "I'll explain tomorrow."

Chapter Eight

Mike opened the door early the following afternoon with an odd combination of anticipation and wariness. He wasn't quite sure what Varga's cryptic call last night would pull him into next, but he knew her well enough by now to expect the unexpected.

She didn't disappoint him.

The creature with the loose, tumbling fall of brown hair and cheeks flushed pink from the November air bore little resemblance to the angry woman who'd stalked out of his house last night. In a tan leather jacket, black turtleneck, and well-worn jeans, she radiated an almost palpable excitement that put Mike instantly on guard. After a quick report on Trish's unchanged condition, she shoved both hands in her jacket pockets and rocked back on her heels.

"I know what the bastard was after!"

Mike stooped to greet the dog dancing around his ankles. "The bastard being the person who broke into your apartment?"

"Yes!" He was after a disk. It's the only thing . . ."

She stopped abruptly, her nostrils flaring. She sniffed the air appreciatively.

"What's that?"

"Texas Red Five-Alarm Chili, with a few of my ingredients thrown in for variation. You'll have to try some later." He included the mutt wiggling obsequiously on his back. "Both of you."

"We might take you up on that," she said, heading for the great room. Mike and Commodore followed. The dog made himself at home on the just vacuumed sofa.

"So what's this about a disk?" Mike asked.

Jennifer whirled, yanking at the buttons of her jacket. "It was in my purse. I didn't realize it was gone until last night. I couldn't sleep after our, ah, discussion, and decided to play around on my PC."

Mike hadn't been able to sleep, either. Their brief confrontation had left him edgy and restless and too damned aware of the woman on a purely physical level. She was having a similar effect on him now. Just the sight of her was enough to make him sweat a little under his V-necked blue sweater. Those damned jeans hugged her rear like a Band-Aid. When she threw off her jacket and tossed it over the back of the sofa, Mike saw that the black turtleneck hugged everything else.

"When I looked for the disk, I couldn't find it," she exclaimed, dragging Mike's attention away from the turtleneck. "I know it was in the side pocket of my purse. Whoever broke into our apartment must have taken it. It's the only thing that's missing."

"Are you sure?"

"I've been through the whole place, including all my closets and drawers." She shuddered. "That's *not* a chore I want to repeat anytime soon."

Mike refrained from comment. From what he'd seen of her room when he went up to get her purse the night of the break-in, he could attest to the fact Jennifer Varga's talents didn't include housekeeping.

"The creep also planted a virus in my system," she added, her mouth curling in disgust. "When I booted up, hordes of slimy, phosphorescent worms popped out of a can. They ate everything, including my operating system. I couldn't even try to reconstruct the records that were on the missing disk."

"You lost me. What records?"

"The ones I found among Ed James's files."

"Whose?"

"Ed James. The civilian who died."

While Mike digested that, she pulled out the chair in front of his computer and toggled the power switch. The screen fizzed to life.

"Good, you've got Internet access."

Watching her beat a staccato rhythm on the keys of his new and very expensive computer system, Mike felt a stirring of alarm.

"Wait a minute. Any chance that you might open another can of worms here?"

"Not to worry. The virus was planted deliberately in my operating system. Yours should be clean."

That "should" didn't exactly reassure Mike, but at that point the system activated with a small, shrill screech. Seconds later, a bong and a round yellow face with a downturned mouth signaled that the connection wouldn't take. Jennifer tried again, with the same results.

"Damn! I can't get on!"

"What did you expect? It's Saturday afternoon. Every kid in the country is surfing the net right now."

"We'll have to wait for the lines to clear," she grumbled.

"I've got some Corona in the fridge," Mike commented. "Let's have a beer, and you tell me what the hell this is all about."

She followed him into the kitchen, her nose twitching at the aroma of supercharged chili bubbling on the island cooktop. While Mike retrieved two bottles and a lime from the fridge, she perched on the same kitchen stool she'd occupied the night before.

Disdaining a glass, she pushed a narrow wedge of lime down the bottle neck with a tip of her pinkie. She drank her beer the same way she did everything else, Mike observed. Impatiently. In small, quick swallows. As though she had to get it down and get on to something else.

He took a satisfying pull on his own Corona, then propped a foot on the stool next to hers. "Tell me about these files."

She set her bottle aside. "I backed up Ed James's work the day he had his heart attack. I used my own system ID, thank goodness, since I couldn't access his desktop the next day using his ID, even though Major Cernecki swore it hadn't been activated."

"And?"

"And I found some records. Military personnel records. They all pertained to people in or projected for training. I noticed that the record for one, a Staff Sergeant Gerald L. McConnell, was only half-complete. When I bumped his name and social security numbers against the Master Personnel File, nothing matched."

"So he wasn't in the Air Force MPF?" Mike lifted his beer. "Maybe he's in another branch of the service, or another agency."

"That was my guess, too. I sent out a few queries, but . . ."

He lowered the dew-streaked bottle. "Are you telling me that you tapped into personnel systems maintained by other federal agencies?"

"I tried."

"Did Major Cernecki approve that?"

"I didn't ask her." She caught his sudden frown. "Okay, I might have stretched regulations a bit."

The Corona hit the counter with a thud. "Stretching Air Force regulations is one thing. Violating federal law by breaking into protected personnel systems is another."

"Well, I didn't break in, so you can relax. None of the queries I sent out took. I didn't get a single response. Not one. I can't figure out why."

The disgust on her face made Mike suspect that she'd had better luck in previous attempts. Jesus!

"I copied the records to a floppy disk and took it home with me," Jennifer continued. "I'd planned to take another look at them and run a few queries on my own, but then—"

"I'm not sure I want to hear this!"

She shot him an impatient look. "Then Trish got hurt and I spent the next few days at the hospital and now the floppy's gone and the same creep who took it trashed my system."

Mike counted to ten. Slowly. In the process, he sifted through what she'd told him. The idea that someone might have resorted to burglary to retrieve a disk containing military personnel records bothered him enough to temporarily shelve his concerns over his subordinate's attempts to hack into other systems.

"Do you remember any of the other names on the disk besides this Staff Sergeant McConnell?"

"All I remember is a tech sergeant named Rosalie. Oh, and a Captain Steve Something. I skimmed through the records so quickly I can't remember anything or anyone else."

"Did you tell Detective Gutierrez about this?" Mike asked slowly.

"I called him from the hospital, but he hasn't gotten back to me yet. In the meantime, I want to search a few civilian databases to see if I can find this McConnell character."

Instantly wary, Mike set his beer aside. "What kind of civilian databases?"

She ticked them off on her fingers, one by one. "Credit histories. DMV records. Family genealogies. Birth and death certificates in some states. Student rosters at some high schools and most universities. Employment records."

"That's all available on the net?"

"It is, if you know where to look for it."

Mike hesitated. Varga had already skirted the edge of the law. His gut instinct told him that she wouldn't need much encouragement from him to plunge over the edge.

She took a step closer, her brown eyes shadowed behind their thick lashes. "I need to do this. I owe it to Trish."

With those soft, determined words, she took Mike right over the edge with her.

She went at her task with a single-minded thoroughness she didn't seem to bring to any other facet of her life. Mike could only marvel at her skill and almost intuitive ability to extract information from the seemingly limitless public domain.

Her initial search turned up an incredible two hundred sixty-seven Gerald L. McConnells. The next step, she informed Mike, was to narrow the list to only those who currently met the age, citizenship, and other general criteria for military service and/or training.

Mike watched for a few moments, but soon got left in the cyber dust. He retreated to an armchair to catch the last quarter of the University of Texas game. Instantly the little mutt leaped from the sofa onto his lap. Resigning himself to the role of stomach-tickler, Mike and his self-appointed buddy watched UT stomp the Texas Aggies into the turf.

Jen paid little attention to the sounds behind her. Absently, her mind recorded the announcer's histrionics over a miracle touchdown. Vaguely, she heard leather creak as Page rose during a commercial break to take Commodore outside.

She didn't realize how much time had passed, though, until she entered a final key sequence and waited for the data to sort. Linking her hands behind her head to ease the ache in her neck, she swirled the chair around to find the dog once more on his back in his host's lap. Legs bent, eyes closed, the terrier quivered in pure ecstasy as Page lightly stroked its belly.

Jen's gaze caught on the blunt-tipped fingers moving slowly over the dog's flesh. When she remembered the way those same hands had held her and stroked her the night Trish was attacked, an odd sort of tightness formed in her chest. A moment later the tightness dropped without warning to her stomach.

Shocked by its intensity, she tore her eyes from Page's hands and focused on the flickering TV screen. Belatedly, she realized that the football game had given way to the evening news.

". . . no word as yet about the missing American," the announcer intoned gravely. "A source at the State Department insists that the Turkish government is cooperating in the search. Cherbanian's family can only hope that they hear from him or his abductors soon. In other news, the president . . ."

"Who's missing?" she asked, more from a need to shatter the eerie, erotic moment than from any real curiosity.

"An American doctor. He was on some kind of one-man medical mission to aid the Kurdish refugee camps."

The underlying note of disgust in Page's voice snagged her attention. "So what's wrong with aiding Kurdish refugees?"

"Nothing. But the way this guy went about it wasn't smart. He put himself smack in the middle of a political hornet's nest without the backing of either government."

At Jen's blank look, Page cut the sound with a click of the remote. Easing Commodore off his lap, he rose and stretched.

"The Turks used to be our strongest allies in the region, but relations between the U.S. and Turkey have been strained since the Gulf War."

"I thought the Turks supported the Gulf War? Our planes flew out of Turkish bases."

"They did. But at the same time we were staging out of Turkey, the CIA armed the Kurds in northern Iraq . . . over the Turks' strenuous objections. The Kurds obligingly gave Iraq hell, then, to no one's surprise but the CIA's, turned those same U.S.-supplied arms on their old enemies, the Turks."

"I can see how that might piss off our allies."

"To put it mildly. To make matters worse, the Kurds in Turkey and Iraq have joined forces to fight for a separate state."

Jen was impressed. "How do you know so much about the political situation in that corner of the world?"

"I spent fifteen months in Turkey. I got to see a lot of the country."

That explained all those copper pots in the kitchen. It also gave Jen some ammunition for a return shot after his lectures last night.

"You only spent fifteen months in Turkey? An unaccompanied tour normally lasts eighteen months. What's the matter, Colonel. Couldn't you stick it out?"

Her teasing little jab went deeper than she'd intended. Slowly, Page stiffened. The warmth in his eyes cooled to an ice-over shale.

"I wasn't on an unaccompanied tour," he replied after a long moment. "My wife and my daughter, Lisa, were in Turkey with me."

His daughter? Jen hadn't noticed any reference to a dependent in his records.

"We left the country early," he continued in a flat voice. "After Lisa's death."

Shock and remorse cut through Jen like a whip. "I'm . . . I'm sorry. I didn't know."

"Not many people do." Deep grooves formed on either side of his mouth. "It happened a long time ago."

Still reeling from the unexpected disclosure,

she followed his gaze to a brass-framed picture on the top shelf of the wall unit.

"That's Lisa. I took that picture just a few months before she died."

Jen stared up at the eight-by-ten photograph of a laughing girl with caramel-colored hair posed against the brilliant mosaics of a Byzantine church. She looked about thirteen or fourteen, young enough to mug impishly at the camera, yet old enough to have shadowed her lids in green and painted her lips a light pink.

Her heart aching, Jen brought her gaze back to the man beside her. His face formed a mask, as closed and distant as she'd ever seen it. Instinctively, she rose and curled a hand on his forearm.

"What happened to her?" she asked softly.

His eyes on the photograph, Page didn't answer for a long moment. When he did, the tightly controlled timber of his words made Jen's throat ache.

"I was stationed at Incirlik, outside Adana. Lisa seemed to enjoy Turkey. She attended an international school, and was always bringing home Brits and Germans or French kids, as well as Turks. She made friends easily. Too easily."

The muscles under Jen's fingertips twisted like steel cables. She didn't speak, didn't take her eyes from Page's rigid profile.

"She started running around with an older girl who'd had some drug problems. We talked to Lisa about it. The girl was clean, she assured us. She needed friends to help her stay that way. My wife and I believed that Lisa was too tenderhearted to reject the girl's friendship, and too smart to let drugs destroy her. We were right on the first count, and wrong on the second. She died of an accidental overdose."

"Oh, no!"

The low exclamation fell into a void. Page didn't hear it, or was so lost in his memories that he paid no attention to it.

"I had just been commissioned. I commanded a unit with detachments at sites all over Turkey. When I wasn't gone, I was up to my ass in work. I didn't see it happening. Neither did my wife."

He stared at the photograph, his eyes locked on a vision of the past that only he could see.

"Our marriage had already started feeling the impact of too many separations and too few happy reunions. Lisa's death ripped it apart."

Jen's stomach lurched as she recalled how close she'd come to throwing his broken marriage in his face last night. She was still thinking of that near miss when his attention shifted from the portrait to her.

"You remind me of Lisa sometimes."

Jen blinked. "I remind you of your daughter?"

"At times?"

He thought of her as a *daughter*? The idea threw her for a moment, but she quickly dismissed it. She possessed enough confidence in her own femininity to recognize that her increasingly complex relationship with this man contained several potentially explosive elements. None of them remotely resembled fatherly, or even brotherly love.

"I wasn't there for Lisa when she needed me," he said slowly. "I shirked my responsibilities to her, and she died because of it."

Rank lay forgotten in the starkness of the moment. Wanting only to give him the same comfort he'd given her the night Trish was attacked, Jen gently moved her hand on his arm.

"Mike . . ."

"You have so much going for you, Jen. Just as Lisa did. I hate to see you waste it."

"I'm not Lisa," she said softly. "Nor am I a teenager. What I do with my life is my decision."

The message was quiet but unmistakable. It broke the grip of Mike's memories. His daughter's face edged to the back of his mind as he focused on the one before him.

Jennifer had it right there, he thought. She wasn't a teenager. She was all woman. Mike recognized that fact only too well. He also recognized that he'd only wade into dangerous waters if he tried to correct himself at this point. He settled for acknowledging her point with a nod.

"I'll remember that."

Her mouth curved a smile that told him she wouldn't let him forget it. "Good."

Her glance went once more to the brass-framed portrait, then swung back to claim his. "She's beautiful."

"Yes, she was."

Silence lay between them for a few moments, then Mike slipped the ache that was Lisa back into the corner of his heart she'd always occupy.

With a nod toward the computer, he directed Jennifer's attention to the data painting across the screen.

"Looks like the results of your latest query have come up."

Accepting his need to change the subject, Jen turned to the computer. Like Mike, she welcomed the distraction. She felt oddly out of sync, off balance. Their relationship had taken another unexpected twist in the past few minutes, she realized, one she'd have to think hard about later. Reclaiming the desk chair, she hooked an ankle under her hips and surveyed the screen.

"Well, there they are. The final contestants."

Page took a position behind her. "What have you got?"

"Nine Gerald L.'s, but . . ." She moved the cursor down the list. "None of them with the rank of staff sergeant. This one's a security guard in Tucson. This one's in his last year of medical school."

She ran through the short list, then slumped back against the chair in frustration.

"None of these guys qualify for military training. Yet Ed James had a half-completed file showing a Gerald L. about to start training at an Air Force training center. Why, for heaven's sake? And why would someone break into my apartment to steal a disk containing that file?"

"You don't know what anyone did," Page reminded her. "At this point, you're still only guessing."

"That disk is the only thing missing from the

apartment. Trish's attacker must have taken it. But why? Why, dammit?"

A sharp, piercing yip swung their attention in the direction of the kitchen. The terrier stood in the entry, obviously impatient to get on with the most important business of the day.

"Let's talk over a bowl of chili," her host suggested. "Commodore's getting hungry."

Jen hit a keystroke command to print out the short list of names. "So am I."

She followed Page into the kitchen once more, feeling surprisingly relaxed and comfortable in the neat surroundings. She could get used to this, she mused.

"I've been thinking," Page said slowly as he dished up heaping bowls of the aromatic chili. "I know you had new locks and dead bolts installed. But I'd feel better if you got a security system."

She glanced at him sharply.

"I also think you should talk to the chief of Comm-computer Security about those files you found. Maybe the Office of Special Investigations."

"The OSI?"

"At this point, we don't know for sure that the person who attacked Trish came after your missing disk, but if he did, the OSI needs to work with the police on this case."

Suddenly Jen didn't feel quite as relaxed and comfortable.

Chapter Nine

The question of why anyone would steal a disk containing Ed James's files nagged at Jen for the rest of the weekend . . . almost as much as her reaction to Page's stunning revelation about his daughter.

By the time she drove to work Monday morning, she was no closer to finding an answer to the puzzle of the files, but she thought she understood her increasing absorption with Lieutenant Colonel Mike Page.

The knowledge that he had loved and lost a child added another dimension to the man. Recalling his face when he talked about his Lisa, Jen wondered how she'd ever considered him emotionless. Even now, her heart ached at the memory of the desolation in his eyes.

When she recalled how he'd compared her to Lisa, that ache swiftly gave way to an altogether different emotion. The idea that Page might view her in a paternalistic light had rocked Jen clear down to her Very Berry-painted toenails. She'd quickly dismissed that ridiculous notion, but she couldn't dismiss as quickly the realization that her own feelings for him were anything *but* daughterly.

Just thinking about the man could cause a spear of heat straight to her womb at the most unexpected moments, she acknowledged with a wry grimace.

Like yesterday afternoon, when he showed up at the hospital in dark slacks and a gray suede bomber-style jacket that had her fingers itching to test its well-worn softness.

And last night, when Commodore had plopped himself in her lap and rolled over for a tickle, reminding Jen of the way Page's strong hand had gently stroked the blissful dog.

And now, when the sight of the Taj Mahal looming above the morning mist generated another of her irreverent, erotic fantasies! In a lightninglike sequence, her thoughts segued from the majestic, red-roofed water tower to phallic symbols in general, to Mike Page in particular, naked and equally majestic.

Groaning, Jen clenched the steering wheel. Heat flushed through her entire body, from her chest to her toes and back up again. When it finally subsided, she admitted the truth. She'd developed a mild case of the hots for Iron Jaw Page. Maybe even a medium case.

She circled the parking lot west of the Personnel Center in search of an empty space. She passed two before she realized that identifying the problem didn't exactly resolve it. If anything, the knowledge that she lusted after her boss made her distinctly nervous about facing him anytime soon.

As it turned out, her only contact with Mike Page was at a brief meeting with the Center's chief of Comm-Computer Security. Unfortunately, Jen had clashed with the major once before over the matter of passwords. She changed hers with religious regularity. She just didn't always use the prescribed combinations of letters and digits that would allow random oversight and access to her work by the security people.

The chief listened with thinly disguised skepticism to Jen's account of the files she'd found on Ed James's desktop, then promised to check into them. She left his office with the firm conviction the task would fall somewhere around the bottom of his list of priorities.

She didn't see Page again for several days. So much work had piled up during the time she'd spent at the hospital the previous week that she stayed glued to her computer, playing catch-up. She didn't even have time to call her insurance company to work a replacement for her chopped-up Cherokee until late Tuesday afternoon. As she'd expected, the agent gave her a ration of crap.

"The Cherokee became a used car the moment you drove it off the lot."

"I know that, but I hadn't even made the first payment when it was stolen."

"Once a vehicle depreciates, fair market value doesn't necessarily equate to the loan amount."

Jen gritted her teeth. "I know that, too. So how much will you give me for a replacement?"

The agent named a figure that made her sputter with indignation.

"You've got to be kidding!"

Unfortunately, he wasn't. Scowling, Jen dropped several unsubtle hints about the Better Business Bureau and the Insurance Adjudication and Appeal Board. The agent countered with another offer. Negotiations came close to breaking down completely before they finally agreed on a figure some two thousand dollars less than the amount Jen owed on the original loan. Fuming, she hung up and vowed to call Harry Waterman the moment she closed a deal on another car.

She squeezed in a trip to the Jeep dealer on her way to the hospital Tuesday evening and picked out a flame red program model with only six hundred miles on the speedometer. Stoically, Jen sacrificed the optional Mopar six-disc CD player and aero-style splash guards to bring the price down to within a hundred dollars of the insurance company's figure.

It took most of Wednesday morning to get the new loan approved. That done, Jen arranged to have her new car delivered to the rental agency that evening. Another call to Harry Waterman resulted in temporary insurance coverage. He promised to put the paperwork in the mail for her signature within a few days.

At six on Wednesday evening, Jen turned in the rented Taurus and took possession of her new Cherokee Sport. The powerful pull of one hundred ninety horses under the shining red hood buoyed her spirits for most of the drive to St. Mary's. One glance at Don Scanlon's lined, tired face brought her back to grim reality.

"There's no change?"

Trish's father shook his head. "Mother's in with her now, helping the nurses give her a bath."

Jen joined the gray-haired professor on the couch.

"We're taking her home tomorrow," he said wearily. "It's all arranged. Mother's going to fly with her in the helicopter, and I'll drive back to Lubbock."

Jen didn't like the idea of him making the trip alone. "Why don't I drive back with you? I'd like to see Trish's hometown."

He smiled at the impulsive offer. "I'd enjoy your company, Jennifer, and you're more than welcome to visit anytime you wish. But you missed enough work last week, and, well . . ." His smile faded. "We'll probably be busy for the next few days getting Trish settled."

"I understand."

"If you don't have any plans for Thanksgiving, why don't you come up then? That's only a week away."

Jen's budget hadn't stretched to a flight to visit her parents in Florida over Thanksgiving. The short drive to Lubbock was easily within her budget.

"I'd love to come up for Thanksgiving, but

Trish will probably be on her way back to San Antonio by then.''

"I hope so."

"I know so!"

Her staunch avowal eased some of the bleakness in Scanlon's face. "You've been a good friend to our daughter, Jennifer. She's often told Mother and me how much she enjoys sharing an apartment with you. And Commodore."

Recalling some of her roommate's less than complimentary remarks about the terrier's parentage and personal habits, Jen smiled and kept silent.

"Bring him with you when you come for Thanksgiving."

"Thanks, I will."

They remained standing together for a few moments, lost in their own thoughts. On the other side of the swinging doors that separated the ICU from the waiting area, the soft ping of life-sustaining equipment marked the passing seconds. Jen suspected she'd hear that faint beeping in her dreams for years to come.

After a while, Don Scanlon sighed. "We have to face the fact that Trish may not recover anytime soon. Even if . . . even *when* she regains consciousness, she may require long-term care. You probably should think about finding another roommate."

Jen reached over and covered his liver-spotted hand with her own. "I'll wait for Trish to get better."

"Mother and I have talked about this. We'll

cover her half of the rent, and if you don't mind, I'll come by the apartment tonight to pick up some of her things. We'll hire a moving company to pack and ship the rest."

"Don't worry about that," Jen insisted. "If necessary, I'll bring it with me when I drive up to Lubbock."

"Are you sure?"

"I'm sure. But it won't be necessary!"

Even Jen's determined faith that Trish would recover faltered the next afternoon. She left work early Thursday to say good-bye to Trish and her parents. The experience wrenched her even more than she'd anticipated.

Trish's fair skin looked bloodless against her silvery blond hair. She lay unmoving as attendants wheeled her out of ICU. The metal stands holding IVs and transportable monitors rattled obscenely in the controlled quiet.

Jen was fighting back tears when Page arrived. He spoke a few quiet words to Trish's mother, who nodded and followed her daughter's gurney into the elevator that would whisk them both up to the rooftop heliport. The doors closed on her caution to her husband to drive carefully.

Jen and Mike walked Don Scanlon to the parking garage. As he'd said he would, Trish's father had loaded his car with his daughter's most personal possessions. The tip of a bright red and white pennant peeked out of one of the boxes piled in the back seat.

Suddenly the tears Jen had been holding back spilled down her cheeks. She remembered the day Trish's junior high girls had won that pennant in a citywide championship. She'd celebrated by treating them all to a feast at McDonald's, and included her roommate in the offer. Jen wouldn't forget the experience of sharing hamburgers and fries with fifteen high-spirited, giggling preteens anytime soon.

Sniffling like a schoolgirl herself, she stood beside Page while Don Scanlon unlocked his car. The door open, he turned and took her hands in his.

"Thank you for everything you did for Mother and me and Trish."

"I wish I could do more." She blinked furiously. "I wish I could help find the bastard who did this to her."

"Detective Gutierrez had promised to keep us informed of any progress on the case." Scanlon's gnarled fingers gripped Jen's. "In the meantime, you be careful."

"I will."

"We'll see you next week?"

"If I can get leave over Thanksgiving," she said with a side glance at Page.

"That won't be a problem."

After a kiss for Jen and a handshake for Page, Don Scanlon drove off. The small cloud of exhaust fumes watered Jen's eyes even more. She swiped them with the back of her hand, grimacing when clumps of mascara mixed with the residue of tears.

She lowered her arm to find Page watching her with an expression that set her stomach fluttering. The fact that she hadn't eaten all day might have had something to do with the sensation, she told herself.

"What do you say to some dinner?" she asked impulsively. "There's a Mexican cantina just a few blocks from here I've been wanting to try."

He hesitated.

"I know it's only a little after four," she admitted, "but I missed lunch. Besides, I owe you for the four bowls of chili my hound and I put away."

A smile touched his eyes. "I think it was five. Commodore cleaned up the remains. Mexican sounds great."

"Good. You can follow me, or"—she took a final swipe at her still-burning eyes and dug in her purse for her keys—"we can leave your car in the garage and pick it up after dinner. We have to come right back by here."

"Good enough." Page extracted a neatly folded handkerchief from his pocket and offered it to her. "But I'd better drive so you can repair the damage."

"That bad, huh?"

"Let's just say you could give the students at Jungle Survival School a lesson in camouflage face painting."

Trading her car keys for the square of white cotton, Jen led the way to the Cherokee. Page ran a quick, assessing eye over the vehicle.

"Nice."

"Very nice!" Jen trailed a possessive hand along the front fender. "With any luck, I'll keep this one at least long enough to make the first payment."

Climbing into the passenger side, she flipped down the mirror. The owl-eyed creature who stared back at her brought a hiccup of half laughter, half dismay.

Grinning, Page put the car in gear and followed Jen's directions to the restaurant. Ten minutes later, he pulled up into the parking lot beside a two-story brick building on Broadway. Jen fumbled with the release on her seat belt, frowning when it resisted her efforts to work it free.

"I think this thing's stuck."

He shoved the gearshift into park and set the brake. "Let me try."

His hands replaced hers on the metal clasp. He leaned toward her, his breath mingling with hers in the close confines of the car.

"I think the hasp is bent. I can't get an angle on it from this side. Hang loose and I'll try from the other side."

He came around and leaned across her to get a grip on the buckle. Jen scrunched against the seat to give him room. Even then, his arm brushed her breast and his hip nudged hers in a way that sent her breath back down her throat.

It took some doing, but he got it open.

"Better get that checked when you take it in," he advised.

She swallowed. "I will."

Shouldering open her door, Jen joined him for the short walk to the restaurant. Although it wasn't yet five, people had already started to gather in anticipation of the cantina's well-known happy hour feast. Eyeing the trendy crowd of professionals, Jen wished she'd taken time to repair more than her eye makeup.

Several stray tendrils had escaped her up-swept hair and now defied regulations by curling over her collar. Her uniform skirt showed the effects of long days at work and evenings at the hospital. She'd traded her much worn sweater for a blue zippered jacket, thank goodness, but suspected that it, too, might sport a few dog hairs.

By contrast, the man beside her could have stepped right off the cover of some slick Air Force publication. In his dark blue slacks, precisely knotted tie, and zippered jacket with its shiny lieutenant colonel's leaves on the epaulets, he turned more than one female head when they walked into the restaurant.

The scent of mesquite smoke and sizzling fajitas greeted them. Jen started salivating even before the hostess led them past a vast, open-flame grill to a spacious booth. She was still breathing in the mouthwatering aromas when their waiter appeared with a heaping basket of tortilla chips and individual bowls of salsa.

His eyes widening, he glanced from Jen to Page and back again.

"Evening, Captain Varga. Colonel Page. How are you doin'?"

Smiling in recognition, Jen accepted the menu he offered. "I'm doing fine, Sergeant Watts. I didn't know you worked here."

"Been here for almost six months," the NCO replied.

The fact that a noncommissioned officer who worked the night shift at the Center's comm center night need outside employment to make ends meet didn't surprise Jen. The Air Force didn't exactly pay union-scale wages.

"I can recommend the shredded beef taco plate," Watts said helpfully. "It's our specialty."

Jen shut the menu with a snap and handed it back to him. "Sounds good."

"And you, sir?"

"Make it two."

"Yes, sir."

A small smile playing at her mouth, Jen watched the NCO cross the room.

"What?" Page asked.

She reached for a chip and dunked it in the salsa. "I pity anyone trying to carry on a clandestine affair in this town. With five military bases in the area, and half of the troops moonlighting as taxi drivers and waiters and motel clerks, no one could get away with anything."

Page eyed her across the table. "I guess it's a good thing we're not trying to get away with anything."

Suddenly the spicy dip set the back of Jen's throat on fire.

"I guess so," she croaked, reaching for her water glass.

Mike cursed as two bright spots of pink appeared in Jennifer's cheeks.

There was no excuse for putting her, or himself, in this situation. He shouldn't have let Jen's tears get to him at the hospital. He sure as hell shouldn't have agreed to her impulsive suggestion of dinner, hoping it would take her mind off Trish's wrenching departure.

Normally, he wouldn't think twice about sharing a meal with a coworker. He and Jennifer weren't co-anything, however. He was her boss, and this was *not* official business. No matter what his rationalization for joining her for dinner, he knew there was more behind it than supervisory concern. He also knew that unprofessional conduct with a subordinate could kill a supervisor faster than a speeding bullet these days, a fact General Daniels hammered home repeatedly. It could also, he realized grimly, mean the termination of Jennifer's already shaky career . . . the same career Mike was determined to salvage.

Christ! How had personal and professional relationships become so damned complicated in recent years?

Well, he'd brought her here and he didn't intend to ruin her dinner by reflecting on his own poor judgment. He'd just make damn sure he kept the appropriate space between him and Jennifer Varga for the foreseeable future.

The future hit him right between the eyes exactly two hours later.

Lazily replete after three shredded beef tacos, charro beans, rice, and cognac-flamed flan, Jennifer suggested Mike drive the Cherokee back to the hospital to reclaim his car. She sprawled comfortably in the passenger seat and used the interval during the short ride to set the station buttons on the as-yet-unprogrammed radio. When Willie Nelson's "Angel Flying Too Close to the Ground" cut through the cackle of static, she joined the country singer in a husky duet. It was a close call as to who sounded more nasal, Mike decided, but Willie at least stayed on key.

Smiling, he pulled into the empty space beside his MG and shoved the gearshift into neutral. Jennifer broke off her singing to thank him for joining her.

"My pleasure. But I wish you'd let me pay."

"I told you, I owed you for the chili. And for the rental car, not to mention arranging to have the apartment cleaned." She tugged at the release on her seat belt. "You can pick up the tab next time."

Mike frowned. This was as good a time as any to make it clear there couldn't be another time.

"Jennifer . . ."

"This thing is stuck again. Can you believe it? I just took delivery yesterday and already something's broke."

Thoroughly irritated, she yanked at the strap.

Mike came around the vehicle to help her. Opening her door, he leaned down at the precise moment the buckle came free.

Off balance, Jennifer lurched sideways. Her forehead slammed into his chin with enough force to knock him backward. He grabbed at her arms to keep from tumbling onto his ass, but his weight proved far more substantial than hers. Instead of halting his fall, he took her with him.

He landed on the pavement.

She landed on him.

Jen would always blame what happened next on the lingering effects of the cognac-based flan and the laughter that shook the body pinned under hers. It started in his stomach, rumbled through his chest, and ended in a rakish, heart-stopping grin.

She grinned back, then, without thinking, lowered her head and covered his mouth with hers.

Chapter Ten

As kisses went, the one Jen laid on Page wouldn't qualify as the world's smoothest.

Her precarious position atop his chest put their chins and noses at awkward angles. She had to grab at his jacket with both hands to maintain her balance and keep her mouth locked with his. In the process, her knee came down between his legs and hit the concrete. It hit more than the concrete, if the way he grunted and jerked to one side was any indication.

Despite these minor inconveniences, the few, breathless moments their mouths joined shoved Jen's medium case of the hots straight into the supersized category. Page lay still beneath her at first, held immobile either by surprise or a rigid, self-imposed restraint. Then her teeth knocked his, and he lifted a hand to anchor her head more firmly. His fingers threaded through her hair, tugging it free of the plastic clip, and his mouth slanted on hers with a driving force that took Jen's breath away.

The man certainly knew how to kiss, she thought before she gave up thinking altogether in favor of simply feeling. His lips were hard and hungry on hers. Giving as much as they took. Heat curled like ribbons of fire along every one of Jen's nerve endings.

She felt him harden against her hip, and a fierce, singing exultation sent her temperature up another dozen or so degrees. Any lingering worries that Page harbored even vaguely paternal feelings toward her disappeared in a haze of sensual delight.

Afterward, she could never decide whether she raised her head first or he clamped his hands on her forearms and lifted her off his chest. She only knew that she was still reeling from his shattering response when he rolled to his feet, bringing her with him.

Under the blue jacket, his chest rose and fell. His breath rasped in the echoing emptiness of the hospital's parking garage. For the life of her, Jen couldn't think of a single thing to say. She settled for digging her fingers into his sleeves and waiting for her lungs to stop wheezing.

She might have known he'd recover first. His arms dropped. Slowly, his face hardened into familiar planes and angles. Jen didn't wait for the ax to fall.

"Sorry 'bout that," she offered with as much savoir faire as she could muster. "For a moment there, I forgot we were in uniform."

His jaw worked. "For a moment there, so did I."

Jen started to suggest that they didn't need to make a big deal out of a simple kiss, but the words stuck in her throat. In the first place, there was nothing simple about that kiss. In the second, it was already a big deal. She knew as well as Mike Page the consequences of what had just occurred.

For all her casual attitude toward rules and regulations, she couldn't dismiss the fact that they'd just engaged in behavior the Air Force would term conduct prejudicial to good order and discipline.

Subordinates just didn't go rolling around on garage floors with their supervisors. It not only wasn't professional, but it could be grounds for a court-martial.

"So what do we do now?" she inquired, eyeing his shuttered, ice gray eyes.

He stared down at her, his face a mask. Here it comes, Jen thought, bracing herself. In the past few days, she'd grown so used to *Mike* Page that she'd forgotten how formidable *Colonel* Page could be. She felt a sharp, lancing regret that the sensual magic of their kiss was about to take a direct hit.

He was silent a moment longer. Then he bent and scooped up the keys that had tumbled onto the concrete.

"You don't do anything. I'll take care of it."

Jen snatched the keys out of the air. " 'It?' I don't think I care for the sound of that."

His mouth twisted wryly. "Sorry. Poor word

choice. What I meant was I'll take care of getting one of us transferred off the team."

"Transferred!" She had expected him to go all stiff and military on her, but she hadn't anticipated anything quite this drastic. "Transferred where?"

"To another duty section. To another building. To another organization on the other side of the base, if I can swing it."

"Look, let's not do anything too drastic. Why not just settle this matter between us?"

He sliced her a hard glance. "How do you propose we do that?"

"I don't know. Agree we crossed the line. Vow never to sin again. Go our separate ways." She cocked her head. "You could approve my waiver request and the whole problem disappears."

"Running away again, are you?"

The low taunt hit home.

"I'll tell you what," she suggested, bristling. "You do whatever you think is right and I'll just pretend the past few moments didn't happen."

Page took a step forward, crowding her against the Cherokee's fender. "It's too late for pretending. Way too late. You know that as well as I do."

As exasperated now as she was aroused a few moments before, she tipped her head, refusing to give an inch. "Is that so?"

"Yes, that's so."

"Yeah, well, you do what you have to, Colonel."

She started to shove past him, but his palms slammed down on the hood, caging her.

"I will."

Jen lifted her chin. "Don't you think we're making too much of something that won't ever happen again?"

For the first time since they'd picked themselves up off the cement, his eyes lost their gunmetal sheen. They drifted down her face, settled on her lips, and slowly reclaimed her gaze again.

"What makes you think it won't happen again?"

Jen's heart jumped into her throat. While she was still trying to force it back into her chest cavity, he set it bouncing again.

"When you're no longer my subordinate, Captain, maybe we'll finish what you started here."

Holy shit! At this point, Jen wasn't sure *what* she'd started.

She wanted to finish it, though. Badly. So badly her knees shook and her mouth went dry and it took everything she had to summon a cool nonchalance that surprised her almost as much as it did him.

"When I'm no longer your subordinate, Colonel, we'll talk about it."

Mike drove in to the base early Friday morning. He knew what he had to do. He just didn't want to do it.

He'd been brought to San Antonio to head

this special team. He wasn't even halfway through his look at what it would take to modernize today's systems for tomorrow's Air Force. He knew darn well that he was more necessary to the effort at this point than Jennifer Varga.

He also knew that he could quietly arrange her transfer off the team. Eyebrows would no doubt raise, especially since he'd taken Captain Varga on against the recommendations of several senior officers familiar with her past performance. Removing her from the team, he suspected, would only add another questionable mark to her record. And when she moved, she would press her new supervisor to approve her waiver.

Either way, Jennifer lost her job, and the Air Force would lose an extremely bright, highly skilled officer who hadn't yet reached her full potential.

Unless . . .

After a night of long consideration, the only solution Mike had come up with to the situation was to talk to the commander who'd brought him to San Antonio to head the team.

Mike had worked for General Daniels at the Pentagon, when she headed the Congressional Liaison Office. The woman was tempered steel under the petal soft magnolia charm that came as naturally to her as breathing. Her petite stature and melodious voice had lulled more than one staffer on the hill into mistaking her for a lightweight. They'd only made that mistake once. Mike had seen her take a Senate staffer apart, rearrange his attitude toward women in general and military women in particular, and put him back together without raising her voice or losing her cool, unruffled smile.

She'd entered the Air Force in the early sixties, during the height of Vietnam, when women were still restricted to support fields like nursing, administration, intelligence, personnel, and communications. She'd chosen personnel and made it to the top by being twice as good at her job as any of her peers or predecessors. Now one of the highest-ranking women in the Air Force, she was on track for another star.

If anyone would understand the need to challenge and direct a woman with Jennifer Varga's talents, General Daniels would.

Mike didn't look forward to the interview, however. He knew his boss would chew him up and spit him out in little pieces for getting involved with a subordinate.

Fortunately or unfortunately, he soon discovered that he might have to wait longer than he'd anticipated to talk to his boss. General Daniels had left last night for Washington, her exec informed Mike, for a no-notice meeting with the three-star director of personnel.

"They're all in a flap at the Air Staff about this doctor who got snatched," Captain Hayes confided.

"The one in Turkey? I heard about him on the news."

"His wife really raised a stink at the White House. Claimed the U.S. isn't doing enough to

find him. In the meantime, the Turks are getting
hot over what they feel is pressure from us to
negotiate with the Kurdish separatists holding
the guy. Iraq's gotten into the act, too, claiming
that the Turks made unauthorized incursions
into their territory to look for the guy. The situation went from bad to worse overnight."

Mike hitched a hip on the exec's desk. "Let
me guess. In the natural order of things, the
whole mess rolled downhill fast. The president's
national security adviser put pressure on the Joint
Chiefs. The JCS tasked EUCOM to beef up its
presence in the area, particularly the communications assets. EUCOM wants additional equipment and personnel to augment its assets. In the
meantime, the Senate Intelligence Oversight
Committee is demanding to know why the hell
the intelligence establishment they've poured
billions into can't locate one American doctor."

"You got it in one," the captain replied with
a grin. "You've done this drill before?"

"Several times," Mike concurred. "I also spent
some time in Turkey. I know how volatile this
situation is. I suspect the boss won't be back for
a day or two."

"Well, she's meeting with the DCS Comm-
Communications and the J-1 folks this afternoon
to review the Air Force augmentation tasking.
She told us she'd call after that to see whether
we needed to clear her calendar for tomorrow,
too. Do you want to talk to the deputy?"

Mike shook his head. He liked and respected
the high-ranking civilian who served as the sec-

ond-in-charge of the Center, but he reported directly to the general.

"I'll wait."

Jen spotted Page's restored MG in the parking lot when she drove in to work an hour later. Its dark green finish, canvas top, and classic lines were hard to miss. Briefly, she wondered how his meeting with the general had gone. She figured she'd find out soon enough.

Impatience to put the artificial barriers of their rank and positions behind them nipped at her like Commodore in his more playful moments. After a restless night reliving those hot, searing moments on the cold concrete, she wanted more. Much more.

Funny, she thought, pulling off her hat and stuffing it in her desk drawer. A week ago, she would have sworn she didn't even like Page!

Now . . .

Now, she lusted after him. A lot. So much so that she stifled a groan when a brief glance at the Center's management information system revealed that the general was on temporary duty in D.C. The system showed no estimated date of return.

She and Page had the whole weekend ahead of them before they could . . . finish.

For once Jen didn't mind the repetitive nature of her task on the team. She clicked through screen after screen, analyzing errors and recommending system changes, while her mind roamed free. A part of her thrilled at the knowledge that a transfer to another duty section would remove the barriers between her and Mike Page. Another part chewed over the possibility that a new supervisor might not prove so recalcitrant about her request for separation. In fact, after Page's interview with the general, that request might very well get expedited. Disconcerted, Jen realized she wasn't quite as anxious to leave the Air Force as she had been a week or two ago.

She was still puzzling over her change of heart when she drove home that night. With her mind drifting between her enigmatic boss, her new, confused feelings about hanging up her uniform, and the undeniably pleasurable feel of her new car under her hands, Jen negotiated the traffic that clogged Loop 410. She opened the front door of her apartment to be greeted by an ecstatically yipping Commodore and the shrill of a phone.

Scooping the dog up under her arm, she dodged his slurpy kisses and answered the phone with a breathless, laughing hello.

"Hi, Jennifer. This is Harry Waterman."

"Hi, Harry. I hope you're not going to tell me there's a problem with the insurance on my car! I told my other agent to take a flying leap into his disclaimers and deductibles."

Rich baritone laughter sounded across the line.

"No, no problems. I'm just calling to see if you're going to be home this evening. I thought

I'd deliver your policy instead of mailing it, and get your signature on the spot."

"Now that's what I call service!"

"At the same time, I could make good on my offer of steak and a fine merlot."

Strangely, the offer didn't even tempt Jen. The idea of steak and fine wine with Harry Waterman didn't hold the same appeal as chili and beer with Mike Page. Calling herself all kinds of an idiot, she begged off dinner and suggested he stop by for a drink instead.

He sounded flatteringly disappointed, but took her up on the offer of a drink. Hanging up, Jen took Commodore out for a quick walk around the complex.

While the terrier happily sprayed every upright object in his path, Jen marveled at the difference one kiss could make. One kiss, and one growled promise to finish what they'd started on the floor of a parking garage. How could any woman enjoy dinner with another man, even a Pierce Brosnan look-alike, with that kind of promise hanging over her head?

When Commodore had marked his territory to his satisfaction, Jen mixed dried dog food with a can of his favorite tuna packed in spring water and left him to chow down. Upstairs, she tossed her purse on her desk and shucked her uniform piece by piece as she traversed the bedroom to the closet. Her panty hose and bra quickly added to the trail on the floor. She pulled on her favorite jeans and a bright red velour sweater.

Deciding that Pierce/Harry deserved fresh makeup, if not her company for dinner, she spritzed a few puffs of Giorgio and went to retrieve her cinnamon-red lipstick from her purse. She was digging through the jumble in her bag when her eyes caught on the list of names taped to her still-defunct computer.

There they were. Her nine Gerald L.'s. So far, the data security folks hadn't come up with anything more that would tie one of them to Ed James. Jen wasn't even sure they'd tried.

What was the connection? she wondered for the hundredth time. Why had Ed had this man's name and half-completed file on his computer? She might never know, Jen admitted. Any more than she'd know why someone broke into her apartment to retrieve a disk containing that file.

She probably should've tossed the list, but she wanted to do just a few more queries when she got her hard drive back. The thing was still in the shop, being dewormed. She hadn't had either the time or the cash to get it out.

Maybe she ought to talk to Harry about a personal property policy, one that would cover computer-eating phosphorescent worms.

She hit him with the question as soon as he walked in.

"High value property items?" Shoulders covered in a fine merino wool lifted in a negligent shrug. "Sure. What do you need . . . ?"

Commodore interrupted with a low growl.

"Behave yourself!" Jen admonished.

Harry hunkered down to let the dog sniff at

his hand. The blue diamond on his ring finger winked in the light. Black gums still quivering, Commodore submitted to a brief tug on one lopsided ear.

Harry rose, dusting his hands. Not a dog lover, Jen decided.

"What was it you wanted covered?" he asked politely.

"My computer. A virus infected my hard drive last week. It's at the computer doctor now. I need medical insurance in case it gets sick again."

Recalling her decision to check out the company a bit more, Jen tacked on an amendment. "I just want a price quote right now. I'm not sure I can afford personal property coverage."

His blue eyes glinted as they drifted over her face. "I'm sure we can come to terms. Give me the model and serial numbers, and I'll fax you a quote."

"The computer's in my bedroom. I'll have to go get the numbers."

Somewhat to Jen's surprise, Waterman followed her upstairs. He paused at the open door to the bedroom opposite Jen's and surveyed the bare walls.

"How's Trish?"

"I talked to the Scanlons last night. She made the trip home okay, but there's no improvement in her condition."

"Too bad," Harry murmured.

Jen's jaw squared. "It's more than too bad. It's criminal."

He trailed her across the hall. "Have the police come up with any leads?"

"No. Not yet."

Sighing, Jen pulled an old dry-cleaning ticket from the assorted scraps of paper on her desk. She jotted down her computer's make, model, and serial number and turned to hand it to Harry. He stood close behind her. Too close. Feeling a bit crowded, Jen edged to one side.

After an infinitesimal pause, his gaze lifted from the computer to lock with hers. He nodded to the scrap of paper clutched in her hand.

"Is that the serial number?"

"Yes."

He tucked the dry-cleaning ticket in his pocket. "I'll send a quote."

Back downstairs, Jen offered him the promised drink. Harry toyed with his scotch, barely sipping it, while she reviewed the policy he'd brought for her signature. She signed the original and closed the door behind him a few moments later.

His mind churning, Waterman drove through San Antonio's streets to his rented southside condo.

How the hell had Varga come up with that list taped to her computer? Who were all those Gerald McConnells? He slammed a palm against the steering wheel. Why wouldn't the stubborn bitch quit?

The dark miles sped under the tires. With an exercise of self-discipline, he brought his fury under control. He'd been in the business too long to allow emotion to interfere with his thinking.

Varga must have run some queries that slipped past the watchdogs in Special Projects. She couldn't have found anything significant, or their built-in safeguards would have triggered an alarm. Still, Anderson wasn't going to like this.

The prospect of having to report this latest development to MEI's chief of staff raised a light film of sweat under Harry's silk turtleneck.

Chapter Eleven

The call from Waterman caught Andy Anderson in the middle of an operations planning session.

His blood thrummed with the adrenaline charge that came with the prospect of action. Even the damaged nerve endings under the scars on his face tingled. He thrived on the challenge of serving as Russ Murdock's chief of staff, but coordinating Special Projects operations like this one fed his soul.

Surrounded by a small select staff, he sat at the head of a conference table in the nerve center buried deep under MEI's Denver headquarters. Phones buzzed in the background. A printer whirred out the latest intelligence data. Lights blinked as computer-generated status boards flashed the status of team members across the country.

Three green.

Two still red.

Five amber, awaiting further instructions.

The secure signal from the White House had

come in less than an hour ago, and already three team members were good to go. The other two still had eleven minutes to verify their availability. If they hadn't responded affirmatively by then, Andy would give their backups the green light.

He'd anticipated the White House signal, of course. The moment news of Dr. Cherbanian's abduction had flashed across MEI's twenty-four-hour, worldwide news service, Andy had put one of Special Projects' top researchers to work. Using contacts at CIA and State, as well as MEI's own extensive network of sources, the researcher put together a brief that, Andy would bet, rivaled the one that the president himself had reviewed.

Russ Murdock had gone over the brief three days ago and directed Andy to devise a contingency ops plan. The coded signal from the White House confirmed the possibility that the plan would soon translate into action.

Andy's eyes narrowed on the map of Turkey projected onto the floor-to-ceiling screen. A few clicks of a button in the console magnified the target area, a mountainous plateau where the borders of Turkey, Iran, and Iraq converged. As the screen zoomed to a startlingly detailed visual, Andy swore silently.

He'd seen worse target areas for the type of operation they envisioned, but not many. Peaks reaching elevations of fifteen thousand feet rose from barren, lava-covered high plains. Snow blew across the slopes in white, swirling gusts.

Andy suspected the bitter cold would cut like a knife.

He enlarged the satellite image once more, until a tumble of stone huts huddled at the base of one of the peaks came into focus. Smoke curled from the chimneys of two, he saw with intense satisfaction. Highly sensitive intelligence sources had tipped the U.S. that the Kurdish rebels who'd kidnapped Dr. Cherbanian had taken him to this remote mountain stronghold just inside the Iranian border. Apparently, the rebels were still in place.

The terse communiqué from the White House indicated negotiations with the guerrillas had all but broken down. The Turks adamantly refused their demands for release of Kurdish rebels in Turkish prisons. The Iranians shrugged aside U.S. requests for intervention. Frustrated, the rebels had demonstrated their deadly seriousness by cutting off their captive's right hand. Dr. Cherbanian's wife had come apart at the seams when she viewed the grainy videotape of his mutilation.

This was the kind of mission that fired the resolve of every member of Special Projects select headquarters cadre, Andy included. They weren't sending in a team to eliminate a Latin American drug lord, or to arrange the "accidental" death of an American arms dealer financing his exotic lifestyle by under-the-table sales to enemies of his own country. They were going in to rescue an innocent citizen caught in a political crossfire.

Every member of the team knew that the United States government wouldn't, couldn't, claim them if anything went wrong. They'd carry no identification. Their fingerprints wouldn't register with any national data bank. They'd been specially selected so that their coloring and skin tone would match those of the population in the area. They'd either fight their way back to the rendezvous and extraction point, or they'd die anonymously on that high, rocky plateau.

The phone on the console in front of Anderson buzzed. His eyes still on the satellite image of the mountain huts, Andy lifted the beige instrument.

"There's a call for you, sir," the comm specialist informed him.

"From Mr. Murdock?"

His gaze lifted to the bank of clocks over the screen. It was just past seven in D.C. Russ should have left for dinner at the White House by now.

"No, sir. From our operative in San Antonio."

Anderson frowned. He'd left strict orders for no interruptions unless the call was urgent.

"Put him on."

A series of discreet clicks activated the secure voice link. Andy listened to the brief report without comment. A slow twitch started to pull at the scarred skin on one side of his face.

When the operative finished, Anderson made a swift, unilateral decision. This wouldn't wait until Russ returned from D.C.

"Take care of it. Do it quietly, and quickly."

Chapter Twelve

Jen couldn't sleep.

She'd just drift off, then Commodore would twitch and pull her awake. The little stinker had crept under the covers sometime during the night and now lay curled in the bend of her knees. Every so often his whole body would twitch in the throes of some doggy dream. Blunt claws would scratch against the back of her leg. Once or twice he yipped.

Between those high-pitched little cries, silence lay like a thick, oppressive blanket over the apartment. With nothing to distract them, Jen's thoughts returned again and again to a deserted parking garage.

She'd just dozed off for the third or fourth time when the dog jerked once more. Only this time, he came wide awake. Nosing his way out from under the covers, he planted his front legs on Jen's chest. His wiry little body quivered from front to back as he stared at the black patch of hallway beyond the open bedroom door.

Jen shifted to ease the bite of his nails on her T-shirt-covered breast. "What's the matter, fella?"

His lips curled back. A low, menacing growl raised the hair on the back of Jen's neck. Her gaze flew to the door. The utter blackness of the hallway defied penetration.

Oh, God! Had the intruder come back? Didn't criminals always return to the scene of the crime?

Fear exploded in her chest and raced through her body with paralyzing intensity. For a moment Jen couldn't move, couldn't think. Her breath rustled like dried, broken leaves in her throat. Another long, spine-tingling snarl from Commodore snapped her paralysis.

Shoving him off her chest, she threw the covers aside. Her bare toes dug into the carpet as she spun in a frantic circle, searching the dark corners of her room for a weapon. She would have sold her soul at that moment for one of Trish's softball bats, or even a tennis racket.

Suddenly the night erupted.

With a volley of ear-piercing barks, Commodore flew off the bed and raced into the hallway. A flash of red split the darkness. Jen heard a yelp of pain and the thud of a small body hitting the floor. She grabbed the back of her desk chair just as a darker shadow appeared in the doorway. With a strength born of terror and mindless, ravaging fury at the assault on her dog, she swung the chair at the patch of darkness.

The metal base smashed into the shadow on an upward swing. The intruder staggered and crashed into the wall of the hallway. A muted pop sounded. Another red flash stabbed through the darkness at a crazy angle. Jen swung again,

slamming the chair into flesh and bone and dry-
wall. Her target hit the wall with a thud and
slid to the floor.

Jen dropped the chair and groped behind her for
the light switch. Fear clogged her nose and throat.
Her wildly shaking hand passed over the wall plate
once, twice, before finally connecting with the
button.

Light flooded the hallway. A male figure
wearing black slacks and turtleneck and ski
mask lay sprawled at her feet. He'd toppled
sideways, onto his stomach, one arm flung out,
the other trapped under him.

Nearly sobbing, Jen looked beyond him to where
Commodore lay in a spreading crimson pool.

A low moan yanked her attention back to the
figure at her feet. Shed had only a fraction of a
second to decide her next move. She could roll
him over to get his gun, or smash the chair
down on his head again.

She groped for the toppled piece of furniture
at the same instant his free hand shot out and
grabbed its base. She tried to yank it away, but
he held on with surprising strength, groaning
and shaking his head to clear it.

Jen wasn't about to wrestle with an armed
man, even one still woozy. Scooping Commodore up in her arms on the run, she raced down
the stairs and across the living room. Fingers
slick with the dog's blood, she fumbled with the
deadbolt on the front door.

"Come on!" she panted, scrabbling for a grip
on the slippery metal. "Come on!"

Fear sliced like razor blades into her throat and lungs. Her heart ricocheted around her rib cage like a bullet. Finally, she wrenched the door open and tore outside. As she ran, she searched the windows of the surrounding apartments for a glimmer of light, some sign that the occupants were awake. She found none.

She didn't dare stop to hammer on a neighbor's door. Her night visitor could appear at any second, before she woke anyone with her pounding or shouting. She had to get away from him. Hide, or . . . or flag down a passing car.

Clutching Commodore to her chest, she raced across the parking lot and cut a path through the dark, silent apartment clusters toward Harry Wurzbach Road, just fifty or so yards away. Stones cut into her bare feet. The cold night air combined with her terror to raise goose bumps on every inch of her body.

Harry Wurzbach Road stretched dark and empty in either direction. Nothing moved. No cars. No trucks. Not even the leaves of the live oak trees lining either side of the four-lane thoroughfare. Three or four hours from now, Jen thought on a rising note of hysteria, rush-hour traffic would line up bumper to bumper!

She raced along the edge of the asphalt, heading for the twenty-four-hour convenience store where she sometimes stopped for gas. She'd taken less than a dozen steps when headlights beamed behind her.

Sobbing with relief, Jen spun around. The oncoming light blinded her. Eyes squeezed almost shut against the glare, she waved an arm madly over her head. She could only pray that her wild appearance wouldn't frighten off the late night traveler. Not everyone would stop for a woman who appeared suddenly out of the night, her feet and legs bare, her thigh-high sleep shirt stained with blood, clutching an animal to her breast.

Thankfully, the vehicle slowed to a halt a cautious twenty or so yards away. Pinned by the brilliant white light, Jen flung up an arm.

A window whirred down. After what seemed like a small eternity, a reedy, teenaged voice came to her through the darkness.

"Do you, uh, need help?"

The careful, almost reluctant question brought an instant, croaked reply.

"Yes! Please!"

She stumbled forward, panting with relief and accumulated fear. Her rescuer climbed out of his car. Thin, gangly, almost enveloped by an oversized blue and gray Dallas Cowboys starter jacket, the boy met her halfway.

"Someone broke into my apartment and tried to kill me," Jen gasped. "We've got to call the police."

"I've . . . I've got a cell phone in the car."

"Thank God!" She rushed past him. "We can call on the way."

"The, uh, way where?" he asked, tripping after her.

She spun around and opened her arms. The little dog lay across them, limp, furry, motionless.

"I've got to get him to a vet."

The boy gaped at Commodore for all of two seconds, then whipped into action. He peeled off his jacket and draped it around Jen's shoulders. Yanking open the rear passenger door, he dived inside to retrieve a wadded-up basketball jersey.

"Here, let me wrap him in this."

Jen surrendered her burden and scrambled into the front passenger seat. Holding out her arms, she demanded the return of her pet.

"You drive. I'll hold him."

The boy hesitated. "He's dead, ma'am."

"No, he's not! Give him to me, dammit, and drive!"

An hour later Jen sat huddled on her living-room sofa. Wrapped in a warm, woolly blanket, she listened numbly while Detective Gutierrez conferred with the uniformed officers who'd responded to the scene.

She couldn't seem to stop shivering. Every time she got a grip on herself, something would set her off again.

Like the police officer's kindness in getting the blanket for her.

Or the memory of the small, bloody bundle wrapped in a silver and black San Antonio Spurs basketball jersey that the vet took from her, his face grave.

Or the hesitant, stammering farewell from her rescuer. The teen, Jimmy Something, had given the police his statement and now had to pick up the bundles of newspapers he delivered before school each morning. Clearly uncomfortable with his role as a hero, the boy shifted from one sneakered foot to the other.

"Uh, I've gotta go."

Jen summoned a weak smile. "If you leave your jacket, I'll get it cleaned for you."

"That's okay. My mom will wash it."

"I'll get your address from the police. To send you another Spurs jersey."

"Yeah. Thanks."

"Thank you. For stopping. For everything."

"You're welcome."

He left with a hurried, nervous good-bye to the police officers.

A few minutes later, Detective Gutierrez claimed the chair next to the sofa. Dark whiskers stubbled his cheeks and chin. Under his tan sport coat and loosely knotted Mickey Mouse tie, his shirt looked as tired as he did. He'd been at another crime scene when her call came in, he'd told her on his arrival.

"The lab folks are on their way."

Jen nodded.

"I doubt we'll lift any prints this time, either, but it's worth a shot. You sure you didn't see his features, or any distinguishing marks?"

She shook her head. "It happened so fast. He was wearing a mask. One of those ski masks you pull over your head. And gloves."

"What kind of gloves? Those thin, plastic ones, like a med tech might wear?"

"Black gloves. Everything he had on was black."

Gutierrez rasped a palm across his chin. "How about his voice? Did he have an accent? Use any peculiar phrases?"

She gave him the same answer she'd given the uniformed police officers. "He didn't say anything."

"Nothing?"

"Nothing. The only sound I remember him making was a groan." She lifted her head, her eyes savage. "I hope I broke the bastard's face. Into *very* small pieces."

"I hope so, too. We've got a call in to Central Dispatch to run a check of the hospital emergency rooms."

Jen could tell Gutierrez didn't hold out much hope that the check would produce results. He started to rise, then hesitated.

"You've been through a lot here, Captain. Maybe you should stay with friends for a few days."

Her heart thumping, Jen met his steady gaze. "You think he'll come back, don't you?"

"I think it's a possibility," he replied carefully. "At this point, we don't know what he was after. He could've come back for something he missed the first time, and your dog spooked him into firing those shots. Or he could have come after you."

"Why? Why would he come after me?"

"Maybe he gets his kicks from attacking women. Maybe he figured you were alone and thought you'd make an easy mark." The detective's thick, black brows slashed into a straight line. "Maybe he thinks you know more about those files on the missing disk than you do."

Nausea churned in Jen's stomach. The same possibility had tumbled through her mind the past hour. Hearing it aloud made her feel sick.

"What good will staying with friends for a few days do? If it's me he wants, he'll find me."

"We just need to buy a little time."

"Time for what?"

"For Ballistics to ID the bullet we dug out of the wall. And the one that wounded your dog."

"His name's Commodore."

"Commodore. Right. We also need time to run a check of the hospitals. To canvas your neighbors. Maybe, just maybe, someone saw something."

She clutched at the folds of the blanket wrapped around her shoulders. "If they didn't? If the hospitals don't report anyone with facial injuries?"

"Then we need to talk again about why someone might be trying to kill you."

Jen didn't reply. She couldn't.

"Call a friend, okay?" He pushed himself to his feet. "We'll take you wherever you need to go when the lab folks finish up here."

Jen nodded, still trying to absorb the fact that she needed sanctuary. A safe place away from her own home.

She thought of the friends she could call. Between them, she and Trish had a large circle of acquaintances, but they weren't especially close. Only one place she could think of offered the kind of sanctuary she craved. Without conscious thought, an image formed of vaulted ceilings and dried spices hanging next to copper pots and strong, safe arms. She rocked back, pierced by a shaft of need so strong it left her dizzy.

"I'll call Mike Page," she told the waiting detective.

"Your colonel?" His dark brows slashed together. "Let me call him first. Check out his alibi for tonight."

Stunned, she stared up at Gutierrez. "Check out his alibi?"

"It's my job, Captain."

Jen stumbled to her feet, almost tripping over the blanket. The terror of the past few hours gave way to one absolute certainty.

"I'm scared and confused and not real sure about what's going to happen next in my life, but I *am* sure of Mike Page, Detective Gutierrez. That wasn't him tonight. I would have recognized him. Even masked."

After a long moment, he nodded. "Yeah, well, give him a call. As soon as the lab folks do their job and you get some things together, we'll escort you wherever you want to go."

The first hint of dawn painted the sky purple when the two-car caravan pulled into the driveway of the sprawling stone house. Lights blazed from the brass lamps on either side of the porch and seeped through the wood-shuttered windows.

Jen reached into the back seat for her carryall

and climbed out of the Cherokee. Gutierrez fumbled with the passenger side seat belt.

"It sticks," Jen said apologetically.

"No kidding."

After a few moments of fiddling, the catch finally gave. He shouldered open the door and walked around to her side. Rubbing the back of his neck wearily, he repeated the promise he'd made her earlier.

"You'll hear from me as soon as I get the ballistics report."

His gaze slid to the man who opened the front door and strode outside.

"I don't like this," he said quietly. "I wish I had some way to verify Colonel Page was here all night, as he told you when you called."

"I don't need verification," she reiterated.

She needed exactly what she got a moment later . . . the feel of the strong, sure arms that wrapped around her waist and pulled her into his warmth.

For a few moments, a few precious moments, the terror of the night receded.

All too soon, Mike gripped her arms and eased her away, his body as tense and tight as she'd ever seen it. He curled a knuckle under her chin and tipped her face to the light.

"You sure you're all right?"

She nodded, her throat too tight to speak. Shooting a swift glance at the police car that pulled away, he took her carryall from her hand and ushered her inside. She followed the comforting scent of fresh-brewed coffee into the great room. Jen didn't realize how desperately she craved an infusion of caffeine until that moment. Folding her arms across her stomach, she waited for him to join her.

Page was only a step or two behind. His face etched in sharp lines, he dropped the carryall on a chair and looked her over. She felt a string of tiny pinpricks as his gaze moved from her face to her throat to her chest and lower. It snagged on her sockless feet thrust into untied sneakers, then flew back to her face.

"I'm sorry about Commodore, Jen," he said quietly. "Is he going to make it?"

"The vet said he lost a lot of blood. It's going to be touch and go for a while. He'll . . ." She swallowed. "He'll call me if there's any change. I need to let him know where I am."

"Give me his number. I'll do it."

She still couldn't speak about the terrier without a sting of tears, but listening to Page's deep, sure voice as he made the call, Jen felt her world slowly tip back to a more level plane. He was so solid. So real. So far removed from the horror of the past few hours.

He'd pulled on jeans and a sweater, as Jen had, but the similarities stopped there. She couldn't imagine what her hair looked like. Tears had left tracks on her cheeks and chin. Traces of dried blood still itched in the crooks of her elbows.

Page, of course, was as well groomed as always. From the glisten of damp in his short sandy hair, Jen suspected he'd showered after her call. He'd even shaved, she mused.

"Do you want some coffee?" he asked quietly. "Or something to eat?"

"I need coffee. I could use food."

"Come on, then. You can tell me what happened over a cheese omelet."

To Jen's surprise, the telling came easier in the brightly lighted kitchen. Given the choice between peeling and dicing onions or crumbling blue-veined goat cheese into a small bowl, Jen opted for crumbling. She soon regretted the choice. The cheese's rank aroma overpowered even that of the onions. She sincerely hoped that the stuff tasted better than it smelled.

It did, thank God. In fact, the light, flavorful omelet melted in her mouth. She sat next to Mike at the tall, tiled counter and devoured every bite. Her mind and body restored, she talked and he listened while dawn slowly took the shadows from the corners of the kitchen and infused the copper pots hanging above the cooktop with their cheery gleam.

His body seemed to grow more taut as hers relaxed. Once or twice, Jen saw his fingers flex on his coffee mug.

"The police found nothing?" he asked, incredulous, when she finished. "No clue to his identity or why he came back?"

"Just the bullets. One from the wall and one from . . . from Commodore. Gutierrez is pinning all his hopes on the ballistics report. He should have it in a day or two."

"We need to make sure the Air Force investigators know about what happened tonight," Mike said grimly. "And what happened the night Trish got hurt. I should have called them sooner, when you first told me about those damned files."

"We told the computer security chief," she reminded him.

"I should have called the OSI," he repeated, his jaw working.

The small movement distracted her. Fascinated her. As though it had a will of its own, her hand lifted. Slowly, she traced the strong, square line.

His eyes blanked at her touch. For a brief, confidence-shattering moment, Jen thought she'd made a mistake. That his welcoming hold had been intended to comfort, and nothing more. Then the tension in his neck and shoulders visibly eased. Confidence flowed back into Jen, along with the need that had brought her to him in the first place.

She trailed her fingers along his throat. His skin felt warm and alive under her touch. Her thumb edged along the line of his jaw.

"I thought this might crack during one or two of our more stormy sessions."

"I thought it might, too."

His mouth turned into her palm, and Jen drew in a swift, ragged breath.

"Mike."

"What?" The word was a whisper of warmth against her skin.

"I don't want to wait," she said softly. "Not until you see the general. Not one more hour."

His head lifted. At the look in his eyes, her heart stalled, stopped, and restarted with a little kick.

"No more waiting. What happened tonight changed all the rules, Jen."

She smiled for the first time in what felt like a lifetime. "From here on out, there are no rules."

He pushed off the tall kitchen stool. His thumbs found the niche under her jaw she'd just explored on his. Tilting her head back, he brushed a thumb across her lower lip.

"You sure you're okay?"

"I'm sure." She drew her tongue along the trail he'd just traced. "How about you? Are you sure you want to . . . ?"

"Finish what you started in the garage?" A smile began at the back of his eyes. "I want . . . I want so bad it hurts."

Still smiling, he bent and took her mouth with his.

His kiss soothed and gentled and slowly consumed. The terror and heartache of the past few hours receded. Jen closed her eyes, letting his touch and his taste bring her home. When she opened them again, her heart pounded and a slow heat curled in her belly.

She saw the same heat reflected in his eyes. How had she ever thought them cold? she wondered, sliding her arms around his neck. She arched up to meet him, or maybe he bent down to taste her. She wasn't sure, and didn't care. All she knew was that she gloried in the hunger that stirred to life at the roam of his hands over her body.

Slowly, deliberately, he divested her of sweater and jeans and sneakers. Wrapping his hands around her waist, he lifted her off the stool and deposited her on the counter. The cool tiles under her nylon-pantied bottom didn't distract her for a moment. She was too absorbed in the hot, hard male before her.

His sweater came off and hit the kitchen floor with a disregard for good order that thrilled Jen. Her belly clenched when his hands went to his zipper and it looked as though his jeans might soon follow. She put both palms on the tiles behind her, her pulse pounding with anticipation. The sight of the rust-colored blood caked in the crease of her right elbow brought her racing heartbeat to a sudden, shuddering stop.

Once more, the horror of the night reached out to grab her. The memory of Commodore's limp weight in her arms brought a rush of hot tears to her eyes.

"Mike, I . . . I need a shower."

His hands stilled on his zipper.

"I'm . . . I'm sorry." She snatched up her sweater and scrubbed at the red stain. "It's . . . It's just . . ."

Mike took the wadded garment from her hand. "I know what it is, sweetheart. Let me take care of it."

Jen thought he intended to show her to the master bath.

Or maybe even carry her.

Never, ever, in her wildest imagination would she have dreamed that neat, orderly, every-uniform-crease-knife-edged-perfect Page would calmly turn on the tap, take up the hand spray, and proceed to bathe her right there in the middle of the kitchen.

It was the most soothing, calming, erotic experience of Jen's life.

Lukewarm water trickled over her shoulders. Tiny rivulets ran between her breasts and down her belly. Mike's free hand followed the water's path. Infinitely gentle, he stroked and slicked and washed away the caked blood.

It had been a long time since Jen had submitted to someone's care like this. For endless moments she didn't think. Didn't allow herself to fear. She only felt.

Yet even as she reveled in his tenderness, she had a foretaste of the aggressive male he held rigidly in check. Solid, unyielding, every muscle taut and glistening from the mist thrown up by the spray, his body blocked her instinctive attempt to close her legs to the water trickling between her thighs. She squirmed on the wet tiles, half embarrassed by her exposed position and wholly, breathlessly aroused.

"Relax, Jen. Just relax."

She tried. She really tried. Her head went back. Her eyes closed. She drank in the exquisite ripples of sensation generated by the warm water and his skilled hands. Her skin tingled from the spray. Her nipples peaked at his touch. Then he leaned down and replaced his hands with his mouth, and pleasure streaked from her breasts to her belly and back again.

"I can't relax when you do that," she gasped.

He lifted his head. His breath heavy and almost as fast as her own, he stared down at her.

"Do you want me to stop?"

"No! Please, no!"

The hand spray clattered against the counter. His arm went around her waist, holding her still while he teased her aching nipple with his tongue and teeth. His other hand found her core.

Jen stood it for as long as she could. Bright starbursts of sensation were painting across her eyelids when she pushed at his shoulders.

"Wait!" she panted, wiggling upright.

"I thought . . . we were done with waiting?" he ground out.

"We are. But I don't want to just take."

She shaped his shoulders, his pecs, the ridges and recesses of his rib cage with eager hands. His skin felt slick and hot under her fingertips. When her palms slid lower, his stomach hollowed. He filled her fist, heavy and hard and totally magnificent.

"Mike," she got out through watery kisses.

"What?"

"Did you . . . ?"

He pulled her wet panties down her thighs, her calves. They hit the floor with a soft plop. His jeans followed a moment later.

"Did you ever . . . notice how . . . the Taj . . . ?" She broke off, gasping, as he pushed himself against her.

"The Taj what?" he breathed into her mouth. "Never mind!"

Already straining with raw need, Mike almost lost it completely when Jennifer spread herself for him. None of his sternly suppressed erotic fantasies about Captain Varga came close to matching the uninhibited sensuality of the living, breathing woman. Like everything else she did, she gave pleasure without holding anything back, and took it with greedy impatience.

He primed her, keeping the thrust of his fingers gentle and steady. She squirmed and gasped and primed him, as well, with hands that weren't quite as steady but far more explosive. They were both at the breaking point when he pulled back. His chest heaved. Water and sweat pooled on his skin.

"We need protection," he growled. "Let me get something."

"No!" She looped her arms around his neck. Her legs went around his waist. "I'm okay."

A slide of her hips brought them off the counter and onto Mike's. The penetration electrified them both. Her stunned eyes met his for an instant, then their brown depths filled with a slow, dawning delight.

"I'm better than okay, Colonel. Much, much better."

Chapter Thirteen

Three hours later, Mike gently disengaged himself from a tangle of blankets and long, curved female limbs. Naked and feeling more satisfied than he could remember in a long, long time, he rose.

They'd have to work on their rhythm, he thought, smiling down at the woman sprawled in unconscious abandon across his king-sized bed. Jen's uninhibited, greedy bursts of passion had blown off the top of his head. Several times. Mike had more staying power, though. He'd set the pace the last time, taking it slow and lazy and long. She'd dropped into an exhausted sleep about ten seconds after her climax.

No wonder. His smile disappeared. She'd been up half the night, dodging bullets.

His satisfaction imploded in on itself and slowly disintegrated. He headed for the shower, reliving once again those moments just after her call had pulled him from sleep in the small hours of the morning. As it had then, fury coiled in the pit of Mike's stomach.

A faceless, nameless bastard had attacked Jen. And Trish. And Commodore. If Mike got his hands on the son of a bitch, he wouldn't hurt anyone again.

He lifted his face to the stinging pellets. Grimly, he acknowledged his own culpability in the predawn attack. He should have gone to the OSI, as he'd originally intended. He shouldn't have let the Comm-Computer security chief palm him and Jen off with a promise to "look into" the unexplained files.

Mike slapped a palm against the faucet, cutting off the water. Only Jen could verify that those files ever existed in the first place. Stupidly, he'd stood by and watched while she'd put herself in danger by playing amateur sleuth. He'd rectify that mistake today.

He let her sleep until noon.

In the interim, he made some calls. The first was to the commander's exec, who informed him the boss had returned from D.C. late last night and was now preparing to meet with her senior directors to brief them on the worsening situation in Turkey. Mike's call caught her on her way to the conference room.

Briefly, Mike explained the urgency for his request to meet with her as soon as possible. General Daniels had been around long enough to understand that there was a hell of a lot more behind the reason Captain Varga was now staying at Mike's house than either of them wanted to talk about over the phone.

"Get in here," she ordered tersely.

"Yes, ma'am."

After that short, uncomfortable conversation, Mike contacted the Office of Special Investigations. The agent on call arranged to meet with both Mike and Jen after their session with General Daniels. Mike dropped the receiver into the cradle. Blowing out a slow breath, he went to mop the kitchen.

That task done, he held a coffee mug under Jen's nose and prodded her gently.

"Jennifer. Wake up."

She pulled the covers over her head.

"Come on, Jen. Wake up."

"Go away."

Mike ignored the muffled grumble. Another prod brought a more colorful response. He ignored that, too. Finally, she dug her way out from under the covers. She sat up, clutching the sheet to her chest with one hand while she shoved her hair out of her eyes with the other. The look she shot him wouldn't qualify as friendly in anyone's book.

"For future reference, I think you should know that I am *not* a morning person."

"Noted," Mike replied calmly. "And it's not morning. It's just past noon."

"Of what day?"

Smiling, he handed her the mug. "Saturday."

She took a cautious sip, frowning at him over the rim. "So why am I naked and you're wearing your uniform?"

"Because I've got to go in to the base." He took

the mug out of her hands and set it on the nightstand. "And, as much as I'd like to keep you naked and in my bed for the foreseeable future, you've got to get dressed and go with me."

"Why?"

"Why are we going to the base? To talk to General Daniels and the OSI."

"No. Why do you want to keep me in your bed?"

Coming from another woman, the question might have sounded coy. From Jen, with her brown eyes disconcertingly direct and her forehead still faintly furrowed, it communicated a frank need to know.

Mike answered as honestly as he could. "You don't think we've finished yet, do you?"

She regarded him steadily for long moments. Too long. Mike was starting to feel the need to demonstrate just how unfinished things were between them when her mouth curved.

"Well, at least we got things off to a pretty good start."

He couldn't argue with that.

Jennifer's smug little smile faded as she reached for the phone on the bedside table. "Before I go anywhere, I have to call the vet to check on Commodore."

"I already called. He's holding his own. The doc thinks he's going to make it."

Her brown eyes swung toward him, relief and joy making them huge. "Really?"

"Really."

"Thank God." She blinked away a sheen of

tears. "He's a pest at times . . . Well, most of the time. But I've kind of gotten used to him."

"The doc says he wants to keep him a week or so. The bullet took out part of his liver."

"I hope you told him to lay in a good supply of tuna fish."

"I recommended ground sirloin. Now get moving, Captain. We've got a meeting with the general in half an hour."

She sat straight up. "You're kidding, right?"

"Wrong. You've got fifteen minutes. I put your carryall in the bathroom."

Showered and more or less groomed, Jennifer appeared a short time later in her blue slacks and a wrinkled uniform shirt that made Mike wince.

"Hey, I wasn't the one who made this appointment," she reminded him. "You didn't leave me enough time to get myself in inspection order."

He held out her blue jacket. "Just out of curiosity, how long does it take?"

"I'm not sure," she retorted, grinning. "I haven't passed one of your inspections yet."

They walked out to a cold, drizzly day. The locals kept assuring Mike that San Antonio winters consisted of normally mild seventy-degree days. He'd yet to see those assurances hold true.

"I'll drive," Jen said, bypassing the MG Mike had backed out of the garage earlier for the flame red Cherokee parked in the circular drive. She unlocked the doors and tossed her purse in the back seat. "I want to enjoy this new car smell as long as I can."

She might as well enjoy the trip to the base, Mike reflected. He suspected she wouldn't enjoy the rest of the afternoon.

She didn't.
Nor did Mike.
They got to the Personnel Center a little before one. Even on a football Saturday afternoon, the parking lot across the street from the three-storied stucco building contained a scattering of vehicles. Jen pulled the Jeep into a vacant slot and grabbed at her purse. In her haste, she spilled the contents across the back floor mat.

Mike took one look at the collection of lipsticks, laundry tickets, candy wrappers, old lottery stubs, and jelly beans and shook his head. Ignoring him, Jen scooped most of the contents back in her purse one-handed.

"All right," she said, slinging the strap over her shoulder. "Let's get this over with."

Pushing through the double glass doors, they verified their IDs to the security police officer on duty. A few moments later they faced the Center's commander.

Even after her late flight back to San Antonio and the half day she'd already put in at the center, Faith Daniels looked as contained and as collected as she normally did. Her jet-black hair neat and smooth against her creamy skin, she listened without comment to Jen's description of the files she'd discovered on Ed James's computer. When she finished, the general ran through the same litany of questions Mike himself had when she'd first told him about the files.

Yes, Jen replied, she'd accessed the Air Force Reserve and Air National Guard personnel systems without proper authority.

No, she hadn't obtained permission to query other federal databases.

Yes, she understood the ramifications of her actions.

"Good!" Daniels raked her with a hard look. "Now let's talk about these attacks. I want to make sure I have this straight."

Jen shot Mike a quick, relieved glance. He nodded reassuringly, but knew they hadn't hit the real wall yet.

"Someone broke into your apartment," the general reiterated. "Injured your roommate so severely she's still in a coma. Took a floppy disk."

"Yes, ma'am."

"This same someone came back last night."

"The police think it was the same someone."

The general's green eyes narrowed. "To do what? He already had this disk. If he just wanted to hurt you, as he hurt your roommate, he could have done that the first time. Why did he come back?"

"I've asked myself that a hundred times since last night. All I can think is that he somehow found out about the queries I ran on Mike's . . ." She corrected herself immediately. "On Colonel Page's computer."

No one in the room missed the small slip. Daniels didn't say anything. She wouldn't, Mike knew. Not to Jen.

"More unauthorized queries, Captain?"

Jen flushed at the stinging question. "No, ma'am. They were legit."

"With what result?"

"I came up with a list of nine Gerald L. McConnells."

"Nine," Daniels echoed, her black brows arching.

"Nine, but none of them with the grade of staff sergeant and none on active duty in any of the services. I'm hoping the OSI can narrow the list down and find a connection to the Air Force that I might have missed."

"Do you have this list?"

"Yes." She flipped her purse open and fished around inside. "Oh, hell! It must have fallen out with the jelly beans. It's in the car. I'll go get it."

She sprang up and hurried out of the office. Daniels stared after her for a long moment. Mike let the silence stretch. He knew what was coming long before the general threaded her fingers together and pinned him with a penetrating stare.

"All right. I'm going to sit here and listen. You're going to explain why a man with your intelligence and outstanding record is doing something as monumentally stupid as sharing a house and a computer and, it appears, a hell of a lot more with a captain in his direct chain of supervision."

Mike shifted, squaring his shoulders. He'd anticipated this moment since Jen fell onto him in the parking garage. He'd intended to avoid it by arranging her transfer to another duty section before he went off the deep end and took her with him, but events—and their mutual need last night—had ripped that intention to shreds.

"I don't have any explanation, ma'am. I broke the rules."

Daniels waited for more. When none was forthcoming, her mouth thinned. "That's it?"

"That's it. I'm not making any excuses. I take full responsibility for what happened."

"What, exactly, happened?"

Mike had always kept his private life private. Even after Lisa's death, when well-meaning friends and stricken relatives had tried to offer him and his wife comfort, he could never bring himself to talk about his private agony.

Putting his relationship with Jennifer into words came almost as hard. Particularly since that relationship still left a great deal of room for interpretation by both parties involved and anyone who heard about it.

"I've had dinner with Captain Varga several times." His voice rock hard and steady, he added the kicker that could end his career. "She stayed with me last night."

"Are you saying you slept with her?"

"Yes."

Faith Daniels was far too professional to let loose with any scorching comments about over-sexed, underbrained idiots. She thought them, though. Mike saw the disappointment on her face before she masked it.

"As of this moment, Captain Varga is no longer a member of your team."

"I understand."

"We'll talk about your status as head of the team when I've had time to think about this more."

Mike leaned forward, his face as implacable as the general's. "Right now I'd rather you think about the fact that Captain Varga seems to have stumbled onto an unexplainable little hiccup in the Military Personnel Data System. So unexplainable that some bastard may be trying to kill her to keep it that way. She's the one I'm worried about."

The general drummed her fingers on her desktop. "So I see."

Unaware of the small, intense drama taking place in her absence, Jen hurried out the front glass doors. The cold drizzle that hit her in the face made her wish she'd remembered to grab her jacket. She dashed across the street and wove through the parked cars to the brick red Cherokee.

A quick search through the jumble on the back floor mat turned up the folded, crumpled list. Shivering in the cold, Jen skimmed its contents a final time. In a way, she hated to turn her sketchy findings over to General Daniels and the OSI. This had become her personal quest, almost her mantra. She wanted to finish that quest more than she could remember wanting anything in a long time . . . except maybe another session in the kitchen with Mike Page.

Smiling, she reached for the door handle. She was just about to swing a foot out when the opposite door was pulled open. Startled, Jen jerked around.

Surprise detonated into instant, heart-stopping shock.

The man who slid into the passenger seat couldn't pass for a Pierce Brosnan look-alike now, she thought wildly. His face sported a startling array of black, blue, and green bruises across one cheek and most of his forehead. His right eye had puffed completely shut. Bloodred streaks colored the other. Jen might not even have recognized him if not for the blue diamond winking on the hand that aimed a lethal-looking gun at her midriff.

"Har . . ." Harry? That was you . . . last night?"

He didn't answer. He didn't have to. His bruised face answered for him.

"And . . . And Trish? You were the one who hurt Trish?"

"Close the door, Jennifer," he said gently. "We're going to take a ride."

"I'm . . . I'm not . . ." Swallowing, Jen fought a superhuman battle over the fear arcing through her. "I'm not going anywhere with you."

He raised the gun a few inches, until it pointed just under her right breast. The barrellike silencer gave it a long, hideous reach.

"I'm afraid I must insist."

She dragged her eyes from the evil-looking weapon to his bruised face. "Are you . . . kidnapping me?"

"Just drive."

The swelling around his nose and eyes effectively disguised any expression, but his soft reply told Jen the terrifying truth.

He was going to kill her. The certainty crashed over her with the force of an avalanche. He didn't want to shoot her here, in the parking lot of the Personnel Center. Someone might drive by at any moment. But he would if he had to.

Like a swimmer going under a rushing, ice-filled river, Jen fought her way through waves of panic. Her only hope was to buy time. To play along with him. Maybe she could throw herself out of the Cherokee while it was moving. Or drive it into a tree.

Shaking with fear and cold, she pulled the door shut and stabbed the key at the ignition. Metal scraped against metal once, twice, before she finally got the key in. In her mindless terror, she twisted it too far. The Cherokee's engine whined a grinding, high-pitched protest before subsiding into a well-mannered growl.

Her heart slammed so loudly against her ribs that she didn't hear the seat belt warning bong out its message. Harry did. Holding the gun steady, he pulled his belt around him.

"Buckle up, Jennifer. We wouldn't want the cops to stop us for not wearing seat belts . . . any more than we'd want you to have an accident."

The malicious irony added the first edge of anger to Jen's throat-clogging fear. With a look of loathing, she fumbled the seat belt around her. Her shaking fingers closed over the gear-shift and pushed it into reverse.

She wet her lips. "Where are we going?"

"Straight out the front gate. I'll tell you where to turn after that."

The Cherokee lurched into drive, its tires spinning as Jen's foot slipped on the accelerator.

"Keep to the speed limit!" Waterman ordered sharply. "And don't try any foolish, stuntman heroics. I'll put a bullet between your ribs and take the wheel before anyone even notices you're dead."

The threat cut through Jen's strangling fear like the slash of an ax. To hell with driving into the side of a building, she thought savagely. She'd hurdle him straight into hell if she had the chance.

"What do you want with me? Why did you hurt Trish?"

"Trish was an unfortunate accident. We'll see that she's taken care of. You . . . ? You've become a military necessity."

"What?"

"Just drive," he repeated.

She drove, her mind and stomach churning. Randolph's tribute to fallen warriors rose ahead of them. Drizzle turned to liquid silver the four aircraft sculpted in flight, with a missing wing-man to symbolize those who didn't return from battle.

Jen wouldn't return, either, unless she won this battle. She hadn't paid much attention to strategy and tactics in the Squadron's Officers' course she'd had to take, but a faint recollection of needing to know your enemy penetrated her whirling mind.

She slanted him a swift, sideways glance. His tan camel's hair sport coat, black turtleneck, and charcoal slacks didn't exactly fit her mental image of an assassin's uniform.

"Is your name really Waterman?"

"My name doesn't matter."

She searched desperately for a clue to his identity, his reason for stalking her. "How did you get on the base?"

Something that could have been amusement flickered in his bloodshot eye. "I drove on, right behind you and Page."

Her lungs squeezed in a thin, excruciating breath. "You know Mike Page?"

"I do now. I had to ID the occupant of the house the police took you to last night."

The steering wheel jerked under her hands. "You followed me?" she gasped incredulously. "And the police?"

"I tracked you." His small smile underscored his contempt for her police escort. "You got away from me for a while last night, but I made sure I wouldn't lose you again. I planted a transmitter under the wheel casing of your nice new Cherokee before the police arrived at the apartments."

"You bastard!"

In her agitation, she jerked the wheel. The Jeep swung on the slick pavement, tires squealing. A second later, the silencer dug into her ribs with bruising force.

"Slowly, Jennifer."

"Okay!" she gasped. "Okay!"

The knifing pain in her side eased. Sweating now with fear and grim determination, Jen steered the Jeep around Randolph's main circle and down the flag-lined boulevard. Her eyes darted right and left, seeking help.

The cold rain and Saturday afternoon football games cut the normal weekend traffic to a mere trickle, she saw, her stomach sinking like a stone. A few cars came at them on the opposite side of the divided boulevard. Only one car traveled in the same direction some distance ahead. Its rear tires threw up a spray that obscured the passengers from Jen . . . and her from them.

Desperately, she wondered if she could get enough speed to catch up to and somehow signal the other driver. Imperceptibly, she added pressure to the accelerator. To her swamping disappointment, the car ahead flashed a turn signal and pulled off the main artery. The outbound lanes stretched endlessly ahead, empty of all signs of life.

Except for the guard at the front gate!

Jen's knuckles went white on the steering wheel. Squinting through the mist, she made out the silhouette of a security policeman inside the tile-roofed guard post. Her heart pounding, she gauged the distance to the gate.

A hundred yards. Seventy. Fifty.

If she floored the accelerator at the last moment and swung wildly, she could . . .

"Don't," Harry warned softly. "If you alert that security cop, I'll have to kill him. I don't want to. The chief won't like it, but I will if you force me to."

"Chief?" Jen almost lost control completely. "What chief? Who are you, Harry? Why are you . . . ?"

A loud clanging broke into her strident cries. Jen jumped half out of her skin, gasping when she matched the noise to the flashing red lights that came on just ahead.

The railroad crossing! That's all she needed! A train traveling the tracks just outside the gate. One of those long, lumbering freight trains that took forever to pass. She'd have to sit in a puddle of sweat and fear beside Waterman while railcar after railcar sped by in a blur.

No, she wouldn't!

A draconian plan burst into her brain just as she was breaking to a halt a few yards from the descending black and white barrier. She didn't stop to think. Didn't try to gauge her chances. Gave no thought to whether the tires would spin on the slick pavement. Acting on pure adrenaline, she stood on the accelerator.

The Cherokee shot forward.

"What the fuck . . . ?"

That was all Waterman got out before Jen spun the wheel and sent the Jeep skidding sideways. The passenger side crashed into the lowered railroad barrier. Instinctively, Waterman threw up his arm to protect his face.

The metal barrier shattered the window and crumpled the upper frame. At the moment of impact, Jen stomped on the brake and hit her seat belt release. As the Jeep squealed to a stop astride the tracks, she threw open the driver's door. Waterman slammed back in his seat, snarling with fury.

Jen fell out the door at the same instant the gun spewed a flame of red. A line of fire razored across her shoulder. She hit the train tracks on one knee and one hip and rolled under the chassis.

Blood pounding, ears ringing from the deafening clang of the warning signal, Jen crabbed frantically toward the rear of the vehicle. She had to make it to the guard gate before Waterman freed himself from the tangle of metal barrier and twisted frame. Above her, the Cherokee rocked with his violent movement.

Suddenly thunder rumbled above the clanging signal. The tracks under her stomach began to vibrate. Scraping her burning cheek on the pavement, Jen craned to look up the tracks.

The single, stabbing light in the distance stopped her heart.

It restarted an instant later with a painful lurch. Panting, pawing, scrabbling for a hold on pavement and iron rails, Jen clawed her way to the rear of the car.

A whistle screamed.

"Varga! Jesus, Varga!" Waterman's frantic

shout cut through the cacophony. "The seat belt's stuck!"

The thunder grew to a roar. Someone shouted in the distance. The rough concrete tore the skin off Jen's palms as she shoved out from under the chassis.

"Jennifer! Help me!"

Her breath stabbing at her throat like a serrated knife, Jen crouched below the line of fire through the back window.

"Throw out the gun!" she screamed, her eyes glued to the oncoming train.

The whistle shrilled again. Louder. Closer. Drowning out her words, and the sound of footsteps pounding the pavement. Jen didn't hear the guard's approach until he yelled in her ear.

"Move!"

He yanked at her, trying to drag her away. Jen clutched at his arm with both hands.

"Keep down!" she cried. "He's got a gun!"

The ear-shattering screech of metal brakes hitting the rails tore away her frantic warning. Horrified at the sound, Jen looked over her shoulder at the onrushing bulk of the red and yellow engine.

"He can't stop!" the blue-suited guard yelled, dragging her with him. "Get back!"

Jen clawed a his hold. "Wait! There's someone in the car!"

With a burst of strength, the guard threw her and himself through the air. They hit the pavement with stunning force a single heartbeat before the world exploded.

Chapter Fourteen

Rafael Gutierrez hitched his hands on his hips and gave a long, silent whistle.

"You sure that freight train didn't run right over you? You look even worse today than you did yesterday."

"Thanks," Jen muttered.

She pushed herself up a few inches in the hospital bed, wincing when the small movement tugged at the stitches in her shoulder.

"Use the buttons, Jen."

Mike's calm instruction issued from the far side of the room. Arms folded, hips propped against the windowsill, he stood silhouetted against the bright morning sunlight streaming in through the miniblinds.

She had a vague memory of his arrival in the emergency room yesterday afternoon, shortly after her own. Demerol had already blurred the edges of her mind as well as her pain, but she registered enough of his fierce, unguarded expression when he first saw her to tuck it away in a corner of her heart for future examination.

When the Demerol had worn off, she'd faced a chorus of questioners. Two OSI agents had appeared in her room just moments after she'd been wheeled out of the ER. Gutierrez had appeared an hour later. Even General Daniels had shown up, her expression as fierce as Mike's.

Jen had recounted every detail, repeated every word, retraced every yard of her short journey with Harry Waterman, until the mounting pain in her shoulder and her skinned hands had resulted in Mike's curt observation that she needed rest. Another shot of Demerol had ended the grilling.

Now only Gutierrez, Mike, and a stocky, barrel-chested man ringed the foot of her bed. The shorter man had reidentified himself as Special Agent Allen Kuykendahl of the Air Force Office of Special Investigations.

Using the control buttons, as Mike had instructed, Jen raised the back of the bed a few inches. "What did you find out about Harry Waterman?"

Gutierrez shook his head. "So far, next to nada. His prints didn't match any currently on file in the FBI database. He didn't carry any identification on his person. We haven't found a driver's license or rental agreement or anything else in his name yet. We're still working on it, but as of right now, it looks like the man existed in a vacuum."

"What about his business? Surely someone there had some information about him."

"The name and description check to an agent

of Western Mutual Life Insurance, but from there it's an empty trail. Harry Waterman operated as an independent with no established office or staff. His supervisor's in Austin, new to the company. Claims he never even met the man, just dealt with him by phone and by fax."

"But I called him at his office," Jen protested. "Several times."

"An answering service forwarded his incoming calls."

She picked at the tan-colored sheet covering her knees. "The company's for real, isn't it?"

Okay, so maybe it was crass to worry about her crunched Cherokee when a man had died in it, but Waterman hadn't exactly endeared himself to her and, well, her life would have to go on.

"As far as we know," Gutierrez replied. "I asked one of our guys who works white-collar fraud to check Western Mutual out. He tells me the company holds over two hundred million in insurance in force, whatever that means, and won some kind of a quality award last year for MEI."

"MEI?"

"Murdock Enterprises, Incorporated, Western Mutual's parent corporation. According to our financial whiz kid, MEI's solid as a rock."

Jen nodded, hiding her kick of guilty relief.

"What about his ring?" she asked. "Some jeweler must have a record of a blue diamond that size."

"There wasn't enough of the diamond left for

a gemologist to come up with a viable description."

The blunt reply drained the blood from Jen's cheeks. She still couldn't quite believe the violence that had invaded her life in the past few weeks. She slumped back against the bed, hearing again the shriek of metal against metal.

Mike gave her a sharp look and took over.

"You found the gun, didn't you? And the bullets from Jen's apartment? Don't they tell you anything?"

Gutierrez hesitated. His gaze held Mike's across the foot of the hospital bed.

"They tell us that this man wasn't your ordinary, everyday thug," he said slowly. "He carried a .380 caliber Beretta Model 86. A Cheetah. He also hand-loaded the ammunition to keep it subsonic."

That apparently meant something to Mike, but Jen needed an explanation.

"By hand-loading the bullets," Gutierrez said patiently, "he eliminated the small snap they make when they break the sound barrier that even a silencer can't suppress. This guy was a pro. A highly trained, highly skilled pro."

The knowledge that a professional gunman had come after her didn't exactly soothe Jen's lacerated nerves. Gutierrez eyed her thoughtfully.

"I guess all we need now from you is that list you think Waterman came after. Think you can reconstruct it?"

She nodded. "As soon as I get out of here and get to a computer."

Special Agent Kuykendahl spoke up for the first time. "I'd like to work with you on that, Captain."

She shifted her attention to the stocky agent. With his bull-like neck and barrel chest, Kuykendahl looked more like a professional wrestler than her idea of a special investigator. Jen wondered briefly what he'd done in his Air Force career before he turned to sleuthing. She knew from one of her friends who worked OSI assignments that they drew their agents from all ranks and career fields. The rigorous initial screening and training process eliminated ninety percent of the volunteers. Those who made it through the program had a pretty good fix on a wide spectrum of Air Force operations.

"Since you discovered these mysterious files on the Military Personnel Data System," he said politely, "the OSI needs to stay involved from here on out."

Despite the courteous wording, Jen knew the agent had just translated her personal quest into an official investigation. That was fine by her. She'd jettisoned any desire to pursue it on her own about the same time Harry Waterman jammed his .380 caliber Cheetah into her kidney.

"General Daniels has assured us that you'll have complete access to whatever data resources you need at the Center," Kuykendahl informed her.

"You're kidding! Complete access?"

Forgetting her stitches, Jen twisted to aim a

grin at the man lounging against the windowsill.
The attempt quickly collapsed into a wince.

Across the room, Mike felt his stomach knot.
He wasn't sure when or how Jennifer Varga's
cocky grin had become so much a part of his
existence, but the idea that the simple act of
smiling would cause her pain fueled a small,
solid core of fury in his gut. Every time he
looked at the bandages humped under her hospital gown or remembered how close she'd
come to ending up under that train, his jaw
went so tight his teeth ached.

He suspected that his involvement with this
woman would result in an official reprimand at
least, removal from his job at worst. Mike could
handle that. He'd endured worse in life than the
loss of a job.

What he couldn't handle was the idea that
someone who sounded very much like a professional hit man had snatched Jen right out from
under his nose. On base. In the middle of the
day. Mike wouldn't forgive himself for that for
a long, long time. In the meantime, he wasn't
letting her out of his sight until the police or the
OSI discovered what the hell was going on.

Assuming, of course, she agreed.

He waited until the two detectives departed
to broach the subject. Anticipating her discharge
from the clinic with her usual impatience, Jen
pushed herself off the bed and extracted clean
clothes from the canvas tote Mike had brought
from the house.

"How long do you think it will take you to reconstruct the list?" he asked as she headed for the bathroom.

"A couple of hours," she called through the closed door. "Why?"

"We need to talk about what you're going to do after that."

She emerged from the bathroom a moment later, gingerly buttoning all but the top button of a bright orange sweater. The tapes holding the shoulder bandage in place poked from one side of the deep V neckline.

"My folks want me to come home," she admitted, digging a pair of socks out of the tote. "I didn't give them all the details of what happened when I called last night. Dad's got a heart condition. I don't want him to stress out, but I had to tell them about Trish and Commodore and the fact that my second new car in as many weeks just took a hit from the Santa Fe railroad."

She perched on the side of the bed and lifted a knee, wincing involuntarily at the pull on her shoulder. Mike crossed the room and took the socks from her bandaged hands. With one of her heels braced on his thigh and the other foot warm in his hands, he tugged on a sock.

"I told my folks we had everything under control here," Jen said, curling her toes. "But we don't, do we? I mean, until I know why Waterman came after me, or who sent him, I don't want to go home and put my folks in possible danger, too."

Mike nodded. The same thoughts had kept him awake most of the night.

She tilted him a worried glance. "I don't want to pull you in any deeper, either. Waterman said he followed me to your house, remember?"

How could Mike forget? The knowledge that someone had tracked her like prey ate at his insides.

"Maybe I should move into the Officers' Quarters for a while, like the OSI suggested."

Mike didn't voice the obvious. Waterman hadn't experienced any difficulty gaining access to the base. Nor would any other skilled pro.

"I have another idea." He lifted her other foot. "I talked to Gutierrez and Kuykendahl earlier this morning. We think you should disappear while they work what leads they have."

Her heel jerked in his hand. "How can I just disappear? I've got a job, a sick dog, a trashed apartment, and a mangled Cherokee all waiting for me to get out of the hospital."

"The apartment and the Cherokee will keep. The vet wants to hold Commodore for a while. As for your job . . . you planned to take leave next week. So take it."

"And go where?"

"You told me the Scanlons invited you for Thanksgiving. Did you mention that invitation to anyone else?"

She thought for a while. "Not that I recall."

"Then I think we should go to Lubbock."

"We?"

"We. Don Scanlon invited me to visit, too.

You can't drive with those skinned hands, and I can't let you go alone."

She angled her head. Tangled chestnut waves spilled down one shoulder. A mischievous gleam lit her brown eyes.

"Are you speaking as a concerned supervisor, or someone who didn't quite finish what he started?"

"I'm no longer your supervisor, Jen."

"Uh-oh. You told the general about us, didn't you?"

"Yes."

"Why, for heaven's sake? Why didn't you just quietly work a transfer and get me off the team?"

"That was the plan before you spent the night in my bed."

"So? What changed the plan?"

"You spent the night in my bed."

"Oh, for heaven's sake. You didn't have to volunteer that particular piece of information to General Daniels."

"I didn't volunteer it," Mike said patiently. "She asked the question, and I answered it."

Her face filled with profound disgust. "Right. I forgot myself for a minute there. You always play by the rules, don't you?"

"I try to."

"Well, this time playing by the rules is going to get both our asses in very hot water."

Hooking her white-wrapped hands under her arms, she turned her back on him and stared out the window.

"Come on," he said evenly. "I didn't tell Daniels anything that wouldn't have come to light eventually. Hell, the rumor mill probably started churning the day after our first dinner together. You said yourself no one could get away with a clandestine affair in this town. I'm not interested in one, anyway."

Her spine stiffened under the orange sweater. "Just what are you interested in, Colonel?"

He closed the small distance between them, breathing in the scent of antiseptic soap and warm woman. Mindful of her injuries, Mike curled his hands loosely on her good arm.

"I'm interested in you, Captain."

She turned back around, her stiffness disappearing in a flush that contained anger and dismay and regret. "Look, we need to face the fact that this . . . this *interest* could cost you your job, not to mention your career."

"I knew the rules, Jen, and I broke them. I accept that it may end my career, but it won't end yours. General Daniels understands that you . . ."

"Oh, for . . . ! Do you think I care about my so-called career?"

"No, but I do."

She shook her head angrily. "Oh, no. We're not going to get into that argument again. We both know you've got a hell of a lot more to lose than I have."

"Wrong." He tucked a tangled strand behind her ear. "I'm beginning to think I've got a hell of a lot more to gain."

His touch combined with the quiet declaration to knock the wind right out of Jen's lungs. For a moment she forgot her anger, her worry, her dismay that she'd put Mike's career in jeopardy.

"Mike . . ."

The sound of a throat clearing brought them both around. A white-frocked physician stood just inside the door. He lifted a brow at Jen's jeans and sweater.

"I see you're ready to break out of here, Captain Varga. Take a seat please."

Throwing the man beside her a glance that warned him they hadn't finished their argument, Jen resumed her seat on the bed. The doc tipped her head back and flashed a beam in her eyes.

"Follow the light, please."

Eyeballing the small, bright pinpoint, Jen responded to questions about the pain, which had dulled to a throb, and the dizziness, which had disappeared completely. The physician snapped off the light and dropped it in his pocket.

"Let's take a look at the wound."

Gingerly, Jen peeled back the sweater. With ruthless efficiency, the doc peeled off the bandage. They both peered down at the angry red line running diagonally across the curve where her upper arm rounded into her shoulder.

"You're one lucky woman," the physician commented. "The powder burns caused more damage than the bullet. It only took a couple of stitches to close the skin. They'll fall out when they're ready. In the interim, keep the wound lightly covered to avoid infection."

He replaced the bulky bandage with a smaller, lighter pad not too much bigger than a Band-Aid. After performing a similar inspection of Jen's hands, he pronounced her fit for discharge, if not for any prolonged or strenuous duty.

Across the width of the room, Jen met Mike's eyes. "Guess it's a good thing I'm taking leave."

"Guess so," he replied with a smile.

A call from the clinic alerted Special Agent Kuykendahl to meet them at the Personnel Center. Jen and Mike drove the short, straight shot from the clinic to the Center in his MG. Thankfully, the route avoided Randolph's wide, central boulevard and front gate. Jen wasn't sure she was ready to view the shattered remains of the railroad-crossing barrier.

With the changeability of November, a warm, almost balmy sunshine had replaced yesterday's cold and drizzle. Sunlight painted the tiles on the Center's roof and rounded portico with a bright brick hue. Jen walked up the front steps, deliberately blanking her mind to what had happened the last time she'd walked down them. Special Agent Kuykendahl waited just inside the front doors.

"The general has designated a secure area for us to work with terminals that can access the Master Personnel File, the ARMS database, and any outside systems you used before. We've set up a special password, and one of the senior database managers is standing by in case we need him."

"We won't," Jen said with breezy confidence.

Accompanied by the two men, she traveled down the long, carpeted corridor to C wing. A short climb took them to the third-floor area. The senior civilian, obviously curious about the call that brought him to the Center on a Sunday morning, showed them to the office set aside for their use. He didn't appear too happy when Kuykendahl politely shut the door in his face.

Jen surveyed the flickering screen, already turned on in anticipation of their arrival. At any other time, she would have delighted in a license to steal like this. Her fingers itched to zing over the keyboard. Wrapped in bandages as they were, however, her hands were no use at the keyboard. She could only peer over Kuykendahl's beefy shoulder and grit her teeth in impatience while his equally beefy fingers pounded out her instructions with maddening slowness.

Even with his rhinoceros touch, the same queries that had taken several hours on Mike's PC spun through the Center's powerful computers in less than thirty minutes. Jen scanned the final product with a keen eye.

"These look like the same Gerald L.'s."

Kuykendahl printed two copies of the list, explaining that he'd promised one to Gutierrez.

"We're cooperating fully with the civilian criminal investigation. Now, can you remember any of the other names that you saw on Mr. James's files?"

"There was a Tech Sergeant Rosalie Something, taking a Satellite Communications course at Keesler. And a Captain Steve, but . . ."

Jen shook her head. With all that had happened in the past days, she couldn't remember anything more than his name and rank.

It took only a few minutes to pull up the enrollment list of the satellite communications course and find Technical Sergeant Rosalie Tobias. Jen studied each data entry as it flicked by on the screen. Hispanic. Divorced. Twelve years of service. Currently retraining into satellite communications.

"I don't see anything here that looks suspicious," Jen said, frowning.

"We'll check her out," Kuykendahl replied calmly.

Another pass through the database produced twelve Captain Stevens/Stephens in various stages of training. One was right there at Randolph upgrading to pilot instructor. The others were attending courses at various training centers and institutes across the country.

"It won't take us long to run these guys down," Kuykendahl said. "We'll have it done before you get back from Lubbock."

"You should also check out Mr. James," Mike said slowly. "Maybe there's something in his background that will give us a clue to these files."

"I started digging into his background as soon

as I got your call," the agent replied calmly. "So far, he's clean. No lingering trauma from his military service in Vietnam. No bad debts or addictions, other than to cigarettes. After his wife's death, he socked most of his salary away. His kids inherited a tidy sum, but not enough to raise questions. The only skeleton I could find in the family closet is his son, Ed Junior. He was busted a few years ago for possession, but got off with a slap on the wrist."

"He owns a video store now," Jen murmured, remembering the pictures taped over Ed's workstation with another twinge of guilt.

In the aftermath of the break-in and the attack on Trish, she'd missed the service held at the chapel in Ed's memory. She felt bad about that. He'd been a good man, dedicated to his job. Jen couldn't imagine how the records she'd found on his electronic desktop could be linked to the vicious gunman who'd called himself Harry Waterman.

"I'll keep working it from this end," Kuykendahl promised. "If anything turns up, I'll contact you. And if you remember the other names, or any other details at all, call me. Here, use this."

He pulled a small, thin mobile phone from his pocket and handed it to Jen. She examined the slender instrument, observing a few unfamiliar annotations on the keys.

"This doesn't look like one of Mother Bell's."

"It isn't, but it operates the same way. Here's my number."

Jen tucked both into her purse and followed

the two men down the stairs. To her surprise, Mike steered her to the back door instead of the long, narrow corridor that led to the front of the building.

"We can't ignore the possibility that Waterman bugged my car as well as yours," he told her. "Kuykendahl has arranged another vehicle for us."

Jen stepped through the glass door into the alley. Her eyes widened when she saw the gleaming forest green Cherokee parked a few feet away.

"Go easy on it," the agent pleaded, only half joking. "The lease is in my name."

Chapter Fifteen

"Where are they?"

Russ Murdock asked the question quietly. Too quietly. A muscle jumped under tight, pulled tissue on the right side of his chief of staff's face.

"We don't know," Andy Anderson replied.

"You don't know."

Murdock sat unmoving in his cream-colored leather chair. Sunlight streamed through the wall of windows behind him. The urethane shields developed by MEI's polymers lab tamed most of the glare reflected from Denver's latest blanket of white, but enough filtered through to give his pale blue eyes an opaque sheen.

"We engineer and manufacture the most sophisticated surveillance equipment in the world. At this very moment, our team downstairs is listening to every breath, tracking every step taken by a small cadre of personnel making their way down the side of a mountain in a remote corner of Kurdistan. Yet you're telling me we can't seem to get a lock on one Air Force captain in San Antonio, Texas?"

"At this point, we're not sure she's still in San Antonio," Anderson admitted reluctantly. "She's on leave, but none of her coworkers know where. Her family thinks she's staying with a friend."

"That lieutenant colonel she spent the night with?"

"Possibly. He's on leave, too, but surveillance of his house hasn't shown any movement for the past forty-eight hours. We haven't had a report on either of them since we lost our senior operative in the area."

Anderson knew his boss wouldn't throw in his face the fact that he'd wanted to terminate the San Antonio operative. Russ didn't believe in recriminations. Only results.

Sure enough, Murdock leaned forward, his whole being focused on the problem at hand.

"Are you absolutely certain the representative from the Office of Special Investigations who talked to our woman at Keesler yesterday went away with nothing?"

Anderson drew himself up. He could answer for every one of his Special Projects personnel. "Yes, sir. Rose knows what to say."

"What about our other people? Any contacts or queries about them?"

"No, sir. Not yet."

Murdock palmed a hand across his thinning, reddish hair. The small movement from the usually contained man revealed his inner perturbation. He dropped his hand and folded it together with his other. His gray-blue eyes fastened on Anderson.

"I don't want any more slips."

"No, sir," Anderson promised, the muscle in his cheek twitching.

His boss studied him for a long moment, then switched off his concern over the San Antonio situation with the abruptness that always disconcerted peers and subordinates unused to it.

"How soon will the team in Kurdistan make contact?"

Anderson didn't need to glance at the priceless French clock atop its platform of crossed elephant tusks to answer that one. He knew the team's timetable down to a heartbeat.

"Within the next two hours."

"Call me when you hear something."

"Yes, sir."

"About either operation," Murdock advised as Anderson headed for the door.

Chapter Sixteen

Mike Page would be the first to admit he'd made some mistakes in his time. Bad mistakes. Allowing the demands of his job to come between him and his family topped the list. He'd never forgive himself for becoming so wrapped up in his duties that he failed to notice his daughter's slide into the drugs that killed her. Just the memory of Lisa sent pain slicing through his chest.

The old, familiar ache now competed with a newer, far more immediate one. Hooking his fingers behind his head, Mike raised a knee to ease the uncomfortable tightness in his groin. The thin hide-a-bed mattress beneath him whispered with the movement. Tight-jawed, he stared up at the shadows dancing across the ceiling of Don Scanlon's study.

Suggesting that he accompany Jen on her visit to the Scanlons had to rank right up there on Mike's list of really dumb moves. At the time, he'd been driven by concern for her safety and an instinctive need to get her out of the line of fire while the police and the OSI worked their meager clues. All right, he admitted to the ceiling, he'd also had this quixotic idea that they needed time away from the Center to get to know each other without the baggage of their rank or respective positions.

Now, with only the shadows flitting across the ceiling and the rhythmic ticking of the grandfather clock in the hallway for company, Mike acknowledged that his plan had worked. Too damn well.

The Scanlons had been horrified by the attack on Jen and Commodore, and desperate to talk about their daughter with her friend and roommate. They'd insisted that the visitors stay at their house instead of a motel. For three nights, Mike had bunked down in the cluttered room the retired professor used for an office while Jen occupied Trish's old bedroom upstairs. For three days—four if he counted the drive up from San Antonio—he'd spent long hours getting to know Jennifer Varga.

Accompanied by the Scanlons, they'd visited still comatose Trish at the University Medical Center. Then they'd rambled through the chrysanthemum-lined walkways of Texas Tech, where Don Scanlon had spent almost three decades of his life. Yesterday, they'd shared a Thanksgiving feast that a determinedly cheerful Mary Scanlon had prepared for friends and family.

On their own, they'd sampled Lubbock's cafés. Once or twice they'd taken lazy drives through fields dotted with gray tufts of cotton clinging to winter-browned stalks. Their conversations had ranged from likes in food and music to hobbies and families, including Jen's brief marriage and Mike's considerably longer one.

In the process, he'd watched her bruises fade and the bandages come off her skinned palms and the wind from the open car windows tangle her thick fall of honey-brown hair. He'd reached the point where he could identify her subtle, lemony scent the moment she walked into a room. Without conscious effort, he'd picked out her particular ripple of laughter in the hum generated by the small crowd the Scanlons had invited for Thanksgiving dinner.

And he'd grown hard as a damned rock each evening when she wished him good night, her eyes filled with a regret he couldn't mistake. Their sleeping arrangements had frustrated her as much as Mike, but she'd given in to the Scanlons' insistence that they stay here at the house with a grace that tugged at his heart.

Tomorrow, he thought, his stomach tightening. Tomorrow they'd take their leave of Don and Mary and Trish and start back toward San Antonio. Tomorrow there'd just be Jen and him and the open road.

He wasn't in any hurry to get back to the city, particularly since neither Gutierrez nor Kuykendahl had turned up anything significant. Their lack of progress grated on Mike's nerves almost as much as his physical frustration.

Kuykendahl had confirmed that Technical

Sergeant Rosalie Tobias was in her last week at the Satellite Communications course at Keesler. Her credentials and background had checked out, right down to the little rose tattooed on the web between the thumb and first finger of her left hand.

Kuykendahl's initial screen of the several Captain Stevens hadn't turned up anything, either. All had been contacted except two who were on leave until after the Thanksgiving holidays, but their records checked out. They'd be interviewed as soon as they returned to their bases.

Nor had Gutierrez had any better luck on his end. Almost a week after it had occurred, the mystery of Harry Waterman's attack remained just that, a mystery. At this rate, Jen had admitted wryly during one of their drives through the flat countryside, she'd spend the rest of her life looking over her shoulder and jumping every time a stranger approached her car.

The idea that she might have to live with fear infuriated Mike as much now as it had then. His fingers curled under the back of his head. The dancing shadows took on sharper, more sinister edges.

Tomorrow, he promised grimly. Tomorrow he'd do his best to banish all her fears . . . for a while, anyway. Closing his eyes, he ignored the metal support bar pressing through the thin mattress and willed himself to sleep.

It came finally, just before dawn.

A few hours later Jen's cry cut through his light doze like a blade.

It was a small sound, hardly more than a muted exclamation, but it brought him off the sofa bed in a swift, silent roll. He was out of the study and halfway to the stairs when the sound of voices spun him around. His heart firing like a string of satchel charges, he raced for the kitchen at the rear of the two-story frame house. A hard palm sent the swinging door slamming back on its hinges.

The two women by the sink jerked around. Their startled exclamations echoed Mike's clawing tension as he searched the room. Dim, formless shapes in the alcove by the back door had him doubling his fists before he identified them as overcoats hanging from pegs.

His heart and his lungs still pumping, he turned to the two women. A nightshirt-clad Jen stared at him openmouthed. Mary Scanlon, her gray head helmeted in yellow plastic curlers, clutched a chenille bathrobe to her throat.

"What happened?" he demanded fiercely. "I heard a cry."

Jen recovered first, her expression shifting from astonished to sheepish. "I was going to help Mary with breakfast, but hot skillet handles and skinned palms don't mix, even with pot holders to protect them."

"You burned yourself? Christ, Varga, you're a walking hazard."

She blinked at the unexpected attack.

"Let me see it," he growled, starting toward her.

"It's fine," she retorted, obviously unimpressed by his belated concern. "Mary's already greased it down."

Mike didn't need Jen's tart reply to know he'd overreacted. He had no excuse, other than frustration and worry and the fact that four days with Jennifer had him wound as tight as he'd been in a long, long time.

"I'll help with breakfast," he informed them, still off center. "At least I know my way around a hot skillet."

Her brows soaring, Jen pinned on a wide, sugary smile. "That's fine by me," she drawled. "I like the idea of keeping my men barefoot and in the kitchen."

It was on the tip of Mike's tongue to tell her that he intended to whittle that plural down to a singular when a choke of laughter dragged his gaze away from Jen.

"I'd appreciate the help," Mary Scanlon told him, her green eyes dancing under the yellow plastic cap. "You might want to dress first, though. Don's pretty liberal, but even he might have second thoughts if he found me frying bacon with a young man in jockey shorts."

Mike conceded the point with a curt nod. "I'll be right back."

Neither woman said a word as he stalked out of the kitchen. The door swung shut behind him. For a few moments, the only sounds in the small, cozy room were the hiss of a gas stove burner and the sizzle and drip of the coffeemaker Mary had switched on just before Jen and the hot frying pan parted company.

Twisting off the burner knob, Mary slanted Jen a catlike glance that reminded her forcibly of Trish at her best . . . or worst.

"Well, well," the older woman purred. "I told Don we'd made a mistake when we gave you and Mike separate beds."

Jen eyed the closed door. "At this moment, I'd say you called it exactly right."

With a reluctant smile, she accepted the mug Mary offered. The older woman leaned a hip against a scrubbed pine counter and sipped at the dark, steaming brew.

"You and Mike didn't act as though you shared anything other than a close working relationship when we first met him," she commented with a smile.

"At the time, we didn't."

"Well, well," Mary murmured again.

"And I wouldn't have described our working relationship as close even then." Jen cradled the mug in still tender palms. "When we get back to San Antonio, it won't exist at all."

"Why not?"

"The Air Force has rules about these things," she replied with a grimace, before honesty compelled her to add a reluctant kicker. "I'm not much for rules and regulations, but this one makes sense. I have a hard enough time following orders to begin with. There's no way I'd take them from a man who'd . . ."

She broke off, fiddling with her mug.

"A man who'd stepped out of his supervisory role and into that of a lover," Mary finished, her eyes twinkling. "I know how that works. Don was my teaching assistant at Texas Tech until I seduced him."

"No kidding?"

"No kidding." Mary patted her curlers with a feminine gesture as ageless as time. "He didn't take much seducing, if I do say so myself."

Jen didn't doubt that for a moment. More and more she saw the daughter in the mother, or vice versa.

"I gave up teaching full-time when I discovered I was pregnant," the older woman continued serenely. "Thirty years ago, women didn't have as many choices as we have today. But surely you and Mike can work this out so neither of you has to sacrifice your career aspirations."

"I don't have any career aspirations," Jen confessed. "In fact, until a couple of weeks ago, I desperately wanted out of the Air Force."

Mary cocked her head. "And now?"

"Now, I don't know what I want."

A smile etched a few more character lines on either side of the older woman's mouth. "I know what I'd want if I were you. He's pulling on a pair of pants as we speak. And if I'm not mistaken, he's about as horny as any male I've ever seen."

The droll comment made Jen laugh. "You sound just like Trish."

At the mention of her daughter, the sparkle faded from Mary's eyes. Setting her mug aside, she leaned forward and folded a hand over Jen's.

"Forgive me if I sound like an interfering mother. From what I've seen of you and Mike these past few days, I'd say you had a chance at something rare. Something my Trish may never get to experience. Grab it, Jennifer. Hang on to it." She blinked away a sudden rush of tears. "Hold on as hard as you can, even with your poor skinned palms."

Mary's fierce admonition echoed in Jen's mind as Lubbock dropped out of sight in the Cherokee's rearview mirror. Ahead, the four-lane highway stretched like a black ribbon laid across flat, brown fields. A few cotton balls clung to withered stalks, dotting the fields with gray. Thicker drifts formed filmy, lintlike beards on either side of the road.

Jen paid little attention to the passing landscape. She felt edgy and restless and every bit as frustrated as she guessed Mike was. The trip that was supposed to have relaxed her had done anything but.

The purple and black bruises on her ribs and hips had faded to a mottled brown. The bullet wound on her shoulder now itched instead of burned. Yet she was going back to San Antonio a whole lot more uncomfortable than when she'd left. Those long nights on Trish's twin bed, with Mike lying in the room almost directly below hers, had nibbled away at her enjoyment of the visit. The final, wrenching visit with Trish this morning hadn't helped, either. Nor had her companion's silence since they'd driven out of the city.

He'd apologized for his gruffness to her and Mary over breakfast. He'd helped Jen load her things into the Cherokee. He'd thanked the Scanlons warmly for their hospitality when he'd parted with them at the hospital. He hadn't spoken a word since.

Nor had Jen. She'd been too absorbed trying to figure out how to hold on to something she wasn't sure she had a grip on to begin with.

"You in a hurry to get back to San Antonio?"

The unexpected question broke the long silence. Slewing around in her seat, Jen leaned a shoulder against the door.

"That depends."

"On what?"

She hesitated, thinking of all the answers she could give. Mary's fierce admonition to grab on to whatever it was she and Mike shared cut through any desire to play coy.

"If getting back to San Antonio means spending the rest of the weekend in an empty apartment or a room at the Officers' Quarters, no, I'm not in any particular hurry. If it means another session with you on the kitchen counter . . ."

"Yes?"

"I'd want you to put the gas pedal to the floor."

His knuckles whitened for a moment, then visibly relaxed. "Even after I made such an ass of myself this morning?"

"Especially after you made such an ass of yourself." She tilted her head, studying his profile. "Mary blamed that little overflow of testosterone on the fact that you're horny, by the way."

A smile pulled at the corner of his mouth. "Interesting observation."

"Are you?"

"As hell." His gray eyes settled on her face. "How about you?"

His look speared right through Jen's buttermilk tan leather jacket, wine-colored top, and silky camisole. Her body tightened involuntarily.

"If you hadn't suggested we leave today, I would have," she admitted. "I couldn't take another night on that twin bed."

"You don't have to."

The low promise curled her toes in her boots. "What do you have in mind?"

"Do you remember that inn we passed a few miles outside San Angelo? The one perched above the river? I called and reserved a room with a king-sized bed."

She thought for a moment, then shook her head. "Uh-uh. No good."

He lifted a brow. "No good?"

"San Angelo's too far away."

Grinning, he dug a map out of the door pocket and tossed it into her lap. "Pick a place. Anyplace."

Jen let the map lie, far more interested at the moment in the man she traveled with than in their ultimate destination.

In some ways, she knew him so well now. They'd certainly had plenty of time to talk in the past few days. She might not agree with his conservative view of politics, or share his taste in music, which ran to Kenny G. and his soprano sax, but she'd come to admire his uncompromising sense of right and wrong . . . even if it irritated the hell out of her at times.

In other ways, though, she felt as though they were still strangers. Their one explosive night together had triggered a hunger neither of them had been able to satisfy. She ached to repeat the experience, to know the man who'd brought her to such stunning physical release. Soon, she thought with a sharp leap of her senses. Soon.

Reminded of her appointed task, she trailed a nail down the wrinkled map. Justiceburg. Shyler. Sweetwater. No, Sweetwater was too far. So was Shyler. Any four-way stop with a motel would do, Jen decided abruptly.

She started to refold the map when her gaze snagged on the yellow patch in the upper corner. Wichita Falls. Sheppard Air Force Base. She circled the area with her fingertip once, twice. A faint memory tugged at her mind. Closing her eyes, she visualized the pictures Ed James had pinned above his computer.

His wife. His daughter and her three grandkids. His son . . .

Jen waged another short, fierce battle with herself. She couldn't quite believe it when a niggling sense of guilt and a nagging curiosity won out over her burning impatience to get Mike naked.

"How about Wichita Falls?" she asked tentatively.

He swung her a quick, teasing look. "I thought you were in a hurry? That's a couple hours out of our way."

"I know." Sighing, she refolded the map. "I just remembered that Ed James's son owns a video rental store in Wichita Falls. I feel guilty about missing his father's funeral. We could stop by for a few minutes to offer our condolences."

Mike's eyes narrowed on the road ahead. "And ask a few questions about his father?"

His shrewd assessment of her motives brought Jen up short. Good grief, what was the matter with her? Why couldn't she just let the professionals handle this? A train had almost flattened her, for God's sake. A bullet had creased her shoulder. What would it take to kill her interest in a few misplaced files?

Poor word choice, she thought with a shudder. She'd opened her mouth to retract her rash suggestion when Mike endorsed it.

"We could stop by Sheppard while we're in the area," he said slowly. "I've got a buddy there . . . the commander of the civil engineering training squadron. He's been in the training business a long time. Maybe he could put a new twist on this business, see something that the rest of us have missed."

"Maybe."

Damn. Jen hadn't planned on an all-day excursion. Just a delay of an hour or two. The anticipation that had bubbled to a near boil just moments ago now threatened to choke her. It would be just her luck, she thought ironically, if Mike's buddy insisted they spend the night at his house. She'd probably end up sharing a bedroom with his six-year-old daughter or on a sofa bed in the den.

"We'll call Bulldog from the hotel," Mike suggested. "And Ed James's son."

"Right," she agreed in a rush. "From the hotel."

As it turned out, they didn't have to call Ed's son. Just moments after Mike had turned off Highway 277 and onto the access road, Jen let out a screech.

"Look! There it is. James's Video!"

Excitedly, she pointed to a shop in a seedy-looking strip mall. Bits of paper cartwheeled in the breeze and caught at the base of the cinder-block buildings, all of which sported iron bars over their doors and windows. The video shop sat sandwiched between a liquor store and a pawnshop with the biggest set of drums Jen had ever seen in the window.

It wasn't until after Mike had wheeled into the parking lot that she picked up the fine print on the sign above the video store.

"James's *Adult* Video." Her eyes danced with mischief. "This could turn out to be an interesting stop."

"You do the talking," Mike suggested, shoving the Cherokee into park. "I'll do the renting."

Jen had always wondered what one of these places with the opaque windows and barred doors looked like inside. At first glance, it could have passed for an ordinary video shop. Tall, unpainted metal racks displayed rows of cartons. Hand-lettered labels above the racks identified the sections. A closer look at the stained, much handled covers on the cassettes soon disabused Jen of the notion that there was anything ordinary about the shop

"Good grief," she exclaimed in an undertone to Mike. "There must be fifty different movies here with spanking in their title!"

"Those are my favorites."

Jolted, Jen swung a quick look over her shoulder.

"Right after the bondage flicks," he added with a grin.

She couldn't quite tell from his grin if she'd been had or not. "In your dreams, big guy," she muttered.

He leaned over until his breath stirred the fine hairs at her temple. "I've had enough dreams the past few nights to last me a lifetime . . . I'm ready for the real thing."

With that soft comment thundering in her ears, Jen stammered out a response to the acne-scarred clerk who appeared from a back room.

"I'd, uh, like to speak to Mr. James."

"He's not here."

"You mean he's gone home for the day?"

The disinterested clerk slapped a batch of returned videos on the counter and popped their covers.

"Eddy's gone, period."

Jen's stomach tightened. So much violence had invaded her life of late she was almost afraid to ask the next question.

"Is he dead?"

"Not unless he shot himself so full of shit he OD'd."

The clerk's bored expression suggested that was a real possibility. Evidently Ed's son hadn't kicked his drug habit after all.

"So where is he?" Mike asked coolly, sliding a palm across the counter.

The bill under his hand disappeared into the clerk's pocket in the blink of an eye, but not before Jen caught a brief glimpse of Ben Franklin's oversized portrait. Her mind boggled at the thought of handing over a hundred dollars to this character, but evidently Mike had read him better than Jen had.

"Eddy's down in Mexico," he told them. "His old man kicked the bucket a few weeks ago and left him a wad. A real wad. Eddy sold me the shop and took off for Acapulco or someplace. Said he could buy a lot more shit with his million dollars down south."

"Million dollars?" Jen squeaked.

Special Agent Kuykendahl had told them that Ed James left his children a respectable sum. Either his definition of respectable differed considerably from hers, or Ed had stashed away more than anyone realized. She was about to blurt out something to that effect when Mike's hand slid up her back and tightened on her neck in silent warning.

"What's Eddy to you, anyway?" the clerk asked suspiciously.

She recovered, feigning a shrug. "Nothing. I mean, no one. I worked with his father in San Antonio and wanted to tell his son how sorry I am. I just didn't realize he'd, uh, left his children so well off."

"Well, maybe it weren't no million dollars, but it was a nice pile."

"Are you sure Eddy got this money from his father?"

"Yeah, from some stocks or something his old man had invested in. Some big corporation up in Denver done a split about a dozen times. NMI or MCI or something."

Jen stared at the clerk. Her heart hammering, she stuttered out a quick question.

"Could that . . . ? Could that company have been MEI?"

"It coulda. Look, you folks going to rent something or not? Eddy may be ass high in grass right now. I sure as hell ain't."

Blindly, Jen reached for the closest video. She needed time to think, to talk to Mike, to call Gutierrez and Kuykendahl. Most of all, she needed immediate access to a computer to find out everything she could about MEI . . . the company that had employed Harry Waterman. Then they could come back and grill this little creep for Eddy James's exact whereabouts. Her mind whirling, she almost missed the clerk's smirk.

"Funny how women like that one so much," he commented to Mike.

Jen glanced down just as the cassette slid into a much used brown paper bag. The title, *Vixens in Velvet,* sounded tame enough, but from the look of unholy amusement on the attendant's face she had a suspicion that she'd just pandered to a male fantasy even more revolting than bondage or spanking.

Dickie Christopher watched his customers walk out the door, his eyes on the crease in the bitch's jeans.

Nice ass, he thought dispassionately. Tits too small for his taste, but nice ass.

The door clunked shut, cutting off his view. Shrugging, he pulled open a drawer and lifted out a blue steel Walther .45. Setting the loaded gun on the counter, he pawed through the drawer for the card Eddy had left with him. This was the second time in less than a week he'd had to use it.

The first time, he'd reported those hick Air Force cops who'd come sniffing around, asking questions about Eddy's old man. The two who'd just left weren't no cops, though. Dickie woulda caught their stink the moment they walked in. They weren't no movie buffs, either. Not the kind of movies he specialized in, anyway.

A smile flitted across his pocked face. The

bitch was gonna get an education tonight. He just wished he could be there to watch the fun.

Reaching for the grimy phone that he used to conduct his business, he punched in the number listed on the card. The person who answered on the first ring didn't identify herself.

Dickie didn't care who she was or what she did with the information he passed her. Eddy had told him to call this number if anyone asked any questions, so Dickie called. Besides, it meant another hundred bucks. This was turning out to be a good day, his first in a long time!

Chapter Seventeen

Russ Murdock stood shoulder to shoulder with his chief of staff. Like everyone else in the small cadre that manned the underground ops center, he kept his eyes fixed on the screen that took up one wall. After forty plus years in the electronics business it still gave him a thrill to see the products his worldwide conglomerate produced put to such superb use.

True, the figure on the screen was haloed with the greenish hue peculiar to ultra-long-distance night-vision equipment. The ULDs returned such a precise image, though, that Russ could pick out the bruises marring the figure's face above his scraggly beard, even the bloodstains on the bandages wrapped around the stump where his right hand had been severed. The fact that Russ was seeing those bruises and bandages real time through a technology he himself had helped develop added to the drama of the moment.

Suddenly the figure on the screen went down. The tension that held the Special Programs cadre immobile became a living, breathing presence. When the target shook his head like a dazed, shaggy dog and pushed himself up one-handed, the spine-cracking tension abated, but didn't disappear.

They were witnessing one of the trickiest parts of the mission. Not the most dangerous, but certainly the most nerve-wracking for the team that had put it together. After snatching the target away from his captors and keeping him drugged for most of the journey down the mountainside, they now had to watch while he stumbled the last few yards to safety on his own.

At Russ's side, his chief of staff breathed in swift, shallow gusts. Andy Anderson thrived on these operations, Russ knew. They were his life, his reason for being. Anderson didn't have sex from the day he began a planning session until the mission terminated. It was his own personal code, one that amused Russ and irritated Andy's wife, according to the transmissions from the surveillance devices in their home. Jill didn't know the reason behind her husband's abstinence, of course. She carped about it when the mood struck her, but for the most part she was as solidly committed to Andy as Evie was to Russ.

A sudden crackle of static whipped Russ's attention to the communications tech at the central console. She held up a palm, her Asian-American features rigid with concentration.

"The Turkish patrol is within two hundred meters," she advised tersely.

From the opposite side of the globe, the team captain confirmed her transmission. "Roger that. We have them on our scanner."

The watchers in the ops center stood rigid, their eyes intent on the injured figure.

"One hundred meters and closing."

An all-terrain vehicle appeared on the screen. Misted with green haze, it bounced along the mountainous track like an oversized tortoise.

The target dropped like a rock and cowered behind a hilly outcropping. The drugs were wearing off, Russ knew, bringing a return of the man's self-preservation instincts. He balled his hands into fists, willing the figure to move.

"Come on! They're friendly. Look at the markings!"

"Seventy-five meters . . ."

A second ATV followed the first. The Turkish flag attached to its antenna whipped in the wind.

The target pushed himself upright. Stumbling, tripping, waving madly with his good arm, he ran toward the small convoy. The ATVs slowed, then stopped. The watchers let out a collective hiss of satisfaction.

"Contact!"

The headquarters cadre was too well trained to whoop and shout, but their elation rolled through the ops center like a vapor cloud. Even Russ, whom Evie usually had to tease into a smile, grinned and rubbed a palm over his thinning hair.

"Welcome back to civilization, Dr. Cherbanian," he murmured to the figure who had fallen, sobbing, into the arms of a uniformed Turk.

Russ watched the drama for a few more moments, then gave each member of the elite team his personal thanks for a job well done. With his chief of staff at his side, he headed for the elevator.

"Cherbanian will touch down in Germany within seven hours," Andy confirmed, stabbing the button for the seventeenth floor. "We can expect word of his escape to break before then. Iraq will think a rival guerrilla faction helped the doctor make it to the border. Turkey will garner international acclaim for standing fast against terrorism. And the United States will have slipped out of another mess it created by arming the Kurds in the first place. Washington owes you for this one, boss. Big-time."

Russ fingered his narrow, black silk tie. The drama that had just occurred wasn't about money. Or power. Or political influence. He hadn't created Special Programs to reap personal rewards, although MEI certainly had cornered its share of defense contracts over the years.

From its inception, Special Programs had been designed to slice through bureaucratic and legal and congressional restrictions to preserve America's interests at home and abroad. If his years as deputy director of the CIA had taught Russ nothing else, they'd show him how easily a handful of men with too much power and too little moral conviction could hamstring operations. The CIA might have to put up with that kind of interference.

Russ Murdock didn't.

The elevator carried them to the top floor with noiseless efficiency. When the doors opened onto Russ's private office, the transition from subdued lighting to the brilliant Denver sunshine made both men squint. With the same abrupt transition, Russ shifted his focus from the operation just concluded to the one yet unfinished.

Crossing to the slab of glistening ebony that served as his desk, he picked up the communiqué Andy had delivered just moments before they were both called to the ops center. His pale blue eyes skimmed the brief message.

Captain Varga had turned up in Wichita Falls just before noon, accompanied by a male companion identified as Lieutenant Colonel Michael Page. They'd contacted one Dickie Curtiss to ascertain the whereabouts of Ed James's son, rented a video, then left. A phone survey of area hotels ascertained that they'd checked into the La Quinta Motel at thirteen-fifteen.

Russ checked the flat, gold Piaget strapped to his wrist. One-fifteen. A little more than an hour ago.

"I have an operative en route," Andy told him. "She'll be in place within an hour."

The thin communiqué rustled in Russ's hand. Admiration for the doggedly stubborn captain pushed its way through his determination to eliminate her as a threat. She was resourceful.

He'd give her that. And a scrapper. If her Air Force record of performance hadn't been so spotty, he might have considered recruiting her for Special Programs.

Page, on the other hand, would have made an excellent candidate. Russ shrugged off a twinge of regret at having to destroy the man. He of all people valued courage and service to one's country.

"I'll handle this," Russ said quietly, reaching for the phone. His personal assistant came on the line a moment later. "Elizabeth, get me the White House, please."

Chapter Eighteen

Mike sprawled in the comfortable easy chair provided by the La Quinta. Legs outstretched and hands looped over his stomach, he watched as Jen paced the narrow space between the king-sized bed and the wall papered in a pale southwestern print. She held the mobile phone plastered to her ear with one hand and speared the other through her hair.

"I know, but that's what the guy said," she insisted. "To use his exact words, Ed James left his son a wad. A real wad."

She took another turn, her cranberry top bright against the tan wallpaper and half-opened drapes. Her long legs moved in short, quick strides.

"No, he wasn't one hundred percent sure of the source, but he mentioned MEI. Well, maybe I mentioned MEI. Yes. Yes, I know."

She lifted her thick chestnut mane, twisted it atop her head, then let it drop.

"We'll be here."

Snapping the cellular phone shut, she tossed

it on the bed. Excitement radiated from her like static electricity. Mike could feel it where he sat.

"Kuykendahl's going to run another check on Ed James's finances, and see what he can turn up on Ed Junior. He says he'll get back to us within an hour or two with whatever he finds."

"An hour or two, huh?"

"I know, I know." She shoved her hands in her hip pockets, grinning ruefully. "That barely gives us time to watch the video and get warmed up."

He levered himself out of the chair. "Think so?"

Mike took his time crossing the room. With each step, he savored the sight of her cocky smile. It was the kind that came from the inside out, lighting her face, telling the world that what it saw was exactly what it got. Mike figured he could live off the memory of that grin for a long time if he had to.

Luckily, he wouldn't have to. He planned to make a lot more memories. Very soon.

He cupped a hand behind her neck, sliding his fingers over warm skin and fine silky curls.

"I don't need much warming up."

She came into his arms eagerly. Her head went back. Her hair spilled over his arm. Golden flecks glinted in her eyes as she stared up at him.

She'd been like this since they'd left the video shop. On edge. Filled with anticipation. Wanting pleasure, but wanting answers, too.

Mike felt the same tug. He'd fully intended to

tumble her onto the bed as soon as they'd checked into the motel. Instead, he'd shoved his hands in his pockets and planted his butt in a chair while she searched her purse for Kuykendahl's card.

Even now he couldn't bring himself to do more than take a swift, hard taste. He wanted her. God, he wanted her. But something stronger than want kept him from seeking the release they both craved.

He didn't hold out a whole lot of hope that anything would come of his suggestion that they visit the huge training center a few miles north of the city, but then he hadn't expected much when he'd pushed that hundred-dollar bill across the counter at the smut shop, either. He just knew that he couldn't take Jen back to San Antonio and possible danger without one last effort to find some answers.

"You have a choice," he murmured into the soft, silky hair at her temple. "Movie first, then a quick trip to the base. Or the base first, and all-night movies."

She drew back, wondering. "We have to work food in there somewhere, too."

"Before or after?"

"How about during?"

"That can be arranged."

Laughing, she snatched up her overnight bag and headed for the bathroom. "I'll go freshen up. Then we'll drive out to the base, get some food, and settle in to watch Vixens in Velvet do their thing."

When the rounded curve of her bottom disappeared into the bathroom, Mike called himself ten kinds of an idiot. He didn't need food as much as he needed Jennifer. The side trip to Sheppard would probably be a waste of time. And he damn sure didn't want to watch anything tonight except Jen's face as she arched under him. Not even . . .

Smiling, he slid the videocassette out of the limp, much used brown bag. The tattered cardboard cover depicted three very well-endowed women wearing ankle-high velvet boots and nothing else.

The sound of splashing water from the next room brought an instant, erotic image of Jen naked and wet and wearing similar garb. Mike groaned and picked up the TV remote in a desperate effort to distract himself. He flicked through the channels to the news.

". . . dramatic escape has electrified the world."

CNN's anchor desk faded almost as quickly as it came on the screen. Mike stood still, remote in hand, as he and the rest of the viewing audience were transported from a sound stage to a harsh, desolate base camp in the shadow of tall mountain peaks. He instantly recognized the sickle moon and star on the red flag flying over the camp. He'd never forget the symbol of the country where Lisa died.

"At this point, Dr. Cherbanian is still suffering from delayed shock and extreme exhaustion. He can give us few details on his escape, except that he slipped away from several armed men during the night."

How the hell did the American doctor pull off that astounding feat? Mike wondered. He knew the people in that region. They were hide tough and skilled fighters. The Kurds, in particular, had a reputation for ferocity that made the Turks very nervous about their demands for a separate state. It amazed him that the American got away alive.

He flicked through the channels once more, picking up bits and pieces of the story on other channels until the sound of running water in the next room cut off. Mike's interest in the TV cut off at the same instant. His gaze drifted to the closed bathroom door. The trip to the base wouldn't take long, he assured himself. A half hour. An hour at most. Assuming Jen ever got it in gear.

He could hold out another hour.

Maybe.

When the Cherokee drove through the main gate of Sheppard Air Force Base, Jen surveyed her surroundings with interest. She'd visited Sheppard only once before. She and a friend had spent the night at the Visiting Officers' Quarters en route to a skiing trip in Colorado. They'd arrived late, well after dark, and left early the next morning. Consequently, she'd only viewed the training center through darkened car windows. Driving its gridlike streets in early afternoon, Jen got a much better feel for the immensity of its size and its mission.

For the most part, the buildings on base followed the Air Force's mandated color scheme, an uninspiring combination of mud and tan. The multistoried dormitories in sand-colored brick had a fifties look to them. The newer buildings carried the same bland hues. Even the 82nd Wing headquarters, situated on a rolling rise at the center of the base, sported dark chocolate trim on its plain tan exterior.

Sheppard wouldn't win any architectural awards, Jen decided, but what it lacked in charm it more than made up in energy. The base pulsed with a rhythm all its own, one unique to a twenty-four-hour operation and a large transient population. Airmen and officers in every combination from baggy camouflage BDUs and Air Force blue to the elaborate uniforms of NATO allies popped salutes as they passed each other. Jet engines thundered from the direction of the flight line. Static displays of aircraft and missiles dotted the area, reminding students and instructors alike of their mission.

Jen wasn't sure of the exact number the center trained annually, but she thought that somewhere around thirty thousand students attended courses as diverse as fuels handling, parachute fabrication, biomedical sciences, and dentistry. Watching the activity that surged around her, she didn't have any trouble believing that number.

"It's been a while since I was at Sheppard,"

Mike commented, turning onto a bisecting street. "If I remember correctly, the 366th Training Squadron is this way."

"How do you know the commander?" Jen asked curiously.

"We were stationed together a long time ago. He dug trenches and I strung them with cable."

"Sounds like fun."

His mouth curved. "It was."

Rows of dormitories rolled by on either side of the street. Halfway down the block, road guards in gray sweats and orange safety vests signaled them to stop.

"Uh-oh. Looks like we're going to be here awhile."

Shoving the gearshift into neutral, Mike hung his wrists over the wheel. Moments later, a flight of sweat-suited troops jogged by in loose formation. Another followed, then another.

Just the sight of those rippling gray waves gave Jen goose bumps. She hated exercise of any sort, and forced exercise even more. She'd run exactly two days at Officer Training School, protesting every step, before she sprained her ankle, thank God. That injury had stood her in good stead all the way through her own tech training at Keesler Air Force Base, in Mississippi.

Despite those less-than-pleasant memories, the singsong cadence the troops called out and the sound of hundreds of sneakers hitting the pavement in unison gave her a strange sort of thrill. Propping a heel on the seat, she wrapped her arms around her knee and watched the passing formations.

Okay, so maybe the early days hadn't been so bad. In retrospect, she could remember some fun times during her weeks at Keesler. During her first few years in the Air Force, even. Lieutenants were expected to be stupid, and those who were smart enough to recognize that fact got away with murder. Jen certainly had.

Her first assignments at base level had exercised her newly learned skills as a programmer. Her subsequent selection for a masters' program and an assignment to the Air Force Propulsion Lab had only whetted her appetite for more. Granted, she'd had to adjust to the totally different world of personnel data systems when she'd arrived at the Center, but she'd viewed that as more of a challenge than anything else.

So when had the Air Force stopped being fun? When had the petty rules and endless regulations gotten to her to the extent that she stopped trying to change them or work around them? When had she lost her zest for improving, if not beating, the system?

Not long after she arrived in San Antonio, she realized. Looking back, she could trace her mounting irritation and dwindling patience to a string of lackluster, shortsighted bosses. Of course, not everyone had shared her opinion of the individuals in question. One had been promoted to colonel and taken over a Basic Military Training Group at Lackland. Another had been pulled up to the Air Staff.

By then, Jen didn't care where they went. She only wanted out. Her attitude and her performance reports reflected that fact. She'd put in her request for a waiver and was counting the weeks until she could separate when Mike Page had walked into the Military Systems Division.

In a few short months, he'd turned both her life and her career upside down. Looking back now, Jen recognized that she'd enjoyed their sparring matches. He'd irritated the hell out of her, true, but she'd done her best to return the favor. Then Ed James had died and Jen had gotten caught up in the challenge of his mysterious files and she and Mike had become allies instead of antagonists.

In the process, her burning desire to separate from the Air Force had cooled. All right, it had almost fizzled out altogether. If anything, getting out of the Air Force now took last place in her revised list of priorities.

She tipped a shoulder against the door frame, shifting her attention from the waves of gray-clad troops to the man who now occupied first place on that list.

He watched the passing parade, his eyes narrowed against the sun and his profile a study in strong lines and fine contrasts. He'd shed his suede jacket during the drive and rolled up the cuffs of his blue cotton shirt. Jen caught the glint of sunlight in the fine golden hairs dusting his forearms, and remembered the comfort she'd found in those same arms.

Comfort, and stunning, explosive pleasure.

Her foot slid off the seat and hit the floor mat with a thump. "The last squadron's coming through. Let's get this show on the road."

His sandy brows rose at the abrupt command.

"We've got work to do and a video to watch," she reminded him tartly. "Not necessarily in that order."

"You were the one who wanted to visit the base before we held a private screening of *Vixens in Velvet*, remember?"

"I remember. I didn't think the excursion would take all day, though."

"It won't," he said decisively, and shifted into gear. "Bulldog isn't the type to ask a lot of questions."

Jen discovered the truth of that statement a few moments later. When his clerk buzzed that Lieutenant Colonel Page was here to see him, Dennis "Bulldog" O'Shay came charging out of his office and drove a fist into his visitor's left shoulder. Short, wiry, and completely bald, the man packed enough punch under his starched camouflage fatigues to rock Mike back on his heels.

"Jesus, Page, I couldn't believe it when I got the word you called earlier. Talk about great timing! We just finished our accreditation review. The headquarters toads are on their way off base as we speak." He shagged a ball cap emblazoned with the school's insignia and a shiny lieutenant colonel's leaf from the coatrack beside his office door. "Let's go guzzle some beer."

That was it? Jen thought in amusement. No curiosity about what brought Mike to Sheppard? No demands to know how long he intended to stay?

"Maybe later," Mike replied easily. "Captain Varga and I just came by to pick your brain for a few minutes."

O'Shay's expression didn't alter as Mike made the introductions, but his swift catalogue of Jen's casual jeans and windblown hair told her that he'd formed his own opinion of the fact that Mike was traveling across Texas with a junior officer.

When his beetle-black eyes cut back to the other man, Jen thought she detected a faint warning in them. He didn't voice it, however. In this instance, friendship obviously went deeper than surface appearances.

"I never thought I'd live to see the day you'd rather talk shop than drink a beer," he replied, spinning the ball cap back to the rack. "But come on in and pick away."

He ushered them into a spacious office flooded with light from rows of windows. Between the windows hung a series of framed paintings. Their stark, vibrant slashes of color formed no discernible patterns that Jen could see, but they shouted out an exuberance for life that struck an immediate, responsive chord in her.

And in Mike.

Whistling, he strolled closer to observe the detail work. "Did Susan do these?"

"She did." The colonel's voice rang with pride.

Mike shook his head, chuckling. "Remember how pissed we were the time she and Lisa scribbled all over the hallway wall in your quarters with Magic Markers?"

"I remember," O'Shay said dryly. "I also remember we couldn't match the paint color and ended up having to repaint the entire hallway, the living room, and the kitchen. Hey, Susie's home from Stanford this weekend. You'll have to stop by and say hello. Better yet, why don't you and Captain Varga joint us for dinner." He reached for the phone. "I'll call Melissa and tell her to pull two more steaks out of the freezer."

Jen's heart sank. She didn't think she could take another delay.

To her relief, Mike dodged the invitation. "We can't, Bulldog. But thanks for the invite. Tell Susan and Melissa I'll catch them next time."

The casual response earned Jen another swift, scrutinizing glance, but the colonel didn't press the point. He waved them to a round conference table and hitched a chair out for himself. Folding his hands across his stomach, he listened intently while Mike gave him a quick sketch of the files Jen had found on Ed James's computer. His eyes widened when Mike described the attack on Trish and Jen, then narrowed to black slits.

"Let me get this straight. The records you

found on this civilian's computer all pertained to people in training?"

"All except Staff Sergeant Gerald L. McConnell," Jen explained. "His record showed a class start date, but not much else. When I tried to bump it against the Master Personnel File, I couldn't get a match."

"The other folks matched?"

"I only remembered a couple of names."

"The OSI checked out one," Mike said. "A tech sergeant at Keesler. They're still working the others. All we had to go on was the rank and first name."

"What rank and what name?"

"Captain Steve. According to the OSI, there are twelve of them in training right now."

"With that many in training and only four Air Force training centers," O'Shay drawled, "I'd say the odds are pretty good that at least one of your captains is here."

Mike nodded. "You got it. According to the OSI, he's on leave until after the holidays. They did a background screen, though, and he checked out."

"So what do you want me to do?"

"Take a look at his record. See if anything strikes you as unusual or different. You've been around this business a long time. You might see something the OSI missed."

O'Shay didn't hesitate. "No problem. Let's see what he looks like."

Shoving back his chair, he crossed to the slim, compact notebook computer on the credenza behind his desk. A few quick strokes brought Sheppard's base-level management information system to the screen. A click of a mouse opened the student database.

Mike hitched a hip on the corner of the desk and swung a leg patiently. Less patiently, Jen peered over O'Shay's shoulder and watched while he did a simple search using "Captain" and "Steve" as key words. When that failed to produce a match, he tried "Stephen."

Jen gnawed her lower lip when that, too, came back with no match. Calmly, O'Shay changed "Stephen" to Steven" and hit the search button again. Five seconds later, a record painted across the screen.

"Bingo!"

"Captain Steven Warner," Jen murmured, testing the name against her memory of one she'd only seen for a second or two. "That could be him. I just don't remember."

The colonel scrolled through the record, highlighting each data point with the click of a mouse. Date of birth. Date entered active duty. Date graduated from undergraduate pilot training.

Impatient, Jen skimmed through the service dates and tried to read the information at the bottom of the screen. "What's he doing here at Sheppard?"

The highlighter zipped to the coded course information. "Learning to be a fighter jock. He's in his fourth week of the six-week Introduction to Fighter Fundamentals course. Let's see what he was flying before."

He stroked the keys and brought up an assignment history. "Hmmm, that's interesting."

Jen crowded closer to his shoulder. "What is?"

"This guy's got some holes in his record. He was grounded for a couple of years, on some kind of medical hold. Before that he flew C-21s in D.C. No, wait. Not in D.C. Looks like he was assigned to a classified location. I don't recognize the designator."

Mike's leg stopped its slow swing. "What year was that?"

The odd note in his voice snapped Jen's attention. Glancing over her shoulder, she caught the slow tensing of his jawline.

"Ninety-three. Why?"

He took his time answering. Her curiosity fired, Jen waited while he sorted his reply through in his mind.

"There was a big flap about misuse of Air Force assets about that time," he said at last, obviously weighing each word. "It happened before I got to the Congressional Liaison Office, but I heard about it. The Air Force sorted the mess out eventually, but Congress and the GAO weren't happy about the fact that certain political appointees had secured dedicated air support without proper justification or compensation."

O'Shay snorted. "So what else is new? A few congressmen I could name have done the same thing in their time."

"Maybe, but the Air Force wasn't clean on this one. We had set up a classified detachment and supplied it with both pilots and aircraft to support a few key presidential advisers."

"Like whom?" Jen asked.

"Like the deputy director of the CIA, among others."

She lifted her shoulders. "So?"

"So the deputy director at the time was Russell Murdock."

It took Jen less than a heartbeat to make the connection. Russell Murdock. Murdock Enterprises, Incorporated. MEI.

"Ho-ly shit!"

They left twenty minutes later. Bulldog showed them out, a troubled crease etched down the center of his forehead. Jen was too excited at first to notice that the same crease marked Mike's brow.

"First Harry Waterman. Then Ed James. Now this Steve Warner." She snapped her seat belt in place, leaving it loose enough for her to hook a leg under her hips and sit sideways in the seat. "I bet if Kuykendahl goes back and digs hard enough, he might find some connection between MEI and Tech Sergeant Tobias, too."

Mike buckled himself in and keyed the Cherokee's ignition. Hooking an arm over the back of the passenger seat, he checked behind the vehicle before backing out.

"Russ Murdock." Jen rolled the name around, thinking of what she knew about the man. What everyone knew. "How in the world could someone like Russ Murdock be connected to the files I found on Ed James's computer?"

"We don't know that he is," Mike put in, cutting into the flow of traffic heading for the main gate. "We're reaching here, Jen. Really reaching."

"I know! But this is the first time we've had something to reach for." She wrapped her hands around her ankle, thinking hard. "I mean, I see the guy on TV all the time, and read about him just about every week in *People* or *Time.* Isn't he the one who flew several planeloads of food and clothing to the Bosnian refugees? And funded a whole string of shelters for women after one of his employees was battered by her husband?"

"He's the one."

The tight note in his voice finally penetrated Jen's absorption. She tilted her head, her hair curtaining the side window as she studied his face.

"Do you know something about Russ Murdock that I don't?"

"I know that he's a very powerful man. A friend of presidents and kings. Hell, his corporation provided a good chunk of the capital for a joint government-private sector venture that kept Senegal's economy from going under after a coup attempt a few years ago."

"The same corporation also apparently provided a front for the man who called himself Harry Waterman," Jen pointed out.

"I haven't forgotten that fact."

How could he?

Tension coiled like a snake in Mike's stomach as Sheppard's main gate fell behind them. He'd spent enough time at the Pentagon to understand the power that men like Russ Murdock wielded. He didn't subscribe to the belief that absolute power corrupted absolutely. During his years working Congressional Liaison, he'd seen too many men and women make the right gut-wrenchingly tough decisions to believe that. But he'd also seen men like Russ Murdock influence the definition of what was right, or legal, or necessary to U.S. national interests.

The sense that Jen had stumbled onto something far bigger than either she or Mike had realized sat like a dead weight in his chest. One fist gripped the steering wheel as he drove south toward Wichita Falls, the other stayed locked on the gearshift.

A few moments later, he pulled off the interstate. Driven by a mounting sense of unease, he turned into the parking lot of La Quinta and followed Jen down the short, pebbled walk to their first-floor room.

Inserting the card key in the lock, he pushed the door open for Jen. She stepped inside. Mike started to follow when he noticed, too late, that the drapes they'd left open an hour ago were now closed.

Chapter Nineteen

"**J**ennifer!"

Mike's shout spun Jen around. Blinded by the transition from bright sunlight to the dim interior of the motel room, she squinted at his silhouette in the doorway.

"Captain Varga?"

The sound of a male voice coming from the room behind her provoked two instantaneous responses. She jumped half out of her skin, and Mike launched himself through the open doorway. His broad shoulders blocked the streaming sunlight for a second . . . just long enough for Jen to see the figure that stepped out of the shadows behind the door. Before she could cry out a warning, an arm sliced through the air and chopped into the side of Mike's neck.

He crashed to the floor at her feet.

The unfamiliar male voice spit out an oath. "Jesus, Mathison, what the hell are you doing?"

Jen whirled in the direction of the stranger. She tensed her muscles, preparing to throw herself at him, when a woman's cool tones cut through the air.

"Don't try it, Captain."

The distinctive snick of a gun's safety being clicked off added emphasis to the soft command.

Jen froze.

"Madre de Dios!"

A third voice added to the confusion, but Jen paid no attention to the terrified maid huddled in the corner of the room, crossing herself repeatedly. Nor did she spare a glance for the man standing a few feet from the maid. Her entire being focused on the woman who stepped into the pool of light streaming through the open door.

She held a gun in both hands. The weapon was smaller than the .380 caliber Beretta Harry Waterman had stuck in Jen's ribs only a week ago, as if designed for the more delicate hand that held it. Somehow, that made it seem even more obscene.

Jen's heart slammed against her breastbone as she lifted her eyes from the gun to the woman who gripped it. She wore tailored gray slacks, a silky white blouse covered by a navy blazer, and a smooth, sleek cap of frosted hair. For a sickening moment, Jen wondered when hired gunmen had gone so upscale. First, Harry Waterman's tanned handsomeness and blue diamond pinkie ring. Now this composed, elegant creature who obviously shopped at exclusive boutiques.

As if sizing up her opponent, the woman took

her own swift inventory. Her expression calm and unruffled, she flicked a quick glance over Jen's jeans and stretchy cranberry top. When their eyes locked again, Jen caught a flash of disdain in the shadowed depths. Disdain, and malicious amusement.

She was enjoying this, Jen realized on a burst of fury. The gun. The power. The man at her feet.

In that instant, Jen hated her.

In the next, the woman's companion stalked to her side.

"What the hell do you think this is?" he demanded furiously. "Some kind of B-grade *Rambo* shoot 'em up?"

"No," she replied coolly, the gun never wavering. "This is a takedown of a potentially dangerous suspect."

He shot her a disgusted look and reached into his suit coat. Swinging around to face Jen, he pulled out a small black case.

"Captain Varga, I'm—"

A grunt from Mike preempted him. Ignoring the two strangers, Jen dropped to her knees on the sand-colored carpet. Her hands shook violently as she wrapped them around Mike's arm. Digging her fingers into the leather sleeve, she helped him up.

He staggered for a moment, then steadied. His gray eyes sliced to the woman holding the gun. She took a deliberate pace back, out of his reach.

Mike's lip curled. "Smart lady."

"Yes, Colonel Page, I am."

"Who are you?" His gaze swept to the other man. "Both of you?"

He flipped open the black leather ID case. "Special Agent William White, of OSI Detachment Four-eleven at Sheppard. This is Detective Alicia Mathison of the Wichita Falls . . ."

A scurry of movement from the corner of the room brought his head whipping around. The maid sidled along the wall, her face pinched with fear.

"Can I go, señor? I have let you in, as you ask. Can I go, *por favor*?"

White jerked his chin toward the door. "Yes. Go on."

She turned and almost fell out the door. Her leather-soled shoes slapped against the walkway.

The remaining occupants of the room didn't speak until the sound died away. It was as if they all needed the few seconds for the high drama of the past few moments to fade and reality to take hold. Jen sure as hell did.

These people were from the OSI, she reminded herself. From the Wichita Falls police. They were the good guys. Mike's wild charge through the door must have spooked them as much as it had her. In retrospect, she could understand why the blonde had given him that vicious chop to the neck.

She could understand it, but that didn't mean she liked it. Drawing in a long, shuddering breath, Jen fought to force her heart to a less frantic beat. The sight of Alicia Mathison's unruffled poise didn't help.

"Why don't you put that gun away?" she snapped.

"Why don't you turn around and put your hands against the wall?"

"What?"

"You, too, Colonel Page."

Jen shoved her hair out of her eyes with a shaky hand. "Wait a minute. We need to fall back and regroup here. I—"

"*Now*, Captain Varga!"

Enough was enough. Jen's chin shot up. "Screw you, Detective Mathison."

Above the weapon, the woman's eyes took on a flat, hard sheen. "Cuff them."

"These are Air Force personnel," the OSI agent ground out. "I'll handle this."

"Then do it."

Snapping his ID shut, he thrust it into his inner pocket. "Turn around and place your hands on the wall, please."

Mike didn't move. Jen couldn't.

"We're not turning our backs to either of you until we know what this is about," Mike said softly.

The agent's face tightened. Tall and thin and chasing his late thirties, he stood his ground.

"I've been asked to bring you in, sir. I'd rather not use force to bring you in, but I will if I have to."

Mike's head reared back. "Bring me in? Why?"

"Your commander has probable cause to believe that you've committed offenses that violate the Uniform Code of Military Justice."

"What offenses?"

"Failure to obey a lawful order. Conduct unbecoming an officer. Possession of pornographic materials."

Disbelief slackened Mike's face. A moment later it went rock hard. "What the hell are you talking about? What lawful order? What pornographic materials?"

"The lawful order issued by General Faith Daniels that you were to cease and desist your association with Captain Varga."

"General Daniels didn't issue any such order," Mike shot back furiously.

"I have a communication from Randolph that says she did."

"The charge of possession of pornographic materials is ours," the detective put in with a cool smile. "We got a tip from a local entrepreneur. Our local magistrate was more than willing to issue a search and seizure order."

Mike swore. Jen felt his arm flex to steel under her fingers. He shook off her hold and confronted the law officers.

"That movie was rented over the counter. It's not illegal. Every frat house and truck stop in the country has libraries full of that kind of crap."

"Not this kind of crap, sir."

"Get real, man. That cheap skin-flick doesn't qualify as porn in anyone's book."

"You don't think so?"

His eyes cold, White slid the videocassette out of the crumpled brown bag. He snapped it into the VCR on top of the TV and punched the on button.

Jen felt a bubble of hysteria well up in her chest. Under guard and in the presence of two strangers, she was finally going to see the Velvet Vixens in action.

Only there wasn't anything the least bit vixenish about the grainy black and white movie that flickered to life on the screen. The few seconds Jen watched were stark, sick, and horrifying. A woman jerked frantically against the ropes that tied her to a chair, her eyes wide with terror. A man approached the chair and pulled her head back. He shoved himself into her mouth. A moment later a knife slashed across her exposed throat.

"Oh, my God!"

Jen closed her eyes, fighting a hot, coppery rush of bile. Her head spun, and the floor seemed to tilt under her feet. For a moment she floated in a dark, silent void.

Without warning, the darkness erupted into a maelstrom of movement. Mike pushed Jen aside and lunged for Mathison. Startled, Jen tripped over her own feet and hit the floor with jarring force. Pain shot up her elbow and knifed through her injured shoulder.

She heard a grunt. An instant later Mathison crumpled down on top of her. Frantic, Jen wiggled and pushed and shoved.

"Get off me!"

Panting, she clawed her way from under the limp bundle of silk and wool and expensive perfume. Her lungs bursting and her arm on fire, she scrambled to her feet.

"Mike! My God, what . . . ?"

She gaped at his wide-legged stance. He held Mathison's gun as steady as the detective had only moments before. A few paces away, a furious, grim-faced agent slowly lifted his hands.

"If you move," Mike warned, his voice low and infinitely threatening, "if you even blink, I'll nail you to the wall."

"What are you doing?" Jen cried. "He's with the OSI! We can't—"

"One or both of them switched the video," Mike bit out.

She shot White a wild look.

"Oh, God! You're not with the OSI? You're another Waterman!"

The agent shook his head, his face taut. "I don't know what you're talking about, but you're right about one thing, Captain. You can't do this. If you do, you'll both step out of one mess into another one a whole lot more serious."

"Search the woman," Mike snapped to Jen. "See if she's got handcuffs on her."

Jen swiped cold, sweaty palms down her jeans. Dropping to one knee, she patted the blonde's hips and waist nervously. A lump in the small of her back proved to be a holster.

"Check her front pockets."

Sucking in a ragged breath, Jen rolled her

over. Even unconscious, Mathison retained a cool, composed elegance she could never achieve . . . even if she wanted to, which at the moment she most assuredly did not.

A quick search of the navy blazer's inner pockets turned up an ID case, a spare magazine, and a small, round canister. To her relief, the next side pocket yielded a set of handcuffs.

She yanked on the steel circlet with both hands. It didn't give.

"Dammit, I need the key."

"No, you don't. Just push the bar straight through."

Metal stabbed against metal as Jen's fumbling fingers pushed at the yoke. It swung through, then dangled open in her fingers. When the steel cuff clicked over Mathison's slim ankle bones, Jen was human enough to feel a vicious satisfaction at the sound. She hoped it would take hours, if not days, to cut the damned thing off.

Mike motioned to White with the gun. "Get down on the floor. Stretch out beside her, head to feet."

"Colonel, listen to me! You're committing a serious offense here. Very serious. Obstructing a law enforcement officer in the performance of his duties and assault with a deadly weapon added to failure to obey and the other charges could earn you a stay at Leavenworth!"

"Get . . . down."

The soft command raised the hairs on the back of Jen's neck. It also brought the agent to his knees. Jen scrambled out of his reach as he flattened himself on his stomach next to the police officer.

"Handcuff his wrist to her ankle, Jen. Don't try to touch her, White. Don't even breathe."

Cautiously, she reached across the unconscious woman and clicked the loose cuff around the agent's wrist.

"All right. Back away."

Mike waited until Jen was clear, then went down slowly on one knee. Holding Mathison's gun only inches from White's temple, he relieved the man of his weapon and slipped it into the pocket of his leather jacket.

A small rattling sound issued from Jen's mouth. She gulped, not realizing she'd held her breath trapped in her throat for the past few moments. She swiped her clammy palms down her thighs again and watched while Mike patted the OSI agent down.

With a grunt of satisfaction, he pulled out another set of handcuffs. He made far quicker work than Jen had of attaching White's ankle to the bed frame. That done, he performed a more thorough search of the two agents.

He extracted a set of keys from Mathison's jacket and White's pants pocket, then rose. Two strides took him to the phone beside the bed. One swift yank ripped the cord and the plate it was plugged into out of the wall.

"Grab your things," he told Jen. "We're getting out of here."

She snatched up her purse and stuffed the few things she'd unpacked into her overnight bag.

As Mike's fist closed over the handle of his carryall, White made a last, urgent plea.

"Think about this, Colonel! You're putting your life on the line here. Yours, and Captain Varga's."

Mike whirled. His lips curled back in savage fury.

"I'll give *you* something to think about, Special Agent White. When Captain Varga and I drove away an hour ago, we left behind a skinflick that wouldn't excite a fourteen-year-old having wet dreams twice a night. Someone switched the cassettes."

"That's bullshit. Why would I plant evidence? I had enough to bring you both in without the porn charge."

"Is that right?" Mike bit out. "Then who decided to throw that little twist into the equation? If I was going to bet on it, I'd put my money on your friend here. Or the local magistrate who granted you the search warrant that got you into this room."

The agent's sudden tensing told its own story.

"I'd also be willing to bet," Mike snarled, "that one or more of your suspects might not have made it back to the base, but I'm not going to stick around to collect on that one."

He caught Jen's arm.

"Colonel, wait!"

Ignoring the agent's shout, Mike pushed Jen toward the bright patch of sunlight streaming through the still open door. She ran outside, threw her things in the back seat of the Cherokee. The car doors slammed on another furious shout from inside the motel room.

Gunning the engine, Mike shoved the gearshift into reverse. Tires squealed. Gravel thrown up by the violent movement rattled against the fender. A moment later Jen slammed back against the seat as the Cherokee shot forward.

She waited until they'd hit the interstate to ask the question burning in her chest.

"Where are we going?"

"To see Bulldog."

Mike dug a folded scrap of paper out of his blue shirt pocket and tossed it to Jen. She recognized the motel's cheap stationery and the number he'd gotten earlier from Sheppard's operator.

"Get him on the cell phone. Tell him to meet us at . . ." He thought for a moment. "At the McDonald's just outside the main gate. Tell him I need a favor. He won't ask any questions."

Jen believed that. She fumbled in the back seat for her purse and dragged out the mobile phone Special Agent Kuykendahl had given her. Before she pushed in the numbers, though, she had to ask.

"How did you know they'd switched videos?"

The look he fired her way shattered her few illusions Jen still retained about neat, orderly, by-the-rules Lieutenant Colonel Mike Page. It was pure rogue male.

"I snuck a preview of *Vixens in Velvet* while you were in the bathroom."

Jen couldn't believe it! Her heart was ricocheting off her sternum like a Ping-Pong ball. Her hands were so slick with delayed fright that she could hardly hold the cell phone. She still hadn't figured out quite what had happened back there. Yet, somehow, Mike's swift, rakish look gave her the illusion that the world hadn't completely unraveled at the seams.

That illusion shattered a moment later. Pulling one of the guns he'd taken from the agents out of his jacket pocket, he held it out.

"Put this in your purse. Keep it close at hand from now on."

Jen's stomach clenched. She wiped her lips, eyeing the weapon. Then she reached for the shoulder bag she'd tossed in the back seat.

They pulled into the McDonald's parking lot scant moments before O'Shay did. Recognizing his friend behind the wheel of a late-model Olds Cutlass, Mike climbed out of the Cherokee. Jen joined him by the side of the vehicle. Her purse hung with a heavy and unfamiliar weight from her shoulder.

"I need to borrow your car, Bulldog. I don't know for how long."

Without so much as a blink, O'Shay tossed his keys in a short arc. Mike caught them in midair. "Thanks."

O'Shay's black eyes narrowed. "That's some bruise you have marching up the side of your neck, pal."

"Yeah, well, you should see the other guy." Mike corrected himself with a small grimace. "Gal."

Bulldog shot Jen a swift, startled glance. She shrugged and declined comment. He turned back to Mike, a scowl pulling his forehead into tight lines.

"Look," he said grimly, "I don't know what the hell's going on here, but you'd better come back to the base with me. You and Captain Varga. I'll make sure no one lays any more bruises on either one of you."

Mike shook his head. "I'm sorry I had to drag you into this, even to this extent. I don't want to pull you in any deeper."

Clearly unhappy about the situation, Bulldog took the keys Mike handed him.

"Park the Cherokee away from the squadron. With any luck, they won't track it to you until we've gotten some answers."

Or been apprehended, Jen thought, swallowing a baseball-sized lump.

"Look, buddy . . ."

"We have to go."

"I don't like this. I don't like this at all."

Mike's jaw worked in a way both watchers recognized instantly. "I don't like it, either."

With a terse farewell to his friend, he pulled their gear out of the Cherokee.

"Come on, Jen. Move it."

For the second time in less than ten minutes, she tossed her things into a back seat and buckled herself in. Her purse she kept at her feet. Seconds later, Mike pulled out of the restaurant's parking lot with far more restraint than he had the motel.

Neither one of them spoke. Jen kept her eyes on the road ahead, expecting flashing lights and screaming sirens at any moment. Mike stayed at the speed limit. They passed under the interstate that led to their motel and turned south, heading toward Wichita Falls's downtown area.

A park flashed by on their right. Jen caught sight of a ribbon of muddy blue cutting through the manicured greenery. Moments later, they crossed the river that had given the city its name.

Wanting to know what to expect next, Jen swiped her tongue across dry, parched lips.

"Where are we going?"

"I don't know."

Right. Okay. She could accept that. She had no idea where they were, either. On the west side of the city, she guessed, looping around to the south. She sat tense and expectant for a few more miles. Finally, she couldn't stand the silence any longer.

"Do you have a plan?"

"No." His knuckles showed white on the steering wheel. "Do you?"

Chapter Twenty

A charged silence gripped both Mike and Jen as they drove through downtown Wichita Falls. Turning off the broad, divided boulevard that stretched the length of the business district, Mike took them past a row of stately old homes. The turn-of-the-century Victorian masterpiece set in solidary splendor on a corner would have drawn Jen's admiring attention at any other time. At that moment, she had no interest in its twin rounded porches or pristine candlestick trim.

"We've got to call Kuykendahl," Mike said finally, breaking the silence. "And Gutierrez."

"How do we know we can trust them?"

"We don't. But we can't do this alone and on the run."

"On the run!" Groaning, Jen slumped against the seat. "A few minutes ago, we were Air Force officers on leave. Now we're fugitives on the run. There's something seriously wrong with this picture."

He didn't bother to comment on that obvious fact.

"Get on the phone, okay? We need to make the calls before we leave the city. If that instrument has some kind of tracking device built into the transmitter, it will show us still here."

"We *are* still here," she pointed out testily.

"We won't be for long. Get Kuykendahl. Tell him what happened. See what he found out about Ed James's finances."

Jen's clammy palms had dried and her heart had stopped ricocheting off her ribs, but the knot of fear and anger and confusion lodged in her chest had grown to a solid mass. The knot added another layer when she plugged the phone's charger into the lighter and depressed the specially marked key Kuykendahl had pointed out to her. He answered on the first ring.

"Where are you?" he asked without preamble.

"Not far from where we were when we called you an hour ago," Jen shot back. "Why?"

A taut silence followed. Her throat tight, Jen met Mike's eyes above the console separating the bucket seats of Bulldog's Cutlass. Finally, Kuykendahl responded, his voice flat and hard.

"Captain Varga, I must advise you and Colonel Page to report to the nearest military installation immediately. Your commander has determined that sufficient evidence exists to charge him with failure to obey a lawful order and you both with conduct unbecoming . . ."

"You want to tell me why the commander suddenly decided to prefer these charges?"

"I can't speak to that."

"No, I didn't think you could. Let's not forget that little bit about possession of pornographic materials," Jen snapped.

"What?"

"You didn't know about that one?"

"What porn?" he asked sharply. "What are you talking about?"

She slapped a hand over the mouthpiece. "Sounds like the video is news to him."

Mike's eyes narrowed. "I had a feeling that was a local initiative."

"You'll have a few more charges to add to your list soon," she informed the agent tersely. "Like resisting arrest and handcuffing a couple of law enforcement officers to a bed."

Swiftly she sketched the events at the La Quinta Motel. Ignoring Kuykendahl's incredulous demand to know if they'd both lost their minds, she launched into the reason for the call.

"We need to know what you found out about the money Ed James left his son."

"I can't discuss that with you," the agent replied stiffly, "unless and until you—"

"Tell me! If you don't want me to hang up right now, tell me!"

"I don't respond to demands from suspects."

Jen's already shaky nerves came apart. "You listen to me, Kuykendahl! Someone's tried to kill me! Twice! They shot my dog, and they put my roommate in a coma. Now you're telling me I'm a suspect? I *don't think* so!"

"Captain . . ."

"We don't have much time," she said angrily. "We've got to decide what we're going to do, and this information could make the difference. Tell me what you found out!"

For long, wrenching moments, Jen didn't think he'd answer.

"We haven't found anything so far," he finally clipped out. "I've had people go through Ed James's probate, his bank accounts, his tax records, even the savings funds he set up for his grandkids. There's no record he invested in any stocks, and no record of any payment to his estate from MEI."

"Dammit!"

Fighting a wave of frustration so strong it left a vile taste in her mouth, Jen shook her head at Mike.

"I'll keep digging," Kuykendahl promised grimly. "In the meantime, you've got to—"

Jen cut him off. "Dig hard. Real hard. While you're at it, you might also take another look at Captain Steve Warner's background. Find out what classified location he was assigned to in 1993. Who he flew with or for. And give Tech Sergeant Tobias another screen. If she turns up with a connection to MEI, we've got some serious talking to do."

"Captain Varga . . ."

"I'll call you."

Jen snapped the phone case shut, cutting the connection. Her hands shook so badly she could barely hold on to the phone. For a few seconds, the only sounds in the Cutlass were her swift, shallow breathing and the muted whir of the road passing under the car.

"You did good."

Mike's voice poured over her jagged nerves like soothing oil. Jen wanted to be soothed, badly, but even more, she wanted this nightmare to end.

"Now what?"

"Now we get hold of Guiterrez. Tell him what happened, and ask him to use his police connections to check out Alicia Mathison."

"And then?"

"Then we toss that phone in the Wichita River and get the hell out of Dodge."

The moon hung like a glowing gold ornament in a dark sky when they pulled into the Hungry Cowpoke Truck Stop and Motel some hours later. A hundred miles lay between them and Wichita Falls.

Over the stench of diesel fumes, Jen caught the scent of grease. Hot, sizzling grease. Her stomach rumbled an immediate SOS.

"I want two of everything they're frying in that oil."

Smiling, Mike pulled up to the restaurant/ motel office. "Two it is. Sit tight."

She watched him walk into the office and nod to the man who appeared behind the counter. Tall and loose-limbed in his jeans and well-worn bomber jacket, Mike fit in easily with the few other travelers in the small establishment.

If he felt even half as wired and taut as Jen

did, he didn't reveal it to the clerk. He signed
the register and paid cash for a room. His smile
was casual as he picked up the key and strolled
a few feet to the food counter. He chatted with
the waitress who took his order, acting far more
like a man on a leisurely cross-country trip than
a fugitive.

Oh, God! A fugitive!

Jen still hadn't gotten used to the idea. For
the first few hours, she'd expected to hear the
wail of sirens and see the flash of lights at every
turn. Eventually, she'd stopped tensing every
time Mike looked in the rearview mirror, but
she couldn't keep her racing mind from playing
and replaying the chase scenes from every
movie she'd ever seen. Unfortunately, most of
those movies had ended in gory shoot-outs or,
in the case of *Thelma and Louise,* with the fugitives sailing over the edge of a cliff in a Cadillac convertible.

She wasn't going over a cliff, Jen swore
grimly, in a Cadillac or Bulldog's Cutlass or
anything else. And she'd be damned if she'd let
the nameless, faceless entity behind the attacks
on her and Trish and Commodore destroy Mike
as well. She owed him that much and more. So
much more.

She wouldn't let herself think about the comfort he'd given her, or his support since this
nightmare began, or even those few hours of
explosive sexual satisfaction. She could only
think about the dangerous morass she'd pulled
him into.

Every spurious charge against him sprang from his involvement with her. Failure to obey a lawful order. Conduct unbecoming, for God's sake! Leave it to the military to come up with such a sanitized term for sleeping around. Now, resisting arrest and possibly desertion. Whoever had instigated those charges was using Mike to get her. Jen had been the target all along. She was still the target. The longer Mike stayed with her, the harder it would be for him to pull free of the danger that surrounded her.

She knew what she had to do. She prayed that she had the courage to do it.

She waited until they'd parked the car out of sight at the rear of the motel and carried their bags and their supper into a small, surprisingly clean room to broach the subject. As soon as the door locked behind them, she dropped her overnight bag on the double bed and turned to face him.

"You have to go back to San Antonio, Mike. You can't add desertion to these ridiculous charges."

He deposited his carryall on the green shag carpet and the paper sack from the restaurant on the room's small table.

"We'll go back together, when we're sure it's safe."

"I'm the one they want, not you. I'll—"

"We'll go back together."

Jen taped a foot impatiently while he checked the windows and the bathroom. "We need to talk about this."

"We just did." He lifted a stack of carry out containers from the bag. "What we need to do right now is eat."

Ignoring her stomach's excited leap at the scent of fried potatoes and what smelled like chicken fried steak, Jen paced the room. The shag carpet deadened the sound of her footsteps.

"All right. We'll eat. Then we'll call Kuykendahl and tell him where you are. *Then* I'm going to take the Cutlass and—"

"The hell you are."

She broke off, gasping as he caught her wrist and pulled her against his chest.

"We'll eat," he said tightly, his jaw working. "We'll call Kuykendahl and Gutierrez. *Then* we'll talk about what we do next."

"Mike . . ."

He buried his hands in her hair, dragging her head back. The anger in his flinty eyes told Jen that the iron control he'd exercised for the past four hours was close to shattering.

"We're in this together, Jennifer. We have been since the moment you tumbled out of the Cherokee onto my chest. Hell, probably since the first day you walked into my office with your list of twenty-seven reasons why I should approve your waiver request."

Jen's fear and worry and fierce determination to keep Mike from sailing over a cliff warred with a small kick of joy. For a moment, just a moment, she indulged herself.

"Come on, Colonel," she scoffed. "You practically threw me out of your office that day!"

"I know. But I thought about throwing you down on the couch."

"Ho-ly . . . !" Her breath caught at the back of her throat. "Why didn't you? Not that I would have let you, you understand, but it might have been interesting if you'd tried."

His fingers tightened in her hair. "Rules, Captain Varga. Regulations."

Oh, God! She shouldn't do this. She shouldn't give in to the urge to touch him, to feel his mouth on hers. She should pull out of his hold. Should take her purse and the Cutlass and drive away now, before their pursuers tracked them down. Instead, she heard herself point out what they both already knew.

"The rules don't apply anymore, Colonel Page. Not those rules, anyway."

"Looking back, I'm not sure they ever applied. I wanted you," he admitted, "right from the first. But I wouldn't let myself cross the line. Now, my only regret is that I waited so long."

Jen couldn't help herself. Her hands came up to shape the strong, square jaw that had fascinated her since the first time she'd made it lock. It was warm to her touch and stubbled with a day's growth. The prickly shadow rubbed against her palms, still sensitive from their brutal contact with the pavement.

The stinging sensation narrowed Jen's thoughts to a single, sharp need. She shuddered, remembering how she'd clawed her way from under her brand-new Cherokee only seconds before a train rolled over it. How she might yet lose this desperate battle of wits with an unseen, unknown adversary.

She wanted this taste of life. Only a taste. Sliding her arms around Mike's neck, Jen pulled herself up to meet his mouth.

Even before her lips and her tongue met his, Jen knew she wouldn't stop at a kiss. Nor would he. Desire too long delayed flared into instant need. Fed by danger, that need burst into heat. His hands fisted in her hair. Her body pressed his.

Unlike their first time, there was nothing sweet or slow or healing about this coming together. Mike didn't gentle his hold. Jen didn't want gentleness. She wanted just what she got. The rush of his breath in her mouth. The feel of his hands on her breasts and hips.

She shoved off his suede jacket, trying not to think about the gun that weighted the pocket. The jacket dropped to the edge of the bed, then slid to the carpet with a small thud. His blue cotton shirt followed a moment later. Jen's hands were urgent on his chest and shoulders. She clung to him, her nails digging into the flesh of his upper arms while he stripped her with the same rough need. For all his urgency, his hands moved carefully over her fading bruises.

They stilled for a moment when he'd bared her. Jen looked up to find his eyes on the red crease Waterman's bullet had carved along the curve of her shoulder.

"It doesn't hurt," she insisted, fevered with impatience.

"It hurts me."

Bending, he pressed his lips to the healing scar. Jen groaned when she felt his heat cooling.

"Jennifer . . ."

"No!"

She tumbled backward, bringing him down with her. He propped himself up, his arms stiff in an effort to keep his weight from crushing her. Light from the bedside lamp gleaned on his shoulders and chest.

"If anything happens," he said softly, seriously, "Bulldog. Call him. He'll get you to a safe haven until . . ."

"Nothing's going to happen," she swore fiercely. "I won't let it!"

He anchored her head with both hands. "If it does, call Bulldog."

"All right!" She wriggled her hips into position under his, making her intentions clear.

"I love you, Jen."

That got her attention. She stopped wriggling and stared up at him. In the glow of the bedside lamp, his eyes held no shadows

"I didn't realize it until recently, because you have a tendency to infuriate the hell out of me, but I do."

"Is that right?" She locked both arms around his neck. "Well so do I and you do, too. A lot."

With a small, tight grin he kneed her legs apart, then bent to cover her mouth once more. Her womb clutched at the feel of his hands and his mouth. His touch brought a wet heat between her legs.

A moment later he sank into her. Jen gasped at the swift thrust and lifted herself to meet it. Her ankles tangled with his. Her face buried in the hollow between his neck and his shoulder. She closed her eyes in an effort to memorize every movement, every slide of his body on hers. Too soon, she started to convulse.

She tried to pull back, slow down. It didn't work. He pumped into her only a few more— or maybe a few dozen more times—before she arched and gasped out his name. Waves of pleasure began low in her belly and rippled outward.

Sweat slicked Mike's skin. He gritted his teeth with the effort of holding back his own climax. Wrapping an arm around her waist, he canted her hips upward. He'd give his soul to make this last all night, but they didn't have all night. They had only these few, stolen moments before fear and the realization of danger once more left their mark on Jen's face.

Whatever happened, he vowed savagely, this was how he'd remember her. With her head arched back and her skin flushed with pleasure. A moment later she groaned and peaked and collapsed in great, shuddering sighs. When she opened her eyes, the sensual delight in their brown depths took him right to the edge. But it was her soft, whispered words of love that sent him over.

* * *

Jen had to eat.

Her rebellious, growling stomach demanded immediate attention. She lay amid the disordered covers, listening to water pelt against the plastic shower insert. Mike had given her first shot at the bathroom, but she hadn't been able to move.

She'd have to get up and get dressed. She couldn't lie in the pile of sheets and covers forever, much as she wanted to. The idea of leaving this small, green-carpeted motel room made Jen's nerves bunch and twist. The idea of leaving it on her own made her feel slightly sick.

She hadn't changed her mind, though. She wouldn't walk out on Mike without trying to make him understand one more time. She owed him that much. But she had to leave. Now, more than ever, she couldn't stand the thought that whoever was after her would take him down, too.

First, she had to eat.

Snatching his shirt from the floor, she pulled it on. His scent clung to it, a combination of musky male and starch. He sent even his casual clothes to the laundry. She threw hers in the washer when the piles on her bedroom floor got too high to walk around or through. Smiling, she acknowledged that she and Mike were in for some interesting days ahead. Assuming, of course, they survived the days ahead.

Rolling up the sleeves, Jen padded across the shag carpet on bare feet and popped the top on one of the large, square plastic containers. Her nose wrinkled at the sight of soggy French fries and chicken fried steak lying in a pool of cold gravy and congealed grease. Her stomach, however, had no such scruples. It somersaulted in delight and rumbled out another loud demand.

"Okay, okay," she muttered. "Hang on a sec."

She popped the rest of the lids. Mike had taken her at her word and ordered double helpings of everything. Greasy fries. Greasy steaks. Even the Texas toast carried a thin gray film where melted butter had congealed on its golden brown surface.

The shower cut off as Jen was arranging paper napkins and plastic utensils on the far side of the small table. Mike walked out of the bathroom a few moments later.

Jen's stomach performed another violent somersault.

His unsnapped jeans rode low on his hips. His bare chest glistened with moisture the towel had missed. The dark gold hair that Jen had buried her fingers in such a short time ago curled with wet. He looked thoroughly untamed and so unlike the colonel she'd butted heads with so many times in the past four months she couldn't believe she'd never seen past his starched uniforms to the raw male beneath.

He stopped a few feet away, grinning. "I like you in my shirt. I like you even better out of it, but the way the tail rides up yours when you bend over like that is nice. Very nice."

Jen dumped the handful of plastic utensils on

the table. "Get that look out of your eye, Colonel. We have to eat, then call Kuykendahl and Gutierrez, then talk about . . ."

She broke off, stiffening. The small scratching had barely carried over the sound of her voice, but Jen had heard it. So had Mike. He thrust her out of the way and dived for the suede jacket still pooled on the carpet beside the bed.

The scratching came again, louder this time. Someone was at the door to their room.

Oh, no! Not again!

Jen wanted to weep as fear, swift and icy, dropped over her. Her hands shaking, she fumbled for the purse she'd draped by its strap over a chair back.

"Get down!"

She didn't need Mike's swift, soft command to drop to her knees behind the bed. The small arms training she'd taken so long ago in Officer Training School came to her aid as she fumbled off the safety and gripped Alicia Mathison's weapon in both hands. Arms outstretched, elbows resting on the bed, she aimed at the exact center of the door.

Mike flattened himself against the wall beside the door.

Jen prayed the gun didn't kick too much and throw her aim off.

A few, nerve-shattering seconds later, the scratching came again. This time it was accompanied by what sounded like a whoosh of air. A dozen different explanations for that small gust slammed into Jen's mind, each one more terrifying than the last.

Someone was trying to set fire to the place, she decided in panic. Or blow it up!

"Mike!" Her scream ricocheted off the walls. "Get down!"

When he ignored her warning and reached for the door, fear for him brought her off the floor and onto the bed. Holding the gun in one hand, she grabbed for the bedspread with the other. If nothing else, she could shield him with the spread and her own . . .

"Mike, no!"

She couldn't get to him in time. He yanked the door open and aimed his gun at the creature on the stoop.

Chapter Twenty-one

It was a dog . . . or a small horse!

In the first, startled instant, Jen wasn't sure which. Then the creature dropped to its belly and flashed a set of yellowed fangs. Those sharp incisors settled the question in her mind.

"Is . . . ? Is that what we heard?" she asked Mike, still shaken.

He took a quick look in either direction. "Apparently."

Jen's knees buckled. She collapsed in a heap on the bed in a near hysteria of relief.

The animal tensed at her abrupt movement, its whole body quivering. Only then did Jen notice its barrel-staved ribs, the bloody scratches on its mottled yellow hide, and the open sores on its neck and withers. It looked like it had tangled with a roll of barbed wire and lost.

The animal performed a swift inventory of its own. Its eyes flicked back and forth between the humans, then fixed the table with an awful intensity. The thing was starving, Jen realized.

She didn't want to move. She was so weak

with relief, she wasn't sure she could. But she couldn't stand the sight of those awful ribs and running sores.

"He can have my dinner."

She edged off the bed, keeping the spread wrapped around her bare legs and bottom.

"Be careful!" Mike held the gun pointed at the animal. "Move slowly."

The dog watched her every move. It looked ready to spring at any second. Jen only wished she knew which way.

"You might as well give him all of it," Mike said, his eyes on the animal. "We'll get something else."

Jen dumped everything into a single container. Holding the blanket with one hand and the heaping mound of cold fries, white gravy, and steak in the other, she approached the door cautiously.

The dog's gums curled back even farther. Obviously torn between its need for food and wariness of the approaching human, it let out a half growl. Its matted, burr-filled coat twitched, dislodging a small cloud of gnats and, Jen suspected, fleas.

"It's okay," she murmured. "It's okay."

Afraid to get too close, she lowered the container to the floor and pushed it across the threshold with her foot. Mike toed it the rest of the way out the door.

Yellow fangs flashed, but the creature didn't move. Mike slowly closed the door. A second later the sounds of ravenous wuffling came through the panel. When it disappeared, the silence grew almost as loud.

Jen faced Mike across a few feet of green shag carpet. After the pumping, adrenaline-shot fright of the past few moments, she wanted desperately to walk into his arms and stay there for the rest of her life. She couldn't do that to him.

"I'd better get dressed."

Mike nodded, his mind already on the call they'd make in a few minutes. Not from the room. He didn't want to go through switchboards. He'd scouted the location of the pay phone in the restaurant earlier. They'd use that. He'd been out of the wire business for a while now, but he knew enough of current technology to calculate how long it would take for a commercial trace to kick in.

His thoughts on the questions and answers they'd have to ask, he watched Jen dig through her bag. Black tights spilled out, joining the assorted garments on the floor. She fished out her makeup kit, scooped up her jeans, and disappeared into the bathroom.

Absently, Mike straightened the bedcovers and picked up the remaining articles. The fact that they'd created such chaos in the short time they'd occupied the small room didn't surprise him. After almost a week in Jen's company, he'd grown used to the trail of maps, sunglasses, shoes, sweaters, diet drink containers, and laughter she left wherever she went. He stacked her scattered belongings beside her canvas tote bag and dug in his own carryall for a clean shirt.

Both he and the room were neat and tidy by the time Jen emerged from the bathroom.

She'd brushed her hair until it gleamed and added a wash of pink to her cheeks and lips, but the color only emphasized the stubborn set to the rest of her face. She was determined to send him back to San Antonio, he knew, to get him out of the line of fire.

He also knew he had no intention of going anywhere without her.

"Let's walk over to the restaurant," he suggested calmly. "While we eat, we'll talk about how we handle the contact with Kuykendahl and Gutierrez."

Pulling on the suede bomber jacket, he slipped Special Agent White's Beretta into the pocket. The weight felt familiar in his hand now. Motioning Jen to wait, he unlocked the door and opened it only enough to let in a slice of night.

A quick glance in either direction showed a few dusty cars parked in front of other doors. Mike started to step outside when his gaze caught on a dark shadow crouched some yards away. He froze, swearing under his breath.

"What?" Jen's nervous demand came from just behind his shoulder.

"We might have made a mistake here. Our friend is waiting for another meal."

"Poor thing," Jen murmured.

He locked the door behind her, keeping an eye on the animal as they crossed the dirt and gravel parking lot. It followed, staying in the shadows, too wary or too wise in the ways of humans to trust even the ones who'd just fed it.

Mike felt a tug of kinship with the half-wild creature. Right now, he didn't trust anyone, either.

Eyes narrowed and nerves tight, he swept the truck stop for signs of danger. With the onset of night, traffic had picked up. Rigs rumbled down the dirt access road and pulled up at the lighted pumps. Diesel fumes mixed with swirling dust to give the air a heavy scent. The restaurant's windows glowed like sheets of white-gold in the darkness.

The crowd inside, Mike saw, formed a representative cross-section of travelers cutting across the open country that was once home to buffalo and wild mustangs. The men kept their baseball caps and straw Stetsons firmly in place while they ate. For the most part, the few women present wore snug jeans and tank tops similar to Jen's.

Mike snagged a couple of menus from a rack by the counter and followed Jen to a booth. From the cloud of smoke swirling around the plastic globes above each table, it was obvious the Hungry Cowpoke Truck Stop and Motel catered to few nonsmokers.

Jen decided to try the chicken fried steak again . . . a double order, she told the waitress with a sheepish glance at Mike.

"If I have any left, I'll give it to our friend."

Mike opted for chili, discovering too late that it was even hotter than his own. The serious business of eating occupied them for fifteen minutes or so. Jen scarfed down her meal and made a serious dent in the extra gravy and fries she'd ordered for the dog. His mouth burning, Mike finished off the chili and two pieces of pie.

Cradling a coffee mug emblazoned with a tall, booted cowboy in both hands, he met Jen's eye across the booth.

"Ready?"

She drew in a deep breath. Her breasts rose under the square-necked scarlet tank top. Mike saw a small, purplish vein pulse in the side of her neck.

"Ready."

"There's a pay phone over there, by the rest rooms. We'll use that. We have to talk fast," he warned. "Until we know what or who's behind these attacks, we can't give them time to run a trace."

"If . . ." Jen wet her lips. "If Kuykendahl doesn't have any answers for us, we're back to square one."

"I know."

"You'll have to go back to San Antonio. Maybe you can . . ."

He pushed out of the booth, his jaw hardening. "I'm not going anywhere without you, period. Let's make the call."

He dropped a handful of coins into the pay phone and punched in the number the agent had given them. Bending slightly so Jen could hear the exchange, he waited tensely while the call went through.

As he had the last time, the agent answered on the first ring. Mike barely gave him time to identify himself.

"What do you have to tell us?"

Kuykendahl countered with a swift demand to know where they were.

"You've got thirty seconds to tell us what you found out," Mike bit out. "Then we hang up."

"Thirty seconds!"

"Twenty-nine and counting."

"All right! The Mexican authorities are tracking down Ed James's son. I contacted his daughter personally. She didn't want to talk at first, but she finally admitted her father had set up a secret trust fund for his grandkids. She thought he was trying to avoid inheritance taxes. We've traced the source of the funds through several holding accounts."

"Any connection to MEI?"

"Not yet, but we're still—"

"What about Tobias?"

The agent hesitated. "I don't think we should discuss this on an open line."

"This open line is going down in fifteen seconds."

"Colonel . . ."

"Twelve. Eleven. Ten."

"She doesn't exist."

"Sure she does. You said your people checked her out."

A taut silence ate up two or three precious seconds. Mike swore and jabbed the receiver at the hook.

"Wait!" Kuykendahl shouted. "She doesn't exist as Tech Sergeant Rosalie Tobias!"

Mike hung up.

Jen gave a small shriek. "What are you doing? He had some information for us!"

Heads turned. Through the haze of cigarette smoke, Mike saw several truckers check out Jen's flushed face and long, slender jeans-clad legs. One of the men nudged a buddy in the ribs, then caught Mike's eyes. The diner turned his attention back to his plate.

"We have to find out what he meant about Tobias!" Jen exclaimed.

"We'll call him back in a few minutes," Mike said far more calmly than he felt.

Jen spun around and threw her shoulders against the wall. "How could Rosalie Tobias not exist? I saw her record. She was in school at Keesler last week. Kuykendahl said he'd combed through her background with a wire brush. Everything checked, right down to the rose tattoo in the web of her left hand!"

Mike didn't have an answer to that one. He only hoped to hell Kuykendahl did. He fished another handful of coins out of his pocket and dropped them in. Jen had her ear to the phone before the last quarter hit with a clunk.

"Thirty seconds," he warned when the agent answered. "Talk fast."

"Tobias finished school last Tuesday and dropped out of sight. Her records dropped off the Master Personnel File the same day. Just like Captain Warner's did this afternoon."

"What!"

"I'm guessing your queries triggered some kind of dump, but so far, no one at the Personnel Center's been able to explain what happened. The general's hot," he added. "Real hot."

Mike smiled grimly. He'd only seen his boss lose her cool a couple of times. As her staff knew only too well, it wasn't a pretty sight.

"We're running both Tobias and Warner through the National Crime Center's computers," Kuykendahl said quickly. "We've got their vitals and general descriptions, down to and including blood types and the rose tattoo on Tobias's left hand. If they've been stopped for so much as a traffic ticket, we'll find them."

"What about Alicia Mathison?"

"We're still checking on her. She came out of Dallas PD when her husband took a job as chief engineer at an oil company in Wichita Falls. She has a reputation among the locals as a hot shot with a mouth on her."

"No kidding," Jen muttered.

"I also checked the magistrate who issued the search and seizure order."

"And?"

Kuykendahl's professional cool heated up. "And he's one of several select members of the judiciary who shoot quail every year at a private hunting preserve in Colorado."

"Let me guess. The preserve belongs to Russ Murdock."

"You got it, Colonel."

Mike hung up.

"Stop doing that!" Jen wailed, punching his arm in sheer frustration.

"We'll call him back."

Mike's reply came out with more of a bite this time. Jen shot him a tight look and slumped against the wall.

"This is crazy," she muttered. "How could Tobias and Warner have dropped out of the system? Military records don't just disappear. You know as well as I do how many safeguards are built in. We have backup tapes, for Pete's sake, and periodic reconciliation runs. Why don't they just . . ."

She broke off, frowning in sudden, intense concentration. Mike could almost hear the thoughts tumbling through her mind.

"What day is this?" she asked slowly.

"Friday. The day after Thanksgiving, remember?"

"No, what date?"

He checked the calendar on his watch. "The twenty-ninth."

She was silent for another moment, then thrust herself off the wall with a burst of explosive energy.

"Come on! We've got to get back to San Antonio!"

"Tonight?"

"Tonight."

"Jen . . ."

"I'll explain as we go!"

Hurrying to their table, she scraped the remains of their meal into the plastic container she'd requested from the waitress earlier and waited impatiently while Mike tossed some bills on the table.

"There's no way those records can just disappear," she told him in a breathless rush when the restaurant door thudded shut behind them. "Anytime vital data is added or deleted from the Master Personnel File, the record is flagged and a copy goes into the blob space."

"Okay, I'll bite. What's the blob space?"

"Binary large object space. It's like a holding pen. In effect, we create a second record without the changes. It remains in the blob space until Quality Control verifies the additions or deletions and deflags the master."

She hurried across the parking lot to their room, too caught up in her explanation to notice the shadow darting between cars to her right. Mike saw it, though. He took the container of scraps from her hands and left it on the stoop.

"Are you saying this holding pen might contain copies of the missing records?" he asked, following her inside.

"That's what I'm saying." Jen tossed her purse on the bed and stuffed her things into her overnight bag. "But only if we get to it fast."

"How fast?"

"Before the system runs an end-of-month purge and dumps the temporary files currently in the holding pen."

She started for the door. Mike caught her arm. "Let's talk about this, Jen."

"What's to talk about?"

"It might be safer for you to tell Kuykendahl about this blob space and have him search it."

She shook off his hold, her eyes fierce. "No! I found the records the first time. I'm going to find them again. When I do, I'm also going to find the connection to MEI."

"Jen—"

"I've got to do this, Mike. I'm tired of looking over my shoulder. I'm tired of people popping guns on us. And I'm damned if I'm going to let anyone, General Daniels included, lay a charge of conduct unbecoming on you or me!"

They pulled out of the Hungry Cowpoke Truck Stop a few minutes later, following in the wake of a lumbering semi. Mike held the Cutlass in check while the truck made a wide turn onto the access road.

"How long will it take us to get back to San Antonio?" Jen asked over the grind of the semi's gears.

"Six or seven hours."

She checked the digital clock. "That will put us in around three a.m. Four at the latest. We'll have to . . ."

Suddenly Mike braked.

Jen stiff-armed the dash, bracing herself against the movement. "What's the matter? What did you forget?"

"Nothing," he said grimly, his eyes on the rearview mirror. "We're being followed."

With a swift, indrawn breath, she twisted

around in her seat. "I don't see any headbeams. Are they running without lights?"

"They aren't. He is."

"He . . . ?" She squinted back toward the restaurant. "Oh, no!"

Her heart wrenched at the sight of the mongrel loping down the gravel and dirt access road. The yellow monster couldn't be more unlike friendly, gregarious Commodore in size or temperament, but he tugged at Jen's compassion, just the same.

Mike shoved the car into park and left the engine running. Legs spread, hands on hips, he stood beside the open door.

The dog slowed its run. It padded a few more yards, then dropped to its haunches twenty or so yards from the car.

"Go on!" Mike shouted. "Get out of here."

The animal didn't move.

Mike bent and picked up a stone. He hefted it in his hand a few times menacingly. To Jen's relief, but not surprise, he didn't throw it.

Cursing, he got back in the car and shoved it into drive. His foot hit the accelerator. The Cutlass shot forward with a spit of gravel.

Jen didn't say a word. They were on the run, she reminded herself. Their commander had laid charges against them. She was beginning to believe that one of the most powerful men in the country wanted to destroy them, or her anyway. They had to get back to San Antonio as quickly as possible if they wanted to preserve the only records that linked the mystery to that man.

This was no time to think about taking on a passenger.

Besides, she wasn't exactly sure she wanted to share the close confines of the Cutlass with an animal that raised a cloud of gnats every time it twitched. Still, her eyes went to the rearview mirror as often as Mike's. A few moments later, his fist hit the wheel.

"Dammit!"

The car screeched to a stop. His face tight, Mike climbed out again.

Jen twisted in her seat just in time to see the dog lope out of the shadows behind them. Even from a distance, she could see the way its sides heaved. Its tongue almost dragged the ground. Its gait wasn't quite as smooth this time. Her throat closing, Jen saw that it had developed a limp.

As it had before, the creature dropped to its haunches a safe distance away. Jen pushed open the passenger door and joined Mike. Shoving her hands into her pockets, she stood beside him and observed the yellow mound in the middle of the road.

"Do you think he's going to follow us all the way to San Antonio?"

"I think he's going to try."

"So . . . ?"

"So I guess we'll have to convince him otherwise."

She tilted her head. In the dappled moonlight, Mike's face might have been carved in granite.

"Convince him how?"

"I suppose I could run over him."

Jen knew the man behind the hard mask now. "Yeah, sure."

"Or shoot him."

"Right."

His breath left on a disgusted gust. "Or coax him into the car."

Chapter Twenty-two

Even at four-twenty in the morning, the Air Force Personnel Center showed a scattering of lights in its long, three-story facade.

Mike pulled into the parking lot across the street and cut the engine. The Cutlass died with a well-mannered hum. Jen gripped her hands together, almost afraid to reach for the door handle. The next half hour would either turn up the link to MEI that she was now convinced lay behind the series of attacks that had driven her out of her home and made her a fugitive or . . .

Or she and Mike would have to call Kuykendahl and answer to the absurd charges laid against them.

The prospect dropped like a rock in the hollow pit of Jen's stomach. She wanted this nightmare over. She wanted her life back. Even more, she wanted to know who was playing these deadly games with her and why. What had begun as a puzzle and segued into a quest was now a grim war, and she was determined to see the end of it.

A rustle of movement behind her drew her attention from the facade of the Personnel Center. She shifted, eyeing the passenger in the back seat. The yellow-furred mongrel returned her stare.

"What are we going to do with you?" Jen muttered as she had a dozen or more times in the past few hours.

Mike gave a snort of disgust. "We've already run through all the options."

"As I recall, bringing him along was your idea."

"As I recall, you didn't have a better one."

Whoever's idea it was, it had taken some doing. Every time Mike or Jen had approached, the dog backed off. Soothing tones didn't work, nor did brisk commands. Yet when they tried to speed off, the animal followed.

Finally, they'd driven back to the restaurant, the dog loping behind, and obtained another order of chicken fried steak. After long and careful deliberation, their reluctant guest had crept up to the food, belly to the ground. It hadn't fought when Mike slipped the length of rope he'd obtained from the truck stop around its neck and urged him into the back seat.

For the first few miles, the hair on Jen's neck prickled every time the creature shifted. Eventually, it had grown accustomed to their presence in the front seat and settled down to sleep. They, in turn, had grown used to its smell.

What they hadn't grown used to was its baying howl. The few times they'd stopped for coffee or gas, it had let loose with an ear-shattering cry when they climbed out of the car. The dog didn't like being left, and didn't mind letting them know about it.

"Do you think we can get him past the security police officer on the desk?" Jen asked, reaching for the rope looped around the animal's neck.

"I'm just hoping we can get ourselves past the guard," Mike replied grimly.

They'd already discussed the possibility that their names had been tagged in the computerized listing of personnel authorized access to the Center after duty hours. If so, their predawn appearance could trigger an alert. They had to take that chance. They couldn't wait until the start of the duty day, when access wasn't as tightly controlled. Jen had to get into the system before the scheduled purge, which normally ran early on the last day of the month. She only prayed it hadn't already been processed.

"Ready?" Mike asked, his voice quiet and steady in the darkness.

Jen drew in a deep breath. "Ready."

She could imagine the picture they presented to the startled security policeman when they walked through the glass doors. She and Mike had been traveling hard since yesterday morning. His five o'clock shadow had added another eleven hours of bristly growth. Tension and lack of sleep had no doubt left its mark on Jen's face as well. The dog padding between them on a rope leash only added to their less-than-sharp appearance.

"Morning, Sergeant," Mike said easily.

"Morning, sir."

The security policeman who took their IDs didn't exactly do a double take, but he did scrutinize their pictures carefully while he waited for their names to come up on the computer. Jen's heart thumped painfully at the interminable wait. Finally, the SP passed Mike back his ID. Jen held her breath until hers, too, slid across the desk. Her hands slick, she slipped it into her purse.

"That's some sorry-looking hound," the cop commented.

"We found him, or rather he found us, beside the road," Mike replied. "We're taking him to the vet as soon as we finish here."

"I'll call the base animal control officer," the sergeant offered, reaching for his radio. "He can take him off your hands."

"That's okay. We've got it under control."

Jen felt the guard's eyes on her back all the way down the hall. At any moment, she expected to hear him call out or pick up the phone. When Mike opened the door to his office and flipped on the lights, she slumped in relief.

"God! I feel like a criminal, slinking in here in the middle of the night."

"I just hope we're able to slink out again."

"You and me both!"

While Mike tilted the blinds to shield the lighted office from the outside, the dog in-

spected the room. After a few moments of interested sniffing, it settled under a chair.

Jen glanced around, wondering how many
times she'd reported to this very office in the
short, turbulent months she'd worked for Mike.
As always, the plaques on the wall hung in perfect alignment. Not a speck of dust had dared
settle on the surface of the furniture. The misty
blue upholstered chairs sat at precise angles to
his desk. Jen could remember tucking her skirt
under her and taking one of those chairs the
morning after her Cherokee was stolen . . . the
same day Ed James had suffered his heart attack
and her world suddenly began to spin out of
control.

Shivering, she moved to the terminal on his
desk. "Let's see if there's anything left in the
blob."

After the tension of the past twenty hours,
getting into the temporary file proved no challenge at all. Jen's worries that security might
have terminated her password disappeared with
the first few commands. Within moments, she'd
navigated through the introductory screens and
accessed the binary large object file. Her fingers
flew as she typed in a search for Technical Sergeant Rosalie Tobias.

"There she is!"

Elated, Jen clicked on the file. It flowered open
to show standard Air Force personnel data entries pertaining to Technical Sergeant Tobias.
Another click sent an instruction to the printer.
A few seconds later the printer/copier on the

credenza behind the secretary's desk started humming. While sheet after sheet slid into the tray, Jen made a backup copy of the file.

"Now let's see if we can find Captain Steve Warner." She hit the keys. "Yes!"

She scribbled the classified code that masked his duty location for the years from 1992 to 1994, then made a paper and backup copy of that record, too.

"This could get a bit tricky," she admitted to Mike after a moment. "That classified code is no longer in use. I'll have to break into a history file to verify the location."

"No, you won't," Mike replied. "I've got access to all history files as part of the study. We can use my ID and password."

"Good, let me just get out of the blob space and . . ."

Jen paused, her fingers curved over the mouse.

"You know," she said slowly, "Ed James had a dozen or so records on his computer that day. Maybe I should do a general pass and pull out any people in training status. Just to see what turns up."

What turned up were thirty-three records, including the half-completed record of Staff Sergeant Gerald L. McConnell that had launched Jen on her odyssey. She bounced them against the Master Personnel File, one after another. Twenty-six matched, showing data that had been corrected and verified before the temporary file dumped. Seven didn't match. Like Gerald McConnell and Rosalie Tobias and Steve Warner, these seven people didn't exist on the master file. On any file, Jen discovered.

More confused than ever, she stared up at Mike. "This is crazy. Each of these people completed an Air Force training course during the past month. Their records were updated to reflect course completion. Yet as soon as the change was verified by QC, the master records disappeared. The only evidence those seven people ever existed at all are these temporary files, and they'll disappear today, when the reconciliation-to-record runs."

"What kind of training were they in?"

She skimmed the records. "Explosive ordnance disposal. Satellite communications. Power production. Electronic countermeasures and surveillance. Combat rescue."

"Combat rescue?" Mike shook his head. "That's a small community. No one can spend weeks training with those guys and just drop out of the system afterward. Unless . . ."

"Unless what?"

He hesitated, frowning.

"Unless what, Mike?"

"Unless they've been assigned to some kind of a covert ops unit," he suggested slowly.

"Covert ops?"

"Look at the skills of these seven people. They could form a hell of a strike team. They've got a communicator to direct them in and out of a target zone. An electronics expert to suppress surveillance."

"Someone who knows how to handle explosives," Jen added in a rush of excitement. "I don't know what a power production man would contribute to the team . . ."

"The ability to hit the enemy in one of his most vulnerable spots . . . his electrical subsystems." Mike's frown etched deep grooves in his forehead. "Think of the confusion and chaos a single individual could create by blacking out a city or a base or a section of a country where a covert operation was scheduled."

Jen stared up at him, her mind whirling. "Does the Air Force employ covert teams like that?"

He shook his head. "If we do, we classify them at a higher level than I'm cleared for."

"This sounds like something right out of James Bond, for heaven's sake!"

"Or the CIA," Mike said slowly.

"Or the CIA," Jen agreed without thinking.

A second later the words sunk in.

"Oh, my God!" she gasped. "Do you think these people could track back to Murdock and his days at the agency? Could he have set up some kind of a cross-agency covert unit, one that's still operating today?"

"I don't know," he said thoughtfully.

She jumped up, too gripped by the idea to sit still. The dog lifted its head and watched her every move.

"Ed James was a trusted employee, one of the few at the Personnel Center authorized to make changes to the Master Personnel File. He could have created whole sets of phony records. Given people detailed histories and sent them through training, then dropped them off the master file."

"Jen . . ."

"These seven people only showed up because they completed training in November." Her gaze went to the windows. Beyond the tilted blinds lay a deep, silent darkness. "What if there are more than seven? What if we're training a small army of people for Murdock? People like Harry Waterman?"

Mike didn't answer. The same questions had been spinning in his own mind with each thread that formed another tentative link to Russell Murdock. A friend to kings and confidant of presidents, Murdock moved in the highest circles of power. He also, Mike knew from the countless articles and news magazine reports about the self-made billionaire, held to a rigidly conservative view. According to his public statements, it was the moral imperative of every citizen to battle the enemies of the United States, both foreign and domestic.

The idea that a man as powerful as Russ Murdock might build his own private army to conduct that battle didn't seem as far-fetched to Mike as it might have a few years ago. If nothing else, the fiery shoot-out with the Waco Branch Davidians and the Oklahoma City bombing had opened the public's eyes to the existence of heavily armed, well-organized right-wing militia groups.

"I think it's time we contacted Kuykendahl

again," he said slowly. "He was going to run the physical descriptions of Tobias and Warner through the National Crime Center computers. We need to know if he tagged them."

He had.

In the thirty seconds Mike allowed him, the special agent spilled a hurried report. Mike listened intently, then hung up. His eyes cold and hard, he faced Jen across the desk.

"They traced a woman who matches the description of Rosalie Tobias, down to the tattoo on the web of her left hand. Her name is Sandra Rose Johnston. She lives just outside Atlanta."

"And?" Jen asked breathlessly.

"And she works as a signals monitor at a commercial satellite telecommunications firm."

"Which is owned and operated by MEI!"

"No." Mike's jaw tightened. "It's owned and operated by StarNet . . . which is a subsidiary of MEI."

Jen wrapped her arms around her middle. Above the wine red top, her face was washed of all color.

"How big is this?" she whispered

"I don't know," he grated in a low voice, "but I have a feeling you were right when you speculated there might be more than seven people out there. The question is, how do we find them?"

"I know one way," Jen said slowly. "But we can't do it alone."

*   *   *

They waited until the first streaks of dawn painted the sky. Mike knew the general well enough to guess that she'd be among the first to arrive at the Center.

Her executive officer beat her in by ten minutes. He was sorting through the previous night's messages when Mike and Jen strode into the executive suite. The young captain's eyes popped.

"Colonel Page!"

His eyes widened even more at the sight of the animal padding in between Jen and Mike.

"What . . . ? Where . . . ?"

He caught himself. Straightening, he flipped the message file shut.

"I have to notify the general immediately and advise her that you're here."

At Mike's nod, he groped for the phone and punched a single button. He hung up a moment later, his face expressionless.

"The general said to plant your . . . selves in a chair and wait. She's less than two minutes out."

The sound of the private door opening in the corridor next to the executive suite a few moments later brought the exec scrambling to his feet. His sudden movement alerted the dog. Patchy yellow fur bristling, it sprang upright. Mike's grip tightened on the rope halter.

General Daniels walked into the office, whipping off her flight cap. Her green eyes flicked from Mike to Jen and back again before settling on the dog. She shook her head, not even bothering to ask for an explanation.

"Is the coffee on, Pete?"

"Yes, ma'am," the exec replied.

"Bring us a full pot. And hold all calls."

Predawn darkness streaked with a faint pink showed in the tall windows of the general's office. She tossed her cap with its single silver star on her desk and unzipped her jacket. Smoothing a hand up the sleek back twist at the back of her head, she waited until the exec had departed before nodding to the leather sofa and chairs grouped around a low glass coffee table.

"We might as well get comfortable. I have a feeling this is going to take some telling."

Jen was more than willing to take her up on the offer, but Mike held back. With the dog hunkered down at his side, he faced the general across a few yards of carpet.

"I'm not sure I can get comfortable until I understand just why Special Agent White was waiting for us when we got back to our motel room yesterday afternoon. He tossed out some interesting phrases, like failure to obey a lawful order and conduct unbecoming."

"I understand the locals threw another possible charge into the mix," the general said calmly.

"Yes," Jen put in, her mouth thinning at the memory of the snuff film. "They did."

"What's going on, General? You and I both know that you removed Captain Varga from my team, but you didn't issue any order for me to cease and desist our relationship."

"You know it and I know it, but the White House staffer who called the Air Force Inspector General yesterday morning didn't."

Jen gulped. "A White House staffer! Holy shit!"

General Daniels smiled. "My sentiments exactly."

The women regarded each other a moment. Mike thought he'd never seen two less similar in either temperament or appearance. Petite, precisely uniformed, and in control, the general exuded the calm confidence that came with command. Jen, as usual, was a bundle of barely contained impatience. Her chestnut hair tumbled in wayward curls. The makeup she'd freshened hours ago at the truck stop had long since disappeared. She sat on the edge of the chair, her hands fisted in her lap.

General Daniels's gaze swung from Jen to Mike. Her eyes hardened to green glass.

"The IG had all the details of your liaison with Captain Varga, including the fact that the two of you were sharing a room at the LaQuinta in Wichita Falls. I agreed with his suggestion that we bring you in immediately for one reason, and one reason only. I want to hear from you what's going on, Mike. I want to know who's behind these attacks on Captain Varga, and I want to know who the hell involved the White House."

"I'll tell you who involved it," Jen said fiercely. "A certain influential campaign contributor, philanthropist, and former deputy director of the CIA."

General Daniels stared at her for a long, silent moment. Then she reached for the coffee carafe and filled three mugs.

"You talk. I'll listen."

Jen talked. In short, swift sentences, she brought the general up-to-date on all that had happened since the train accident less than a week ago. Some of it General Daniels already knew. Special Agent Kuykendahl had kept her apprised of the status of his investigation, as well as the fact that the records of Tobias and Warner had dropped from the personnel system. But the possibility that Warner, if that was his name, might have piloted Russell Murdock at one time was news to General Daniels, as well as the information that Tobias had been tracked to a civilian in Mobile, who also worked for MEI.

The general frowned at each reference to Russ Murdock. When Jen and Mike finished outlining their findings, her frown had deepened to a tight, unsmiling mask.

"That's absurd! A man like Russ Murdock could recruit, train, and equip a private army using his own funds if he wanted to. Why would he go to such elaborate measures to send his people to military training courses?"

"We don't know that he did," Mike admitted. "But Jen's just found seven additional records that need to be checked out."

"Seven!"

"We suspect there may be more," he added quietly.

The general's eyes narrowed. "How many more?"

"I don't know," Jen admitted. "But if the blob space held seven . . ."

"The blob space?"

"It's a technical term," Mike explained dryly. "Only those who work in the bowels of the Data Systems Directorate are familiar with it."

Jen waved a hand impatiently. "The point is, I caught these seven before the November purge wiped them out. How many completed training before November? How many are *still* in training? There's only one way to find out."

"And that is?" Faith Daniels asked.

"We could shut the system down and run a onetime reconciliation-to-record."

"Shut it down!"

"Only for twenty-four hours. Thirty-six at the most. We'd have to turn everyone off. The Guard and Reserve. The Finance and Accounting Center. All eight military subsystems. Then we run a comparison of the current records to the backup tapes made, say, two or three months ago."

The general slammed her mug onto the table, sloshing coffee onto the glass top. "You don't know the magnitude of what you're suggesting, Captain!"

Jen stiffened. "Yes, ma'am, I do. Shutting all those subsystems down for thirty-six hours would cost the Air Force close to a million dollars."

Sudden, crackling tension leaped through the quiet office. Everyone felt it, even the dog. A slow, rumbling growl issued from deep in its chest.

"Let me get this straight," Daniels snapped. "You're talking about a complete shutdown of the personnel system?"

Jen lifted her chin. "Yes, ma'am."

Her rapier-sharp eyes went to Mike. "Which I'm supposed to authorize on the recommenda tion of a lieutenant colonel who exercised extremely poor judgment with regard to a subordinate and a captain whose record of performance is questionable at best?"

"Yes, ma'am," he replied softly.

The reconciliation took thirty-one hours and twenty-two minutes.

Jen was sure she would remember every minute of every hour for the rest of her life . . . mostly because she had so little to do during that endless stretch of time. Once the general's order went out to stop all batch updates to the system and perform a reconciliation-to-record, the mainframes at the Defense Information Systems Agency located on Kelly Air Force Base across town shuddered, stopped, then whirred back to life.

All Jen could do was wait.

She paced Mike's office. She drove to the Visiting Officers' Quarters on base to shower and change into the uniform Mike had retrieved from his house, along with his own. She ate the meals brought from the cafeteria adjacent to the Personnel Center. She made several calls to the off-base vet to check on Commodore, who was slowly gaining strength. She even coaxed a very large, very reluctant animal into Special Agent Kuykendahl's car for a trip to the vet on base.

"He was *not* happy about being left overnight," the stocky, wide-shouldered OSI agent reported upon his return. As she had when she'd first met him, Jen wondered what he'd done before he went into investigative work. With his bull-like neck and barrel chest, he could have made a living thumping professional wrestlers to the mat.

Shaking his head, Kuykendahl deposited a briefcase on the table. "That dog has a set of lungs on him that won't quit."

"We've heard them," Mike said wryly. "I hope you remembered to tell the doc to hose him down."

"And spray him," Jen put in.

"I did. I'll have to spray my car, too, before I let the kids in the back seat. Where did you find him, anyway?"

"He found us," Mike replied. "Did you bring your case file?"

"Yes, sir."

"Let's get to work."

Using the small conference room that the general had ordered set aside for their use, they sifted through the information they'd already assembled and the additional intelligence they gathered from a host of sources. Slowly, day faded into night. Even more slowly, the night ticked away.

Gradually, a chilling picture began to form.

Murdock had chosen George "Andy" Anderson, a former Special Forces commander, as his trusted second in command. The scarred veteran appeared only rarely in print, but the few articles written about him stressed his patriotism . . . and almost fanatical loyalty to Russ Murdock.

MEI and its many subsidiaries offered substantial employment incentives to veterans, which in itself seemed admirable enough. When two more of the seven records Jen had pulled out of the blob space matched to MEI employees, however, it became apparent that some of those vets hadn't quite severed their ties to the military.

Even more disturbing was the extent to which the U.S. military employed technology developed by MEI. From classified and unclassified sources, it became apparent that Murdock Enterprises, Incorporated, constituted the third largest supplier of communications equipment in the world. Four nations, the United States among them, had built their military networks using MEI-produced systems.

Mike's expertise in this area awed Jen. She'd forgotten that he'd worked his way up from a no-striper stringing cable to an officer with a masters in engineering and years of Pentagon experience under his belt. Where her knowledge was localized on computers and the individual data systems she'd worked with, his was much broader and more globally oriented. He soon lost her with his description of telemetry encoders, transmitter measure voltages, and narrow beam frequency bands.

How did he do it? she wondered, leaning back in her chair to watch him pull facts and figures out of an incomprehensible MEI report. Even now, after almost forty-eight hours with little more than a catnap, he looked alert and sharp and so darned *neat!*

Her fingers itched to shag in his sandy hair and disorder its strict discipline. She wanted to tug his tie loose and unbutton his top shirt button and put her mouth to the pulse that beat at the base of his throat. Even more, she wanted to curl up in his arms and forget for just a few moments the violence and terror that had invaded her life in the past weeks.

As soon as she recognized the insidious impulse for what it was, Jen pushed it aside. She'd dragged Mike into this mess. She'd put his career on the line with the same carelessness she'd offered up her own. She owed it to him to finish the fight. She just wished she could shake the sense that she was going up against a mighty, unbeatable Goliath.

The more she learned of Russ Murdock's extensive holdings and political connections, the more nervous she got. She traced a fingertip on the conference table, wondering who would confront him . . . and when.

"Jen?"

She glanced up to find the two men looking at her.

"Sorry. I was just thinking about Murdock. When does he find out what we've uncovered?"

Kuykendahl rolled his muscled shoulders, easing the kinks from long hours of work. "It depends."

"On what?"

"On what we turn up in this reconciliation. On what this Sandra Rose Johnston has to say to the investigators who are talking to her now. On whether the FBI and the U.S. Attorney's Office feel they have enough to take to a grand jury, or whether they'll subpoena MEI's corporate accounts and employee records first. The process could take days, or months."

Jen stared at him, appalled. "Months!"

Kuykendahl rasped a hand across his jaw. He was as tired as she, Jen saw, and almost as tense.

"I'm sorry, Captain. I can't give you a more definitive answer until the FBI has a chance to review all the evidence. In fact . . ." He glanced at his watch. "I'd better get back to the office. The money-laundering experts thought they'd have something on the transfer of funds to Ed James's heirs by this evening."

Jen pushed out of her chair. Disturbed by the thought that she might have to dodge trains and bullets and shadows for weeks yet, she moved to the window. The crepe myrtle trees on the street in front of the Center formed darker shadows against the night.

After a murmured farewell, muffled footsteps

sounded on the carpeted floor. Jen felt Mike's presence behind her. His arms slid around her waist. Gratefully, she leaned back against his solid warmth.

"You should go back to the Officers' Quarters," he said quietly. His breath fanned the small hairs at her temple. "You need sleep."

"So do you."

He rested his chin on the top of her head. "I don't think I've had a full night's sleep since you talked your way onto my team, Captain Varga."

She smiled at his image in the darkened windowpane. "If you remember, I also tried to talk my way off it. Several times."

"I remember." His arms tightened. "I wouldn't let you go then. I don't want to let you go now."

Her hands folded over his arms. "I like it fine right where I am."

They stood in the quiet sanctuary of the conference room, content with the simple contact. Funny, Jen thought. A few weeks ago, she only wanted out of the Air Force. Now, her world had narrowed to an intense inquiry, a small conference room at the Personnel Center, a room at the Visiting Officers' Quarters, two dogs, and this man.

At that moment, it was enough.

More than enough.

Chapter Twenty-three

Ever afterward, Jen would smile wryly when she remembered Allen Kuykendahl's warning that the evidence gathering and grand jury process might take weeks, or even months. For her, events seemed to move with the speed of light.

The reconciliation run finished at two-thirty the following afternoon. The Defense Information Systems Agency took another two hours to prepare and deliver the results. Jen, Mike, Allen Kuykendahl, and a trusted agent from the Data Systems Directorate spent the rest of the day and a good part of the night sorting through the thousands of anomalies identified in the run.

With hundreds of millions of transactions posted each year in the eight major subsystems, Jen wasn't surprised at the number of anomalies. In fact, she was astonished at how small the overall error rate actually was.

Most errors had been caused by simple input mistakes. Misspelled names. Incorrect service dates. Wrong gender or ethnic codes keyed in.

Those would have been caught eventually in routine record reviews.

A number had more serious ramifications. One senior master sergeant had supposedly retired more than a year ago, yet still received full pay. A physician serving time in Fort Leavenworth for selling drugs had somehow been promoted to major.

But it was the growing stack of error reports concerning people in training that riveted the small team. As the night wore on, they found record after record in the reconciliation run that didn't match to the current master file.

Each one, Special Agent Kuykendahl ran through the OSI and National Crime Center's databases. By the time the team finished its initial review, they'd identified an additional thirty-five unauthorized civilians trained by the Air Force . . . six of whom had direct links to MEI.

After a few hours of snatched sleep, the team reported to General Daniels early the next morning.

In preparation for the meeting, Special Agent Kuykendahl showered and shaved and changed into a charcoal gray suit. As usual, Mike looked razor-sharp in his uniform. Even Jen got caught up in the drama of the moment. She'd used the facilities at the Officers' Quarters to press her skirt and long-sleeved blue blouse. Her black heels carried a rare shine, and for once her hair stayed swept up in its neat twist. Back straight and shoulders square, she stood at the head of the conference table and reported the team's findings to the unsmiling general and her civilian deputy.

When Jen finished, a charged silence fell over the room. Finally, General Daniels pinned the OSI agent with hard green eyes.

"Have you briefed your headquarters on these findings yet?"

"No, ma'am," Kuykendahl replied. "Given the political ramifications of the case, I plan to fly up to D.C. this morning and update the OSI commander in person."

She nodded. "You can fly up with me. I've got a MilAir flight laid on for nine-thirty. Captain Varga, you and Colonel Page will accompany me, as well. You're scheduled to brief the director of personnel at two, and be on standby to brief the chief of staff after that."

Jen blinked. "The chief of staff of the Air Force?"

"If this gets the chief's attention, which I'm sure it will," the general drawled, "I suspect we'll be taking the same briefing to the White House. This could prove to be an interesting day."

A succinct, if colorful, endorsement to that little understatement trembled on Jen's lips. She caught it just in time and snapped to attention, more or less, as the general swept out of the conference room with an order to be at base ops by ten-fifteen.

Jen stared after her. "I can't believe she laid on a flight to D.C. and set up these briefings before she knew the results of the run."

"Don't kid yourself," Mike replied, smiling.

"General Daniels wouldn't have authorized a total shutdown of the personnel system if she hadn't believed we'd find something significant."

The OSI agent shuffled a stack of papers into his briefcase. "I'd better make a quick call to OSI headquarters to advise them that I'm coming up. And I promised Rafael Gutierrez I'd let him know what's happening. I'll meet you at base ops in . . . Damn! Forty minutes!"

Allen Kuykendahl was waiting for Jen and Mike when they pulled up at the red-tiled, stuccoed building that served as Randolph's base operations center. His short, stocky body radiated a barely suppressed excitement.

"I called Gutierrez," he told them, raising his voice to be heard over the high-pitched whine of jet engines from the end of the runway. "I also called my contact with the FBI. The Bureau's been keeping loose tabs on Russell Murdock since I first alerted them to the investigation."

A sleek white T-38 Talon roared down the runway and launched into the air. Mike waited until the earsplitting sound had died before he asked the obvious.

"And?"

"And Russell Murdock left Denver early this morning for Washington. He's having lunch with the president, then he's driving out to Andrews."

Jen's stomach jumped. "Andrews Air Force Base? Isn't that where we're flying into?"

"You got it!"

The idea that she might cross paths with the man she was now convinced was behind the attacks on Trish and Commodore and herself made her heart skip a few beats, then kick into overdrive.

"Why is Murdock driving out to Andrews?" she asked.

"He's part of the official party that will welcome home Dr. Cherbanian."

Mike's brows slanted in a quick frown. "What's his connection to a hostage who just escaped the Kurds?"

"Officially, Murdock made his private jet available to Mrs. Cherbanian to fly to Germany for a reunion with her husband," Kuykendahl reported. "Unofficially, he deflected some of the heat Mrs. Cherbanian was giving the White House for failing to rescue the man."

"How?"

"I don't know. He had something to do with special equipment provided to the Turks for the search. I didn't have time to get the details."

"What time is Dr. Cherbanian supposed to arrive?" Mike asked tersely.

The special agent's eyes glinted. "About ten minutes after our own ETA."

A bumpy flight added to a nervousness that had wrapped itself like a noose around Jen's stomach. The small twin engine C-21 passenger jet bucked and dipped and dropped far too often for her comfort. Strapped in facing the general, with Mike and Allen Kuykendahl across the narrow aisle, Jen prayed she wouldn't disgrace herself and her uniform by throwing up.

Thankfully, the general used the four-hour flight to go over the findings again and pepper Jen with the questions she could expect from the three-star deputy chief of staff for personnel and the four-star chief of staff. Jen had an answer for them all except one . . . why? Why would a man like Russell Murdock use the military to train his people? Why would he resort to murder to cover the scheme up? Why . . .

"We're cleared on final to Andrews," the co-pilot advised over the intercom. "They're letting us slip in before an inbound C-141. Please buckle up in preparation for landing."

The quick, swooping descent didn't help Jen's shaky stomach. Nor did a glimpse through the port window of the crowd waiting outside the air terminal. The bright winter sunshine and Cherbanian's dramatic escape had drawn a huge crowd to welcome him home. Hand-lettered signs and pennants rose above the crowd on poles. Flags whipped in the breeze. Sunlight glinted on tubas and trombones of what looked like a high school marching band.

But it was the knot of dignitaries at the front of the entourage that held Jen's interest. She leaned forward, studying the cluster of top-coated VIPs as the C-21 rolled to a stop a hundred yards or so from the terminal. Somewhere among them was Russell Murdock.

The side hatch door opened, letting in a gust

of aviation fumes and cold winter air. The general exited the plane first, returning the salute of the pilot, the crew chief, and the leather-jacketed colonel waiting to greet her. Mike went next, turning to offer Jen a hand as she stepped through the hatch. Her high heels clicked on the metal steps, and her breath clouded in the air. After San Antonio's fifty-degree temperature, D.C.'s frigid air shocked her lungs and raised shivers under her zippered Air Force jacket.

Radio in hand, the colonel escorted them to a waiting blue Air Force sedan.

"We've got the secretary of state, most of the Washington media, and half the population of Baltimore here to welcome Dr. Cherbanian home," he told the general. "The doc's become a local hero."

General Daniels nodded. "I can understand why."

"With all the VIPs here, we've had to beef up security and secure the flight line. I'll call and clear a—"

A crackle of static and a call for Eagle One cut him off. He raised the radio and acknowledged the message that the Code Four was on final.

"Roger that."

"I want to see this," the general told the harried commander. "You go take care of your VIPs. We'll watch from the lounge."

The colonel tipped her a grateful smile and a crisp salute. "Yes, ma'am."

With a murmured farewell, Kuykendahl

headed for a second staff car. It would take him to OSI headquarters at Bolling Air Force Base, across the Potomac from downtown D.C.

Mike walked around the rear of the car and took the front passenger seat. The driver held the rear door open for Jen. She was about to slip into the sedan when she caught sight of the man whose picture she'd studied so intently the past few days. She froze, staring at him over the top of the car.

He was so short, she thought irrelevantly. He almost got lost in the cluster of dignitaries. But Jen couldn't mistake his thinning reddish hair, nor did she miss how the other men bent obsequiously to catch his every word. What Murdock lacked in inches, she thought grimly, he obviously more than made up for in power.

At that moment, his glance strayed down the runway and snagged on the Air Force sedan. Jen stiffened as his eyes seemed to lock on hers. From this distance, she couldn't see their color, but she knew they were blue. Pale, almost colorless blue.

Bastard! she thought fiercely. *If you're the one behind Trish's injuries, I hope we bring you down so far and so fast your teeth hit the ground before your butt. I hope you rot for what you've done to her, and to me, and to the Air Force.*

Her legs trembling, she slid into the back seat. "I saw him."

"I did, too," Mike said, his jaw working. "He's hard to miss, even at . . ."

The roar of jet engines and the screech of tires

on tarmac drowned out his words. A wild cheer went up from the waiting crowd. The huge C-141 rolled onto the taxiway just as Jen and Mike and the general stepped out of the sedan at the entrance to the terminal. Inside, a welcome warmth wrapped around them, while the floor-to-ceiling windows gave a clear view of the ceremony. Mike stood beside her, stiff and unmoving. His gray eyes never left the small man in the tan overcoat and plaid Burberry scarf.

The cargo jet taxied to a stop in front of the crowd. Its four engines whined, then died. A ground crew rolled a metal stairway to the side door. When a uniformed crew member shoved back the hatch, controlled pandemonium broke out. Camera crews and news reporters jostled each other for position. The band boomed out a rousing rendition of "Happy Days Are Here Again."

A rustle of movement behind Jen signaled the gathering of another crowd, this one comprised of terminal workers and uniformed personnel who hadn't wanted to brave the cold. Jen felt their presence at her back, but her whole focus was on Murdock.

Why? she wondered again. Why would someone with his power, his wealth, play such dangerous games? Why?

A figure appeared in the 141's open hatch. Pale and wan and carrying his truncated arm in a sling, Cherbanian appeared startled by the flash of camera lights and whistles and cheers. He held back until his wife appeared and slipped an arm around his waist. Gently, she steered him down the stairs.

Still, Jen watched Murdock. He walked forward beside a man Jen recognized but couldn't name. His reddish hair ruffled by the breeze, Murdock waited at the bottom of the stairs for the returning American.

Dr. Cherbanian's wife went up on tiptoe and whispered something in his ear. The former hostage stopped in front of Murdock and threw his good arm around him. Murdock returned the fierce hug, then stepped aside while Cherbanian greeted the other dignitaries.

Good God! Jen stared incredulously as Murdock took a surreptitious swipe at his eyes. He was crying!

Were they wrong about the man? she wondered wildly. Had they followed false leads back to MEI? Was he ignorant of those leads?

A moment later Murdock stepped to the microphone. He gave a simple speech welcoming Dr. Cherbanian home and extolling his values as an American . . . values that took him to a remote corner of the world to help a troubled people, and gave him the courage to fight free of the terrorists who threatened American interests at home and abroad.

Murdock's voice rang with sincerity. Pride and patriotism shone in his face. He gave a stirring, emotional performance that moved everyone present.

In that moment Jen's doubts disappeared. She knew without even having to think about it that

Russ Murdock considered himself an unquestioned arbiter of American interests at home and abroad. Suddenly wretchedly sick, she couldn't stand to listen to him another moment.

"You okay?"

She glanced up to find a frown creasing Mike's brow.

"No," she murmured. "He makes me feel ill. Him, and the bumpy ride up here. I'm going to the ladies' room."

She edged back through the crowd of spectators. Mike's gaze and Murdock's ringing phrases followed her to the bathroom at the rear of the VIP lounge. He saw her safely inside, then turned back to the drama on the flight line.

The door swished shut behind Jen, thankfully cutting off the sound of Russell Murdock's voice. She turned on a tap and splashed her face with cold water. That done, she stared at her reflection in the mirror.

"This is *not* the portrait of an officer about to brief the chief of staff," she muttered.

Her skin carried a gray tint under her eyes. Stray tendrils had worked loose from her plastic hair clip and curled on her neck. Even the captain's bars on her jacket's epaulets tilted at an angle.

Sighing, Jen turned off the tap and reached up to unpin the silver tracks on her left shoulder. She was just about to reposition the insignia when the door opened behind her.

Jen immediately recognized the svelte redhead who came in. She'd seen her often enough on TV, reporting from the White House. Helen McKinley Dawes dumped her notebook and small tape recorder on the shelf above the sink, pulled off her black leather gloves, and smiled at Jen.

"It's a bitch out there, isn't it?"

"It's pretty nippy," Jen agreed.

"I can't take the cold anymore. I pee in my pants every time I sneeze."

With that, she swept into the stall.

Smiling, Jen repositioned her rank insignia and left the bathroom. She was on her way back to the crowd at the window when she glanced out the glass door that led from the VIP lounge to the parking lot. The long row of gleaming black limos parked at the curb snagged her attention. If it weren't for the flags flying at the antennae, she might have thought they'd assembled for a funeral.

Suddenly she frowned. She was still standing there, staring at the two men deep in conversation beside one of the limos when the bathroom door opened behind her. She stopped Helen Dawes.

"Do you know who that man is?"

The reporter peered through the glass. "Sure. That's Andy Anderson, Russ Murdock's chief of staff. He doesn't get to Washington as much as his boss, but he's pretty well known around town."

Jen's pulse jumped. She thought she'd recognized Anderson from the pictures Kuykendahl had gathered. With those scars puckering the left side of his face, it wasn't difficult.

"What about the other man?" she asked breathlessly.

"That's H. Paulson Jacoby." The reporter's mouth curled. "He's a low-level White House national security staffer who thinks he's at the center of the universe and acts accordingly. The man's got an Ollie North complex that won't quit."

"Ollie North complex?"

"He'd love to work secret deals and save the world, but personally I don't think he has the balls."

Maybe he didn't, Jen thought in a rush of nervous excitement, and maybe he did. The reporter started to drift away. So did the two men. With a kick of certainty so strong she tasted it, Jen knew this might be the only chance to catch Anderson off guard.

For once, just once, Jen wanted to attack. She was sick to death of sitting back and being a target.

She grabbed Dawes's arm. "Can I borrow your tape recorder? Please! Just for a few minutes!"

"Sorry, Captain. I've got an interview with Dr. Cherbanian after the ceremony."

"If I capture what I hope to capture on tape, you'll get a story a whole lot bigger than Cherbanian!"

The reporter's instincts went on full alert. "What kind of a story?"

Jen snatched the small instrument out of her hand and stabbed at the red record button. Over the heads of the crowd, she caught a glimpse of Mike's profile.

"I can't tell you now," she said, shoving the recorder into her jacket pocket, "but I promise you an exclusive. Just tell that lieutenant colonel there by the window where I am and what I'm doing."

"What *are* you doing?"

"My duty," Jen said grimly.

Well, not exactly her duty. As she jammed her flight cap on her head, she suspected this might go above and beyond the call of duty. But she was damned if she was going to let Russ Murdock and company terrorize her anymore.

Shoving open the glass door, she stepped into the frigid cold. Head high and hands swinging in loose fists at her sides, she hurried down the covered walkway.

To a casual observer, she might have been any officer departing the ceremonies to get back to work. To the man with the scarred face and suddenly narrowed eyes, she was obviously more.

His head lifted. His shoulders squared under his black wool overcoat. Over the shoulder of his companion, he met her eyes.

Jen halted. She didn't have to feign the sudden rush of nervous dread that froze her in place. What the hell was she doing? Was she crazy?

She spun on one heel and started back to the

lounge. After two steps, she stopped again. She turned, more slowly this time.

Anderson stood at attention beside the limo. His eyes never left Jen's face. The man with him glanced over his shoulder, frowned. Muttering a few words, he hurried away.

He couldn't shoot her here, Jen reasoned. Not in the middle of the afternoon, with several thousand people a few yards away, and a high school band playing "The Stars and Stripes Forever," for God's sake!

Could he?

No, his hands were in plain view. They stayed that way as Jen slowly approached. She stopped a few feet away, making no effort to disguise the fact that she knew his identity.

Nor did he. His face registered a fleeting emotion that might have been amusement or admiration or even regret. Jen was too nervous to decide which.

"Hello, Captain Varga."

"Mr. Anderson."

Her breath formed a cloud of vapor between them. The cloud lifted on the breeze and evaporated before either of them spoke again.

"You're a very persistent young woman."

She almost didn't hear the soft comment above the rousing beat of the march.

"Yes, I am."

He waited.

Jen waited back.

Behind her, she heard the click of heels on the walkway. Two civilians hurried by, their shoulders hunched against the cold. Jen had just about decided Anderson didn't intend to say more when his lips stretched in a thin smile.

"That was quite a feat, convincing General Daniels to shut down the personnel system."

"You know about that?"

"We knew about it three minutes after the computers stopped running batch updates," he replied calmly.

"Bastard!"

The single word slipped past Jen's taut nerves and tight throat.

"Just tell me why!" she demanded in a low, passionate rush.

Anderson's eyes flicked over her face. "That's all you want to know, Captain Varga? Just why?"

Her hands clenched into fists. "Yes, damn you! You owe me that much!"

"We don't owe you anything."

"The hell you don't! Your people put my friend in a coma and tried to kill my dog. They almost killed me. At least you can tell me why Russ Murdock used the military to train his private army. He could buy whatever expertise he needed and train his people himself!"

Anderson folded his arms across his chest.

"Tell me!" Jen demanded fiercely.

A muscle twitched under the puckered tissue on his neck. "First, you have no solid evidence that connects Russ Murdock to whatever you found in your review of the personnel database. There is none. Second, what makes you think this army you're talking about needed training?"

"Why else would your people attend military courses?"

"Perhaps . . ." The drawn-out pause mocked her. "Perhaps to become familiar with U.S. military operations and procedures and frequencies . . . so they can avoid a takedown of friendly troops during a mission."

"What missions?"

In answer, he glanced beyond her to the crowd lining the fence.

Jen gasped "Are you . . . ? Are you saying your people rescued Dr. Cherbanian?"

"I'm not saying anything, Captain. I'm just giving you the 'why' you so desperately want."

The door whooshed open behind her. Jen stiffened. She guessed who came running down the walkway even before Mike's angry voice cut through the cold air.

"What the hell's going on here?"

Anderson dropped his arms. "Just a friendly discussion, Colonel Page. It's over now."

He started to turn away, then paused for a final parting shot.

"Think about this before you go any further. Mr. Murdock's too powerful and too well respected for anyone to give credence to a crazy conspiracy theory concocted by a captain who's a half step away from getting thrown out of the Air Force and a lieutenant colonel who can't keep his pants zipped. You can't bring him down."

His face impassive, he turned and walked away.

"Maybe not," Jen whispered with fierce exultation. "But you can. Wait till Helen Dawes hears this."

She unclenched her fists and slipped them into her jacket pocket. Her numbed fingers closed around the tape recorder just as Mike grabbed her arm and spun her around.

"Are you out of your mind?" he snarled, as furious as Jen had ever seen him. "How the hell many times are you going to put yourself in the line of fire?"

"I . . ."

"You had no business taking Anderson on by yourself, dammit!"

"I just . . ."

His hands dug into her upper arms. "Don't ever, *ever*, go off half-cocked like that again, Captain!"

This was the time, Jen thought on a rush of relief, adrenaline-charged nerves, and still soaring tension. If Mike Page's granite jaw was ever going to crack, this was the time.

"I don't take orders from you anymore, Colonel," she said with a shaky attempt at a grin. "You're not my supervisor, remember?"

He gave a growl of sheer male fury and hauled her up against his chest. Jen barely had time to register the fact that orderly, precise, do-it-by-the-book Mike Page was about to disregard every dictum of military propriety before his mouth came down on hers.

Chapter Twenty-four

Five weeks and three days later, a small crowd of uniformed officers and civilians filled the command conference room at the Air Force Personnel Center. The murmur of their voices carried to Jen as she waited with Mike in the commander's office for the ceremony to begin.

Petite, sleekly beautiful, and every inch a general, Faith Daniels faced the individual who would receive an award in the next few minutes. Her green eyes traveled from the recipient's unruly, upswept chestnut hair to her uncharacteristically spit-shined shoes.

"I had to chose between court-martialing you and agreeing with Helen McKinley Dawes's impassioned piece in the *Washington Post* that you deserved a medal, Captain Varga. It was a close call. A very close call."

"Yes, ma'am."

"I still can't quite believe I'm doing this."

Nor could Jen. She was still reeling from all that had happened in the weeks since her ladies' room encounter with Helen Dawes. A grand jury had returned indictments against Russell Murdock, George "Andy" Anderson, and a White House staffer by the name of H. Paulson Jacoby for conspiracy to commit murder, misappropriation of government resources, illegal transfer of funds, and a host of lesser charges. No one could even hazard a guess when any of the defendants would be brought to trial. But Helen McKinley Dawes had run a series of articles in the *Washington Post* exposing MEI's supersecret Special Programs unit. The entire country now watched and waited to learn the fate of a man so patriotic, so dedicated to his country, that he'd break any law to protect and preserve it.

As a result of her role in the stunning events, Jennifer Varga was about to be decorated.

But Mike Page wasn't.

Mike considered himself lucky that he'd received only a written reprimand for his unprofessional conduct with a subordinate. The reprimand was now filed in his promotion folder . . . right below the letter on White House stationary commending Lieutenant Colonel Michael Page for his role in unraveling a conspiracy that had reached the Office of the National Security Adviser. The president also recommended him for immediate promotion to full colonel. Jen didn't doubt which would hold the most sway with the promotion board.

Still, it rankled her that the man who had slipped a engagement ring on her finger the night they brought Commodore home from the vet wouldn't stand beside her at the ceremony about to take place. Nor was she reticent about saying so.

"I still think Mike—Colonel Page—should receive a medal, too."

Faith Daniels lifted one perfect brow. "We've discussed this, Captain."

A stubborn glint came into Jen's eyes. "Yes, but if you ask me . . ."

"I didn't," the general drawled.

Mike moved to Jen's side, his gray eyes smiling. "Let it go, sweetheart. I believe in playing by the rules, remember?"

"How could I forget?"

Despite her disappointment on his behalf, Jen's heart swelled with pride at the sight of Mike Page in his blue service dress uniform. He stood so tall and proud, his shoulders square and his uniform coat decorated with rows of ribbons and shiny badges. He was the kind of officer she'd never be, Jen acknowledged, even if she remained in the Air Force for another two or three decades . . . which she certainly didn't intend to do.

After a long, heated discussion with Mike she'd decided to apply to join the Reserves. Either she or Mike would have to leave the Center anyway, Jen had argued, and she had no illusions about who was more valuable to its operation. As a part-time Reservist, Jen could start her own Internet-based business. And, she'd reminded Mike wryly, she could still pay the Air

Force back for her computer training during her Reserve duty days.

Jen wasn't ready to admit, even to Mike, that she would miss the Air Force if she hung up her uniform for good. Duty called to her, however faintly. But first, there were the matters of a decoration, a marriage, and a honeymoon to take care of. She decided it was time to get this show on the road.

"I'm ready if you are, General."

"In a hurry, Captain?"

"Yes, ma'am." She shot Mike a quick, private smile. "We have two dogs and a long drive waiting for us. We're going to swing by Lubbock to check on Trish—"

"Your roommate? How's she doing?"

Jen's smile tipped into a happy grin. "She wiggled a toe! Her father called to tell us a few nights ago. She's still unconscious, but she definitely wiggled a toe in response to his voice."

"Good!" General Daniels rolled her shoulders to adjust the impeccable fit of her jacket and started for the conference room. "Where are you heading after Lubbock?"

Laughing, Mike held the door for both women. "We're driving up to Colorado so Jen can meet my folks . . . in her new Blazer, by the way. There was no way in hell I was getting into another Cherokee with her."